# THE
# ILLUSTRATED
# KIPLING

# THE
# ILLUSTRATED
# KIPLING

*Edited by Neil Philip*

COLLINS
8 Grafton Street
London W1
1987

"No price is too high to pay for the privilege of owning yourself"
*Rudyard Kipling*

First published 1987 by William Collins Sons & Co Ltd
London · Glasgow · Sydney · Auckland · Toronto · Johannesburg

An Albion Book

Conceived, designed and produced by The Albion Press Ltd
9 Stewart Street, Oxford OX1 4RH

*Designer: Emma Bradford*
*Editor: Jane Havell*
*Picture Researcher: Elizabeth Loving*

© Selection and editorial matter: Neil Philip 1987
© Volume: The Albion Press 1987
The Acknowledgements on page 191 constitute an extension
of this copyright page

*British Library Cataloguing in Publication Data*

Kipling, Rudyard
The illustrated Kipling.
I. Title II. Philip, Neil
823'.8[F] PR4852

ISBN 0–00–217725–0

Typeset by Wyvern Typesetting Ltd, Bristol
Printed in Hong Kong by South China Printing Co

TITLE PAGE ILLUSTRATION: *An Indian snake charmer, drawn by the Rev. W. Urwick, 1891.*
OPPOSITE: Punch *making gentle fun of Kipling's Nobel Prize for Literature in 1907.*

## "A VERRAY PARFIT NOBEL KNIGHT."

[The Swedish trustees of the Nobel bequest have this year awarded the International prize for Literature to Mr. Rudyard Kipling.]

# Contents

# Introduction

No writer's reputation has fluctuated more wildly over the last hundred years than Rudyard Kipling's. He has been both revered and reviled: often, in both cases, for inadequate reasons. What no one has ever denied is the force of his mind, and the exact control with which he set down what he wanted to say.

This book draws from the whole range of Kipling's work, in an attempt to show the curve of his life and thought. To some extent this is impertinent – Kipling would have thought it so – but it is also, I hope, illuminating. For though Kipling was a very private man, he was also a public figure, and the point where those private and public concerns meet is a legitimate point for us to begin to understand this most outwardly simple, most inwardly complex of writers.

That outward simplicity is important: for Kipling addressed himself from the start to the widest possible audience, and not to any coterie. He looked to the world of action for his subject matter and his readership. His characters are soldiers, engineers, civil administrators, doctors; the self-referential world of writing about writing held no appeal for him. Thus his great verse monologue in celebration of a steam ship, "McAndrew's Hymn", drew a letter of appreciation from the Engineer-in-Chief of the U.S. Navy; his "Barrack-Room Ballads" were sung by the soldiers whose patterns of thought and speech they mimicked; the stories and poems of Indian life were, as one of his titles made clear, both of and for "mine own people". This broad base of popular appeal has saved Kipling from the vagaries of fluctuating critical opinion: he has not always had influential admirers, but he has always had readers.

*"The Light that Failed", a cartoon by Scott Rankin, playing on the title of Kipling's first novel, published in book form in 1891.*

Dick, the hero of Kipling's bitter semi-autobiographical novel *The Light that Failed*, says that, "Under any circumstances, four-fifths of everybody's work must be bad." Kipling was a ruthless judge of his own work, and submitted it to the ruthless judgement of others, particularly his father, and not much that he published is frankly bad. A great deal of it is astonishingly good. Any attempt, for instance, to select a single volume of his "best" short stories founders because so many of them share the concentrated brilliance, the taut narrative line, the extreme "economy of implication", which make Kipling so gripping while one is reading him, and so resonant afterwards.

The short story was Kipling's natural narrative mode, from the brittle early anecdotes of Anglo-Indian life to the compressed, oblique psychological studies of his mature years. These later stories, such as "'They'", "The Wish House", "Friendly Brook" and "Mary Postgate" are undoubtedly among his best work: they are highly readable but also highly demanding, for every word, every cadence, every image counts. The closely worked texture of these penetrating stories has perhaps diverted too much attention from the more showy and precocious early work, with its extraordinary vitality and its unerring flair for dramatic shape.

The sombre late stories have also blurred recognition of how much Kipling relished the comic, from the smallest of ironies to the full-blown farce of a story such as "The Village that Voted the Earth was Flat". Laughter was important to Kipling; it was what made us, or kept us, human. The Archangel Jibrail laments in "The Enemies to Each Other": "The last evil has fallen upon Thy creatures whom I guard! They have ceased to laugh and are made even with the ox and the camel."

Joy in life is one of the great distinguishing marks of Kipling's undoubted masterpiece, *Kim*. Yet Kim's irrepressible glee in the sights and sounds on the Grand Trunk Road is matched by the Lama's spiritual search for release from the Wheel of Life, and by the compromised necessities of the Great Game of politics and spying. It is often said that *Kim* is simply a picaresque string of episodes rather than a plotted novel. It seems to me much more carefully patterned than that, and I have not tried to extract passages from it for this selection. But it is true that the chief character in the book, and the directing influence of the story, is India itself, conveyed directly to the eyes, the nose, the touch by Kipling's precise strings of images: "Swiftly the light gathered itself together, painted for an instant the faces and the cart-wheels and the bullocks' horns as red as blood. Then the night fell, changing the touch of the air, drawing a low, even haze, like a gossamer veil of blue, across the face of the country and bringing out, keen and distinct, the smell of wood-smoke and cattle and the good scent of wheaten cakes cooked on ashes."

Kipling's portraits of children, such as Kim, are keenly observed. He retained all his life a vivid sympathy with the rules and rituals of children's imaginative play. In a poignant early tale, "The Story of Muhammad Din", for instance, he describes with great tenderness the play of a solitary Muslim child:

> For some months, the chubby little eccentricity revolved in his humble orbit among the castor-oil bushes and in the dust; always fashioning magnificent palaces from stale flowers thrown away by the bearer, smooth water-worn pebbles, bits of broken glass, and feathers pulled, I fancy, from my fowls – always alone, and always crooning to himself.

Some of the early stories of child life are disfigured for us by baby-talk, as the early soldier stories are disfigured by their phonetic dialect. In both cases, we must read against our prejudices, to discover, for instance, that "His Majesty the King", for all its lisping charm, is a bitterly unsentimental account of emotional deprivation. When "His Majesty's" mother is questioned about his well-being, her answer chills:

*"Rud" drawn by his affectionate father, probably in the early 1890s.*

"I don't know," said Mrs. Austell. "These things are left to Miss Biddums, and, of course, she does not ill-treat the child."

The agony of Kipling's own childhood encounter with mental cruelty still sears in his autobiographical story "Baa Baa, Black Sheep".

Imaginative reading provided Kipling with a means of escape, and he remained grateful all his life to the authors who had sustained him. At the end of his life, he wrote of Juliana Ewing's "Six to Sixteen": "I owe more in circuitous ways to that tale than I can tell. I knew it, as I know it still, almost by heart." Kipling's own children's books would alone put him in the rank of great writers: the incantatory magic of the *Just So Stories*; the fierce excitement and emotional strength of the Mowgli stories; the beautifully modulated essays in historical understanding collected in the Puck books; the vibrant, unvarnished picture of school life in *Stalky & Co.*; the rumbustious fun and aching delicacy of the children's verse.

Kipling's children's books pioneered a method of linking prose and verse which Kipling adopted for all his later books. That, combined with the unfathomably eccentric arrangement of the "Definitive Edition" of his verse, has perhaps retarded perception of the variety and quality of Kipling's poetry. The poems scattered through the late volumes are technically adroit, concentrated statements, and in many of them Kipling's mastery of rhythm and his journalist's instinct for the biting phrase combine to striking effect. Many of the earlier narrative poems, and particularly the Browning-influenced monologues "McAndrew's Hymn" and "The Mary Gloster", also show a prodigious talent. But his reputation as a poet still rests largely on the "Barrack-Room Ballads" which he wrote in 1890, taking the forms, concerns and conventions of the Victorian popular ballad and making something new and potent: the best account of the British soldier since Shakespeare.

Kipling's interest in the "Tommy" was not patronising; he was not trying to sentimentalise, glorify or improve the soldier, but to get inside his skin. He did so with haunting brilliance. "Danny Deever", the first of the ballads to appear, uses an old technique of rhymed dialogue to build an unbearable emotional tension.

Because he worked in this popular tradition for a popular audience, Kipling did not recognise the usual distinctions about what was proper subject matter for his pen. Much of his writing is pugnaciously political. In his own lifetime and since, this has stood in the way of many readers' enjoyment of his work. This is partly because the popular idea of Kipling's "imperialism", for instance, is a crude caricature of his real beliefs. He is judged, very often, not on what he actually wrote but on what people think he stood for. Often, too, what he believed is, as he put it in "If", "Twisted by knaves to make a trap for fools".

Though Kipling's work embodies in its confident surface the

*"Strong Meat for Men"*, *a cartoon by Bert Thomas from* Punch, *November 1922.*

simple credos of imperialism, it provides in its darker implications a sustained critique of its structures, and an awareness of their inevitable fall. No one could read Kipling with sensitivity to those implications and think him either a blind jingoist or a crude racialist, though odd lines taken out of context can make him seem both. Readers should remember, as Mowgli found out, that "the Jungle's full of words that sound like one thing, but mean another."

The over-emphatic rhetoric of some of Kipling's writing is in part a reaction to what he felt was the complete misunderstanding in England of the nature of the Empire:

> They derided my poor little Gods of the East, and asserted that the British in India spent violent lives "oppressing" the Native. (This in a land where white girls of sixteen, at twelve or fourteen pounds per annum, hauled thirty or forty pounds weight of bath-water at a time up four flights of stairs!)

So his work developed into what he aptly called "a vast, vague conspectus – Army and Navy Stores List if you like – of the whole sweep and meaning of things and effort and origins throughout the Empire."

"Throughout the Empire" came, in the end, to mean England too. The history-laden Sussex countryside of *Puck of Pook's Hill* is as important to a full understanding of Kipling's achievement as the teeming spicy India of *Kim*.

Kipling's work forms a whole. He remained throughout his career intrigued by the slow workings of emotion: feelings which are nurtured and hoarded like treasures. He liked all his life to set petty human preoccupations against the background of some great ideal. He explored both the comradeship and the jealousies of closed communities; the idea of belonging both attracted and dismayed him. He always revelled in the slang and technicalities of a particular trade. If his work does show a movement over time, it is away from the theme of revenge towards the theme of healing.

Both of these dominant themes reflect Kipling's fascination with the problem of pain – he even, late in life, after years of gastric illness, composed a sombre "Hymn to Physical Pain". That fascination is not gloating. Some have accused Kipling of brutality, on the strength, for instance, of the cheerful amorality of his ballad "Loot". This is to misunderstand the writer's relation to his art. In his underestimated story of the London slums in the 1890s, "The Record of Badalia Herodsfoot", there is a cold-blooded description of Tom's attack on Badalia which is stark to the point of brutality, but it is, in its context, pitiful rather than brutal or callous:

*"Mr. Kipling as Mr. Nast imagines him", a drawing by Thomas Nast from* St Paul's, *October 1894. Kipling's outspoken views did not make him popular in America.*

> The head drooped to the floor, and Tom kicked at that till the crisp tingle of hair striking through his nailed boot with the chill of cold water, warned him that it might be as well to desist.

The deliberate distancing here – "the head" rather than "her head" –

shows the author refusing to participate in what he describes. The bareness is a reflection of Badalia's emotions, not Tom's.

Economy of language – writing which leaves, as it were, a series of oblique shafts through which the reader can penetrate into the heart of the story – is a feature of all Kipling's work. There is always a great deal more to be grasped than is apparent on the surface, so that an early story such as "Without Benefit of Clergy" or a late story such as "The Gardener" equally repay careful re-readings, and remain with the reader as unresolved experiences.

It is perhaps useful to remember that Kipling's first language was Hindustani; his awareness of the exact values of English words reflects this slight detachment from his mother tongue. He wrote:

> I made my own experiments in the weights, colours, perfumes, and attributes of words in relation to other words, either as read aloud so that they may hold the ear, or, scattered over the page, draw the eye. There is no line of my verse or prose which has not been mouthed till the tongue has made all smooth, and memory, after many recitals, has mechanically skipped the grosser superfluities.

The work he produced is inevitably of varying quality, but the worst of it commands attention at least while one is reading; the best lingers and amplifies in the mind. Kipling was always a craftsman, with a craftsman's respect for the crafts of others, be they soldiers, bridge-builders or hedgers and ditchers. He was always, too, a journalist, with a reporter's gift for soaking up local colour, and a reporter's hunger for detail. Most of all, he was a listener.

He cherished his privacy. His closest friendship, with the publisher Wolcott Balestier with whom he wrote a weak novel, *The Naulahka*, was cut short by Wolcott's premature death in 1891. Shortly afterwards, Kipling married Wolcott's sister Carrie, and she, supporting him with magnificent strength, also shielded him from the world.

Nevertheless, the idea of Kipling as a surly curmudgeonly recluse is a misapprehension. Despite the private sadnesses of his life and the public sadnesses of his times, Kipling's work is full of delight: delight in language – "Aren't those beautiful words, Best Beloved?" he exults in the *Just So Stories* – and delight in "God's great, happy, inattentive world":

> For to admire an' for to see
>> For to be'old this world so wide –
> It never done no good to me,
>> But I can't drop it if I tried!

NEIL PHILIP
*Oxford, 1986*

ABOVE: *Kipling "scouting and reporting along the fantastic skyline of the future", drawn by David Wilson for* The Graphic, *February 1914. The phrase comes from a speech to the Royal Geographic Society.*

OPPOSITE: *Kipling and his creations, a monochrome oil painting by Cyrus Cuneo, from the* Illustrated London News, *October 1910. In the background can be seen the singer of "Mandalay" and his Burmese maiden; Mowgli, Bagheera and Baloo; the Soldiers Three; Kim and the Lama.*

# Early Memories

Joseph Rudyard Kipling was born in Bombay on 30 December 1865. The first five and a half years of his life were spent there; the account below was written in 1935, for Kipling's evasive memoir *Something of Myself*. These early years were an idyll of indulged curiosity, and left him with a deep and abiding love for the vivid restless variety of Indian life and the Indian people at all levels. His father taught at the newly founded Sir Jamjetjee Jejeebhoy School of Art in Bombay, encouraging Indian artists and architects to draw on their own culture rather than mimic the West; his mother, sparkling and elegant, established her claim to his ambiguously aimed dedication in *Plain Tales from the Hills*, "To the wittiest woman in India". Later, Lockwood became director of the Mayo School of Art, Lahore, from which post he exercised a real influence over Indian art and design; an influence traceable, for instance, in the meticulous work of his student Munshi Ghulam Muhammad for J. Ph. Vogel's *Tile-Mosaics of the Lahore Fort* (1920). It was to Lahore that Kipling would return as a young journalist. He never again lived in Bombay, but his last brief visit to India in 1891 ended there, when he saw once more the *ayah* who had nursed him and his younger sister Trix, "so old but so unaltered". The native servants were affectionately remembered for their storytelling ability in "Baa Baa, Black Sheep" and in a charming and little-known story of 1893, "The Potted Princess".

*The first of several versions of this bookplate, drawn for Kipling by his father, Lockwood.*

My first impression is of daybreak, light and colour and golden and purple fruits at the level of my shoulder. This would be the memory of early morning walks to the Bombay fruit market with my *ayah* and later with my sister in her perambulator, and of our returns with our purchases piled high on the bows of it. Our *ayah* was a Portuguese Roman Catholic who would pray – I beside her – at a wayside Cross. Meeta, my Hindu bearer, would sometimes go into little Hindu temples where, being below the age of caste, I held his hand and looked at the dimly-seen, friendly Gods.

Our evening walks were by the sea in the shadow of palm-groves which, I think, were called the Mahim Woods. When the wind blew the great nuts would tumble, and we fled – my *ayah*, and my sister in her perambulator – to the safety of the open. I have always felt the menacing darkness of tropical eventides, as I have loved the voices of night-winds through palm or banana leaves, and the song of the tree-frogs.

There were far-going Arab dhows on the pearly waters, and gaily dressed Parsees wading out to worship the sunset. Of their creed I knew nothing, nor did I know that near our little house on the Bombay Esplanade were the Towers of Silence, where their Dead are exposed to the waiting vultures on the rim of the towers, who scuffle and spread wings when they see the bearers of the Dead below. I did not understand my Mother's distress when she found "a child's

hand" in our garden, and said I was not to ask questions about it. I wanted to see that child's hand. But my *ayah* told me.

In the afternoon heats before we took our sleep, she or Meeta would tell us stories and Indian nursery songs all unforgotten, and we were sent into the dining-room after we had been dressed, with the caution "Speak English now to Papa and Mamma." So one spoke "English", haltingly translated out of the vernacular idiom that one thought and dreamed in.

*A street scene in Bombay, drawn by the Rev. W. Urwick in 1891.*

# Baa Baa, Black Sheep

English families in India sent their children to England to escape the deadly heat and what was seen as the deleterious influence of the Indian servants, and to have them brought up in an English culture and with English values. In April 1871 the Kiplings sailed for England, and when they returned that December they left Rudyard and his younger sister Trix behind. The next five years, from the age of six to eleven, were miserable ones for Rudyard. The children's chosen guardians were strangers, not family; and while Captain Pryse Agar Holloway, who died in 1874, was fond of Kipling, his fierce wife Sarah disliked him, and terrified him with threats of Calvinist hell-fire; their son Harry seems to have been a sly bully. Kipling was undoubtedly a spoilt little boy with a temper – he was remembered storming down the street aged two chanting, "Out of the way, out of the way, there's an angry Ruddy coming" – and a Sahib's commanding ways were out of place in shabby-genteel Southsea. But Kipling remembered his treatment in "the House of Desolation" as "calculated torture". He was beaten and humiliated; Trix remembered Mrs. Holloway telling them that they had been abandoned by their parents "because we were so tiresome and she had taken us in out of pity". "Baa Baa, Black Sheep" was written in Allahabad in December 1888, and draws directly on these painful events, as does the opening chapter of his novel *The Light That Failed*. But while it is closely autobiographical, as later accounts by Rudyard and Trix confirm, "Baa Baa, Black Sheep" is a work of fiction, and the later memoirs are fatally dependent on it. It is undoubtedly distorted, and to some degree marred, by the violence of Kipling's feelings. He wrote it "in a towering rage" and himself dismissed it two years later as "not true to life"; but late in life, when Trix asked him whether the Holloways' house was still standing, he could only reply, "I don't know, but if so, I should like to burn it down and plough the place with salt."

Baa Baa, Black Sheep,
Have you any wool?
Yes, Sir, yes, Sir, three bags full.
One for the Master, one for the Dame –
None for the Little Boy that cries down the lane.
*Nursery Rhyme.*

## THE FIRST BAG

When I was in my father's house, I was in a better place.

**ayah:** nurse
**hamal:** bath-attendant
**Surti:** from Surat

They were putting Punch to bed – the *ayah* and the *hamal* and Meeta, the big *Surti* boy, with the red and gold turban. Judy, already tucked inside her mosquito-curtains, was nearly asleep. Punch had been allowed to stay up for dinner. Many privileges had been accorded to Punch within the last ten days, and a greater kindness from the people of his world had encompassed his ways and works, which were mostly obstreperous. He sat on the edge of his bed and swung his bare legs defiantly.

"Punch-*baba* going to bye-lo?" said the *ayah* suggestively.

"No," said Punch. "Punch-*baba* wants the story about the Ranee that was turned into a tiger. Meeta must tell it, and the *hamal* shall hide behind the door and make tiger-noises at the proper time."

"But Judy-*baba* will wake up," said the *ayah*.

"Judy-*baba* is waked," piped a small voice from the mosquito-curtains. "There was a Ranee that lived at Delhi. Go on, Meeta," and she fell fast asleep again while Meeta began the story.

Never had Punch secured the telling of that tale with so little opposition. He reflected for a long time. The *hamal* made the tiger-noises in twenty different keys.

"'Top!" said Punch authoritatively. "Why doesn't Papa come in and say he is going to give me *put-put*?"

**put-put:** smack-smack

"Punch-*baba* is going away," said the *ayah*. "In another week there will be no Punch-*baba* to pull my hair any more." She sighed softly, for the boy of the household was very dear to her heart.

"Up the Ghauts in a train?" said Punch, standing on his bed. "All the way to Nassick where the Ranee-Tiger lives?"

"Not to Nassick this year, little Sahib," said Meeta, lifting him on his shoulder. "Down to the sea where the cocoa-nuts are thrown, and across the sea in a big ship. Will you take Meeta with you to *Belait*?"

**Belait:** England (Blighty)

"You shall all come," said Punch, from the height of Meeta's

WE ARE ALL     BORN PRINCES.

AYAH & BEARER     N. INDIA.

*A watercolour drawing by Lockwood Kipling, showing a shrewd appreciation of the spoiling affection lavished on Anglo-Indian children by native servants.*

strong arms. "Meeta and the *ayah* and the *hamal* and Bhini-in-the-Garden, and the salaam-Captain-Sahib-snake-man."

There was no mockery in Meeta's voice when he replied – "Great is the Sahib's favour," and laid the little man down in the bed, while the *ayah*, sitting in the moonlight at the doorway, lulled him to sleep with an interminable canticle such as they sing in the Roman Catholic Church at Parel. Punch curled himself into a ball and slept.

Next morning Judy shouted that there was a rat in the nursery, and thus he forgot to tell her the wonderful news. It did not much matter, for Judy was only three and she would not have understood. But Punch was five; and he knew that going to England would be much nicer than a trip to Nassick.

Papa and Mamma sold the brougham and the piano, and stripped the house, and curtailed the allowance of crockery for the daily meals, and took long counsel together over a bundle of letters bearing the Rocklington postmark.

"The worst of it is that one can't be certain of anything," said Papa, pulling his moustache. "The letters in themselves are excellent, and the terms are moderate enough."

"The worst of it is that the children will grow up away from me," thought Mamma; but she did not say it aloud.

"We are only one case among hundreds," said Papa bitterly. "You shall go Home again in five years, dear."

"Punch will be ten then – and Judy eight. Oh, how long and long and long the time will be! And we have to leave them among strangers."

"Punch is a cheery little chap. He's sure to make friends wherever he goes."

"And who could help loving my Ju?"

They were standing over the cots in the nursery late at night, and I think that Mamma was crying softly. After Papa had gone away, she knelt down by the side of Judy's cot. The *ayah* saw her and put up a prayer that the *memsahib* might never find the love of her children taken away from her and given to a stranger.

Mamma's own prayer was a slightly illogical one. Summarised it ran: "Let strangers love my children and be as good to them as I should be, but let *me* preserve their love and their confidence for ever and ever. Amen." Punch scratched himself in his sleep, and Judy moaned a little.

Next day they all went down to the sea, and there was a scene at the Apollo Bunder when Punch discovered that Meeta could not come too, and Judy learned that the *ayah* must be left behind. But Punch found a thousand fascinating things in the rope, block, and steam-pipe line on the big P. and O. Steamer long before Meeta and the *ayah* had dried their tears.

*John Lockwood Kipling and his bride, Alice MacDonald.*

**Apollo Bunder**: the main dock at Bombay

"Come back, Punch-*baba*," said the *ayah*.

"Come back," said Meeta, "and be a *Burra Sahib*."

"Yes," said Punch, lifted up in his father's arms to wave good-bye. "Yes, I will come back, and I will be a *Burra Sahib Bahadur*!"

At the end of the first day Punch demanded to be set down in England, which he was certain must be close at hand. Next day there was a merry breeze, and Punch was very sick. "When I come back to Bombay," said Punch on his recovery, "I will come by the road – in a broom-*gharri*. This is a very naughty ship."

The Swedish boatswain consoled him, and he modified his opinions as the voyage went on. There was so much to see and to handle and ask questions about that Punch nearly forgot the *ayah* and Meeta and the *hamal*, and with difficulty remembered a few words of the Hindustani once his second-speech.

But Judy was much worse. The day before the steamer reached Southampton, Mamma asked her if she would not like to see the *ayah* again. Judy's blue eyes turned to the stretch of sea that had swallowed all her tiny past, and she said: "*Ayah!* What *ayah*?"

Mamma cried over her and Punch marvelled. It was then that he heard for the first time Mamma's passionate appeal to him never to let Judy forget Mamma. Seeing that Judy was young, ridiculously young, and that Mamma, every evening for four weeks past, had come into the cabin to sing her and Punch to sleep with a mysterious rune that he called "Sonny, my soul", Punch could not understand

*Bombay harbour. In "To the City of Bombay", Kipling hymned his birthplace as:*

*Mother of Cities to me,*
*But I was born in her gate,*
*Between the palms and the sea,*
*Where the world-end steamers wait.*

**Burra Sahib**: a big man
**Burra Sahib Bahadur**: a very big man indeed
**broom-gharri**: brougham carriage

**Sonny my soul**: Keble's "Evening Hymn", "Sun of my soul"

what Mamma meant. But he strove to do his duty; for, the moment Mamma left the cabin, he said to Judy: "Ju, you bemember Mamma?"

"'Torse I do," said Judy.

"Then *always* bemember Mamma, 'r else I won't give you the paper ducks that the red-haired Captain Sahib cut out for me."

So Judy promised always to "bemember Mamma".

Many and many a time was Mamma's command laid upon Punch, and Papa would say the same thing with an insistence that awed the child.

"You must make haste and learn to write, Punch," said Papa, "and then you'll be able to write letters to us in Bombay."

"I'll come into your room," said Punch, and Papa choked.

Papa and Mamma were always choking in those days. If Punch took Judy to task for not "bemembering", they choked. If Punch sprawled on the sofa in the Southampton lodging-house and sketched his future in purple and gold, they choked; and so they did if Judy put up her mouth for a kiss.

Through many days all four were vagabonds on the face of the earth – Punch with no one to give orders to, Judy too young for anything, and Papa and Mamma grave, distracted, and choking.

"Where," demanded Punch, wearied of a loathsome contrivance on four wheels with a mound of luggage atop – "*where* is our broom-*gharri*? This thing talks so much that *I* can't talk. Where is our *own* broom-*gharri*? When I was at Bandstand before we comed away, I asked Inverarity Sahib why he was sitting in it, and he said it was his own. And I said, 'I will *give* it you' – I like Inverarity Sahib – and I said, 'Can you put your legs through the pully-wag loops by the windows?' And Inverarity Sahib said No, and laughed. *I* can put my legs through the pully-wag loops. I can put my legs through *these* pully-wag loops. Look! Oh, Mamma's crying again! I didn't know I wasn't not to do *so*."

A *Bombay* rekla, *drawn by Lockwood Kipling.*

Punch drew his legs out of the loops of the four-wheeler: the door opened and he slid to the earth, in a cascade of parcels, at the door of an austere little villa whose gates bore the legend "Downe Lodge". Punch gathered himself together and eyed the house with disfavour. It stood on a sandy road, and a cold wind tickled his knicker-bockered legs.

"Let us go away," said Punch. "This is not a pretty place."

But Mamma and Papa and Judy had left the cab, and all the luggage was being taken into the house. At the doorstep stood a woman in black, and she smiled largely, with dry chapped lips. Behind her was a man, big, bony, grey, and lame as to one leg – behind him a boy of twelve, black-haired and oily in appearance. Punch surveyed the trio, and advanced without fear, as he had been accustomed to do in Bombay when callers came and he happened to be playing in the veranda.

"How do you do?" said he. "I am Punch." But they were all looking at the luggage – all except the grey man, who shook hands with Punch, and said he was "a smart little fellow". There was much running about and banging of boxes, and Punch curled himself up on the sofa in the dining-room and considered things.

"I don't like these people," said Punch. "But never mind. We'll go away soon. We have always went away soon from everywhere. I wish we was gone back to Bombay *soon*."

The wish bore no fruit. For six days Mamma wept at intervals, and showed the woman in black all Punch's clothes – a liberty which Punch resented. "But p'raps she's a new white *ayah*," he thought. "I'm to call her Antirosa, but she doesn't call *me* Sahib. She says just Punch," he confided to Judy. "What is Antirosa?"

Judy didn't know. Neither she nor Punch had heard anything of an animal called an aunt. Their world had been Papa and Mamma, who knew everything, permitted everything, and loved everybody – even Punch when he used to go into the garden at Bombay and fill his nails with mould after the weekly nail-cutting, because, as he explained between two strokes of the slipper to his sorely-tried Father, his fingers "felt so new at the ends".

In an undefined way Punch judged it advisable to keep both parents between himself and the woman in black and the boy in black hair. He did not approve of them. He liked the grey man, who had expressed a wish to be called "Uncleharri". They nodded at each other when they met, and the grey man showed him a little ship with rigging that took up and down.

"She is a model of the *Brisk* – the little *Brisk* that was sore exposed that day at Navarino." The grey man hummed the last words and fell into a reverie. "I'll tell you about Navarino, Punch, when we go for walks together; and you mustn't touch the ship, because she's the *Brisk*."

Long before that walk, the first of many, was taken, they roused Punch and Judy in the chill dawn of a February morning to say Good-bye; and of all people in the wide earth to Papa and Mamma – both crying this time. Punch was very sleepy and Judy was cross.

"Don't forget us," pleaded Mamma. "Oh, my little son, don't forget us, and see that Judy remembers too."

"I've told Judy to bemember," said Punch, wriggling, for his father's beard tickled his neck, "I've told Judy – ten – forty – 'leven thousand times. But Ju's so young – quite a baby – isn't she?"

"Yes," said Papa, "quite a baby, and you must be good to Judy, and make haste to learn to write and – and – and –"

Punch was back in his bed again. Judy was fast asleep, and there was the rattle of a cab below. Papa and Mamma had gone away. Not to Nassick; that was across the sea. To some place much nearer, of course, and equally of course they would return. They came back after dinner-parties, and Papa had come back after he had been to a place called "The Snows", and Mamma with him, to Punch and Judy at Mrs. Inverarity's house in Marine Lines. Assuredly they would come back again. So Punch fell asleep till the true morning, when the black-haired boy met him with the information that Papa and Mamma had gone to Bombay, and that he and Judy were to stay at Downe Lodge "for ever". Antirosa, tearfully appealed to for a contradiction, said that Harry had spoken the truth, and that it behoved Punch to fold up his clothes neatly on going to bed. Punch went out and wept bitterly with Judy, into whose fair head he had driven some ideas of the meaning of separation.

When a matured man discovers that he has been deserted by Providence, deprived of his God, and cast without help, comfort, or sympathy, upon a world which is new and strange to him, his despair, which may find expression in evil-living, the writing of his experiences, or the more satisfactory diversion of suicide, is generally supposed to be impressive. A child, under exactly similar circumstances as far as its knowledge goes, cannot very well curse God and die. It howls till its nose is red, its eyes are sore, and its head aches. Punch and Judy, through no fault of their own, had lost all their world. They sat in the hall and cried; the black-haired boy looking on from afar.

The model of the ship availed nothing, though the grey man assured Punch that he might pull the rigging up and down as much as he pleased; and Judy was promised free entry into the kitchen. They wanted Papa and Mamma gone to Bombay beyond the seas, and their grief while it lasted was without remedy.

When the tears ceased the house was very still. Antirosa had decided that it was better to let the children "have their cry out", and the boy had gone to school. Punch raised his head from the floor and sniffed mournfully. Judy was nearly asleep. Three short years had not taught her how to bear sorrow with full knowledge. There was a distant, dull boom in the air – a repeated heavy thud. Punch knew that sound in Bombay in the Monsoon. It was the sea – the sea that must be traversed before any one could get to Bombay.

"Quick, Ju!" he cried, "we're close to the sea. I can hear it! Listen! That's where they've went. P'raps we can catch them if we was in time. They didn't mean to go without us. They've only forgot."

"Iss," said Judy. "They've only forgotted. Less go to the sea."

The hall-door was open and so was the garden-gate.

"It's very, very big, this place," he said, looking cautiously down the road, "and we will get lost; but *I* will find a man and order him to take me back to my house – like I did in Bombay."

He took Judy by the hand, and the two ran hatless in the direction of the sound of the sea. Downe Lodge was almost the last of a range of newly-built houses running out, through a field of brick-mounds, to a heath where gypsies occasionally camped and where the Garrison Artillery of Rocklington practised. There were few people to be seen, and the children might have been taken for those of the soldiery who ranged far. Half an hour the wearied little legs tramped across heath, potato-patch, and sand-dune.

"I'se so tired," said Judy, "and Mamma will be angry."

"Mamma's *never* angry. I suppose she is waiting at the sea now while Papa gets tickets. We'll find them and go along with them. Ju, you mustn't sit down. Only a little more and we'll come to the sea. Ju, if you sit down I'll *thmack* you!" said Punch.

They climbed another dune, and came upon the great grey sea at low tide. Hundreds of crabs were scuttling about the beach, but there was no trace of Papa and Mamma, not even of a ship upon the waters – nothing but sand and mud for miles and miles.

And "Uncleharri" found them by chance – very muddy and very forlorn – Punch dissolved in tears, but trying to divert Judy with an "ickle trab", and Judy wailing to the pitiless horizon for "Mamma, Mamma!" – and again "Mamma!"

### THE SECOND BAG

Ah, well-a-day, for we are souls bereaved!
Of all the creatures under Heaven's wide scope
We are most hopeless, who had once most hope,
And most beliefless, who had most believed.
*Easter Day. Naples, 1849.*

All this time not a word about Black Sheep. He came later, and Harry the black-haired boy was mainly responsible for his coming.

Judy – who could help loving little Judy? – passed, by special permit, into the kitchen and thence straight to Aunty Rosa's heart. Harry was Aunty Rosa's one child, and Punch was the extra boy about the house. There was no special place for him or his little affairs, and he was forbidden to sprawl on sofas and explain his ideas about the manufacture of this world and his hopes for his future. Sprawling was lazy and wore out sofas, and little boys were not expected to talk. They were talked to, and the talking to was intended for the benefit of their morals. As the unquestioned despot of the house at Bombay, Punch could not quite understand how he came to be of no account in this his new life.

Harry might reach across the table and take what he wanted; Judy might point and get what she wanted. Punch was forbidden to do either. The grey man was his great hope and stand-by for many months after Mamma and Papa left, and he had forgotten to tell Judy to "bemember Mamma".

This lapse was excusable, because in the interval he had been introduced by Aunty Rosa to two very impressive things – an abstraction called God, the intimate friend and ally of Aunty Rosa, generally believed to live behind the kitchen-range because it was hot there – and a dirty brown book filled with unintelligible dots and

*"Ruddy's idea of heaven", a drawing made by Lockwood when Kipling was two.*

marks. Punch was always anxious to oblige everybody. He therefore welded the story of the Creation on to what he could recollect of his Indian fairy tales, and scandalised Aunty Rosa by repeating the result to Judy. It was a sin, a grievous sin, and Punch was talked to for a quarter of an hour. He could not understand where the iniquity came in, but was careful not to repeat the offence, because Aunty Rosa told him that God had heard every word he had said and was very angry. If this were true why didn't God come and say so, thought Punch, and dismissed the matter from his mind. Afterwards he learned to know the Lord as the only thing in the world more awful than Aunty Rosa – as a Creature that stood in the background and counted the strokes of the cane.

But the reading was, just then, a much more serious matter than any creed. Aunty Rosa sat him upon a table and told him that A B meant ab.

"Why?" said Punch, "A is a and B is bee. *Why* does A B mean ab?"

"Because I tell you it does," said Aunty Rosa, "and you've got to say it."

Punch said it accordingly, and for a month, hugely against his will, stumbled through the brown book, not in the least comprehending what it meant. But Uncle Harry, who walked much and generally alone, was wont to come into the nursery and suggest to Aunty Rosa that Punch should walk with him. He seldom spoke, but he showed Punch all Rocklington, from the mud-banks and the sand of the back-bay to the great harbours where ships lay at anchor, and the dockyards where the hammers were never still, and the marine-store shops, and the shiny brass counters in the Offices where Uncle Harry went once every three months with a slip of blue paper and received sovereigns in exchange; for he held a wound-pension. Punch heard, too, from his lips the story of the battle of Navarino, where the sailors of the Fleet, for three days afterwards, were deaf as posts and could only sign to each other. "That was because of the noise of the guns," said Uncle Harry, "and I have got the wadding of a bullet somewhere inside me now."

Punch regarded him with curiosity. He had not the least idea what wadding was, and his notion of a bullet was a dockyard cannon-ball bigger than his own head. How could Uncle Harry keep a cannon-ball inside him? He was ashamed to ask, for fear Uncle Harry might be angry.

Punch had never known what anger – real anger – meant until one terrible day when Harry had taken his paint-box to paint a boat with, and Punch had protested. Then Uncle Harry had appeared on the scene and, muttering something about "strangers' children", had with a stick smitten the black-haired boy across the shoulders till he wept and yelled, and Aunty Rosa came in and abused Uncle Harry for cruelty to his own flesh and blood, and Punch shuddered to the tips of his shoes. "It wasn't my fault," he explained to the boy, but both Harry and Aunty Rosa said that it was, and that Punch had told tales, and for a week there were no more walks with Uncle Harry.

But that week brought a great joy to Punch.

He had repeated till he was thrice weary the statement that "the Cat lay on the Mat and the Rat came in".

"Now I can truly read," said Punch, "and now I will never read anything in the world."

He put the brown book in the cupboard where his school-books lived and accidentally tumbled out a venerable volume, without covers, labelled *Sharpe's Magazine*. There was the most portentous picture of a griffin on the first page, with verses below. The griffin carried off one sheep a day from a German village, till a man came with a "falchion" and split the griffin open. Goodness only knew what a falchion was, but there was the Griffin, and his history was an improvement upon the eternal Cat.

"This", said Punch, "means things, and now I will know all about everything in all the world." He read till the light failed, not understanding a tithe of the meaning, but tantalised by glimpses of new worlds hereafter to be revealed.

"What is a 'falchion'? What is a 'e-wee lamb'? What is a 'base *uss*urper'? What is a 'verdant me-ad'?" he demanded with flushed cheeks, at bedtime, of the astonished Aunty Rosa.

"Say your prayers and go to sleep," she replied, and that was all the help Punch then or afterwards found at her hands in the new and delightful exercise of reading.

"Aunty Rosa only knows about God and things like that," argued Punch. "Uncle Harry will tell me."

The next walk proved that Uncle Harry could not help either; but he allowed Punch to talk, and even sat down on a bench to hear about the Griffin. Other walks brought other stories as Punch ranged farther afield, for the house held large store of old books that no one ever opened – from *Frank Fairlegh* in serial numbers, and the earlier poems of Tennyson, contributed anonymously to *Sharpe's Magazine*, to '62 Exhibition Catalogues, gay with colours and delightfully incomprehensible, and odd leaves of *Gulliver's Travels*.

*Kipling aged about eight: Punch being turned into Black Sheep.*

As soon as Punch could string a few pot-hooks together he wrote to Bombay, demanding by return of post "all the books in all the world". Papa could not comply with this modest indent, but sent *Grimm's Fairy Tales* and a Hans Andersen. That was enough. If he were only left alone Punch could pass, at any hour he chose, into a land of his own, beyond reach of Aunty Rosa and her God, Harry and his teasements, and Judy's claims to be played with.

"Don't disturve me, I'm reading. Go and play in the kitchen," grunted Punch. "Aunty Rosa lets *you* go there." Judy was cutting her second teeth and was fretful. She appealed to Aunty Rosa, who descended on Punch.

"I was reading," he explained, "reading a book I *want* to read."

# SHARPE'S
# London Magazine:

## A JOURNAL OF ENTERTAINMENT AND INSTRUCTION
### FOR GENERAL READING.

No. 19.]                    MARCH 7, 1846.                    [PRICE 1½d.

The Shepherd of the Giant Mountains

See page 298.

## GRAY'S ELEGY, AND STOKE POGES.

THE manuscripts of celebrated men, whether poets who have stirred human souls to action, or philosophers whose lessons have guided nations, must ever possess a peculiar charm for succeeding ages. The places where illustrious men have lived and died, have their natural interest increased by becoming the depositaries of their writings.

Could we enter the room where a Milton or a Shakspere thought and wrote, and gaze upon the very pages over which their fingers have passed, we should enter into a closer fellowship with the poets on whose memorials we reverently gaze. The former homes of men ennobled by lofty thoughts are the appropriate resting-places of their writing.

"You're only doing that to show off," said Aunty Rosa. "But we'll see. Play with Judy now, and don't open a book for a week."

Judy did not pass a very enjoyable playtime with Punch, who was consumed with indignation. There was a pettiness at the bottom of the prohibition which puzzled him.

"It's what I like to do," he said, "and she's found out that and stopped me. Don't cry, Ju – it wasn't your fault – *please* don't cry, or she'll say I made you."

Ju loyally mopped up her tears, and the two played in their nursery, a room in the basement and half underground, to which they were regularly sent after the mid-day dinner while Aunty Rosa slept. She drank wine – that is to say, something from a bottle in the cellaret – for her stomach's sake, but if she did not fall asleep she would sometimes come into the nursery to see that the children were really playing. Now bricks, wooden hoops, ninepins, and chinaware cannot amuse for ever, especially when all Fairyland is to be won by the mere opening of a book, and, as often as not, Punch would be discovered reading to Judy or telling her interminable tales. That was an offence in the eyes of the law, and Judy would be whisked off by Aunty Rosa, while Punch was left to play alone, "and be sure that I hear you doing it".

It was not a cheering employ, for he had to make a playful noise. At last, with infinite craft, he devised an arrangement whereby the table could be supported as to three legs on toy bricks, leaving the fourth clear to bring down on the floor. He could work the table with one hand and hold a book with the other. This he did till an evil day when Aunty Rosa pounced upon him unawares and told him that he was "acting a lie".

"If you're old enough to do that," she said – her temper was always worst after dinner – "you're old enough to be beaten."

"But – I'm – I'm not a animal!" said Punch aghast. He remembered Uncle Harry and the stick, and turned white. Aunty Rosa had hidden a light cane behind her, and Punch was beaten then and there over the shoulders. It was a revelation to him. The room-door was shut, and he was left to weep himself into repentance and work out his own gospel of life.

Aunty Rosa, he argued, had the power to beat him with many stripes. It was unjust and cruel, and Mamma and Papa would never have allowed it. Unless perhaps, as Aunty Rosa seemed to imply, they had sent secret orders. In which case he was abandoned indeed. It would be discreet in the future to propitiate Aunty Rosa, but, then again, even in matters in which he was innocent, he had been accused of wishing to "show off". He had "shown off" before visitors when he had attacked a strange gentleman – Harry's uncle, not his own – with requests for information about the Griffin and the falchion, and the precise nature of the Tilbury in which Frank Fairlegh rode – all points of paramount interest which he was bursting to understand.

OPPOSITE: Sharpe's London Magazine, *1846. This page, engraved by Dalziel from a drawing by Selous, stuck in Kipling's mind. It accompanied a poetic narrative translated from the German by Menella Bute Smedley. Miss Smedley and her sister, Elizabeth Anna Hart, both wrote poems which had a profound effect on Kipling's imagination, including "Wolfie", which sowed the seed of the Mowgli stories:*

> *A wolf took a child in her mouth,*
> *And carried him off to her cave;*
> *And so he grew up among little young wolves,*
> *Who taught him how to behave.*

*Among other favourite books remembered from this period were Mrs. Molesworth's* The Cuckoo Clock, *F. E. Paget's* The Hope of the Katzekopfs, *George MacDonald's* The Princess and the Goblin, *and various stories by Juliana Horatia Ewing, including* Six to Sixteen, *which concerns an Anglo-Indian girl's English upbringing. His parents sent the bound volume of* Aunt Judy's Magazine, 1872, *in which Mrs. Ewing's tale first appeared, to Rudyard at Southsea, and he devoured it with glee: "Here was a history of real people and real things."*

*The Holloways lived in straitened gentility, almost certainly with a single maid-of-all-work to do "the rough". Servants and children were natural allies under Mrs. Holloway's fierce regime. In* Something of Myself, *Kipling recalled: "I had never heard of Hell, so I was introduced to it in all its terrors – I and whatever luckless little slavey might be in the house, whom severe rationing had led to steal food. Once I saw the Woman beat such a girl who picked up the kitchen poker and threatened retaliation."*

Clearly it would not do to pretend to care for Aunty Rosa.

At this point Harry entered and stood afar off, eyeing Punch, a dishevelled heap in the corner of the room, with disgust.

"You're a liar – a young liar," said Harry, with great unction, "and you're to have tea down here because you're not fit to speak to us. And you're not to speak to Judy again till Mother gives you leave. You'll corrupt her. You're only fit to associate with the servant. Mother says so."

Having reduced Punch to a second agony of tears, Harry departed upstairs with the news that Punch was still rebellious.

Uncle Harry sat uneasily in the dining-room. "Damn it all, Rosa," said he at last, "can't you leave the child alone? He's a good enough little chap when I meet him."

"He puts on his best manners with you, Henry," said Aunty Rosa, "but I'm afraid, I'm very much afraid, that he is the Black Sheep of the family."

Harry heard and stored up the name for future use. Judy cried till she was bidden to stop, her brother not being worth tears; and the evening concluded with the return of Punch to the upper regions and a private sitting at which all the blinding horrors of Hell were revealed to Punch with such store of imagery as Aunty Rosa's narrow mind possessed.

Most grievous of all was Judy's round-eyed reproach, and Punch went to bed in the depths of the Valley of Humiliation. He shared his room with Harry and knew the torture in store. For an hour and a half he had to answer that young gentleman's questions as to his motives for telling a lie, and a grievous lie, the precise quantity of punishment inflicted by Aunty Rosa, and had also to profess his deep gratitude for such religious instruction as Harry thought fit to impart.

From that day began the downfall of Punch, now Black Sheep.

"Untrustworthy in one thing, untrustworthy in all," said Aunty Rosa, and Harry felt that Black Sheep was delivered into his hands. He would wake him up in the night to ask him why he was such a liar.

"I don't know," Punch would reply.

"Then don't you think you ought to get up and pray to God for a new heart?"

"Y-yess."

"Get out and pray, then!" And Punch would get out of bed with raging hate in his heart against all the world, seen and unseen. He was always tumbling into trouble. Harry had a knack of cross-examining him as to his day's doings, which seldom failed to lead him, sleepy and savage, into half-a-dozen contradictions – all duly reported to Aunty Rosa next morning.

"But it *wasn't* a lie," Punch would begin, charging into a laboured explanation that landed him more hopelessly in the mire. "I said that I didn't say my prayers *twice* over in the day, and *that* was on

Tuesday. *Once* I did. I *know* I did, but Harry said I didn't,'' and so forth, till the tension brought tears, and he was dismissed from the table in disgrace.

"You usen't to be as bad as this," said Judy, awe-stricken at the catalogue of Black Sheep's crimes. "Why are you so bad now?"

"I don't know," Black Sheep would reply. "I'm not, if I only wasn't bothered upside down. I knew what I *did*, and I want to say so; but Harry always makes it out different somehow, and Aunty Rosa doesn't believe a word I say. Oh, Ju! don't *you* say I'm bad too."

"Aunty Rosa says you are," said Judy. "She told the Vicar so when he came yesterday."

"Why does she tell all the people outside the house about me? It isn't fair," said Black Sheep. "When I was in Bombay, and was bad – *doing* bad, not made-up bad like this – Mamma told Papa, and Papa told me he knew, and that was all. *Outside* people didn't know too – even Meeta didn't know."

"I don't remember," said Judy wistfully. "I was all little then. Mamma was just as fond of you as she was of me, wasn't she?"

"'Course she was. So was Papa. So was everybody."

"Aunty Rosa likes me more than she does you. She says that you are a Trial and a Black Sheep, and I'm not to speak to you more than I can help."

"Always? Not outside of the times when you mustn't speak to me at all?"

Judy nodded her head mournfully. Black Sheep turned away in despair, but Judy's arms were round his neck.

"Never mind, Punch," she whispered. "I *will* speak to you just the same as ever and ever. You're my own own brother though you are – though Aunty Rosa says you're bad, and Harry says you are a little coward. He says that if I pulled your hair hard, you'd cry."

"Pull, then," said Punch.

Judy pulled gingerly.

"Pull harder – as hard as you can! There! I don't mind how much you pull it *now*. If you'll speak to me same as ever I'll let you pull it as much as you like – pull if out if you like. But I know if Harry came and stood by and made you do it I'd cry."

So the two children sealed the compact with a kiss, and Black Sheep's heart was cheered within him, and by extreme caution and careful avoidance of Harry he acquired virtue, and was allowed to read undisturbed for a week. Uncle Harry took him for walks, and consoled him with rough tenderness, never calling him Black Sheep. "It's good for you, I suppose, Punch," he used to say. "Let us sit down. I'm getting tired." His steps led him now not to the beach, but to the Cemetery of Rocklington, amid the potato-fields. For hours the grey man would sit on a tombstone, while Black Sheep would read epitaphs, and then with a sigh would stump home again.

"I shall lie there soon," said he to Black Sheep, one winter evening, when his face showed white as a worn silver coin under the light of the lych-gate. "You needn't tell Aunty Rosa."

A month later he turned sharp round, ere half a morning walk was completed, and stumped back to the house. "Put me to bed, Rosa," he muttered. "I've walked my last. The wadding has found me out."

They put him to bed, and for a fortnight the shadow of his sickness lay upon the house, and Black Sheep went to and fro unobserved. Papa had sent him some new books, and he was told to keep quiet. He retired into his own world, and was perfectly happy. Even at night his felicity was unbroken. He could lie in bed and string himself tales of travel and adventure while Harry was downstairs.

"Uncle Harry's going to die," said Judy, who now lived almost entirely with Aunty Rosa.

"I'm very sorry," said Black Sheep soberly. "He told me that a long time ago."

Aunty Rosa heard the conversation. "Will nothing check your wicked tongue?" she said angrily. There were blue circles round her eyes.

Black Sheep retreated to the nursery and read *Cometh up as a Flower* with deep and uncomprehending interest. He had been forbidden to open it on account of its "sinfulness", but the bonds of the Universe were crumbling, and Aunty Rosa was in great grief.

"I'm glad," said Black Sheep. "She's unhappy now. It wasn't a lie, though. *I* knew. He told me not to tell."

That night Black Sheep woke with a start. Harry was not in the room, and there was a sound of sobbing on the next floor. Then the voice of Uncle Harry, singing the song of the Battle of Navarino, came through the darkness:–

> Our vanship was the Asia –
> The Albion and Genoa!

"He's getting well," thought Black Sheep, who knew the song through all its seventeen verses. But the blood froze at his little heart as he thought. The voice leapt an octave, and rang shrill as a boatswain's pipe:–

> And next came on the lovely Rose,
> The Philomel, her fire-ship, closed,
> And the little *Brisk* was sore exposed
> That day at Navarino.

"That day at Navarino, Uncle Harry!" shouted Black Sheep, half wild with excitement and fear of he knew not what.

A door opened, and Aunty Rosa screamed up the staircase: "Hush! For God's sake hush, you little devil. Uncle Harry is *dead*!"

**Cometh up as a Flower**: a daring novel of 1867 by Rhoda Broughton

OPPOSITE: *The battle of Navarino, 1827, a painting by Charles Dixon.*

## THE THIRD BAG

Journeys end in lovers' meeting,
Every wise man's son doth know.

"I wonder what will happen to me now," thought Black Sheep, when semi-pagan rites peculiar to the burial of the Dead in middle-class houses had been accomplished, and Aunty Rosa, awful in black crepe, had returned to this life. "I don't think I've done anything bad that she knows of. I suppose I will soon. She will be very cross after Uncle Harry's dying, and Harry will be cross too. I'll keep in the nursery."

Unfortunately for Punch's plans, it was decided that he should be sent to a day-school which Harry attended. This meant a morning walk with Harry, and perhaps an evening one; but the prospect of freedom in the interval was refreshing. "Harry'll tell everything I do, but I won't do anything," said Black Sheep. Fortified with this virtuous resolution, he went to school only to find that Harry's version of his character had preceded him, and that life was a burden in consequence. He took stock of his associates. Some of them were unclean, some of them talked in dialect, many dropped their h's, and there were two Jews and a negro, or some one quite as dark, in the assembly. "That's a *hubshi*," said Black Sheep to himself. "Even Meeta used to laugh at a *hubshi*. I don't think this is a proper place." He was indignant for at least an hour, till he reflected that any expostulation on his part would be by Aunty Rosa construed into "showing off", and that Harry would tell the boys.

"How do you like school?" said Aunty Rosa at the end of the day.

"I think it is a very nice place," said Punch quietly.

"I suppose you warned the boys of Black Sheep's character?" said Aunty Rosa to Harry.

"Oh yes," said the censor of Black Sheep's morals. "They know all about him."

*South Parade, Southsea.*

"If I was with my father," said Black Sheep, stung to the quick, "I shouldn't *speak* to those boys. He wouldn't let me. They live in shops. I saw them go into shops – where their fathers live and sell things."

"You're too good for that school, are you?" said Aunty Rosa, with a bitter smile. "You ought to be grateful, Black Sheep, that those boys speak to you at all. It isn't every school that takes little liars."

Harry did not fail to make much capital out of Black Sheep's ill-considered remark; with the result that several boys, including the *hubshi*, demonstrated to Black Sheep the eternal equality of the human race by smacking his head, and his consolation from Aunty Rosa was that it "served him right for being vain". He learned, however, to keep his opinions to himself, and by propitiating Harry in carrying books and the like to get a little peace. His existence was not too joyful. From nine till twelve he was at school, and from two to four, except on Saturdays. In the evenings he was sent down into the nursery to prepare his lessons for the next day, and every night came the dreaded cross-questionings at Harry's hand. Of Judy he saw but little. She was deeply religious – at six years of age Religion is easy to come by – and sorely divided between her natural love for Black Sheep and her love for Aunty Rosa, who could do no wrong.

The lean woman returned that love with interest, and Judy, when she dared, took advantage of this for the remission of Black Sheep's penalties. Failures in lessons at school were punished at home by a week without reading other than school-books, and Harry brought the news of such a failure with glee. Further, Black Sheep was then bound to repeat his lessons at bedtime to Harry, who generally succeeded in making him break down, and consoled him by gloomiest forebodings for the morrow. Harry was at once spy, practical joker, inquisitor, and Aunty Rosa's deputy executioner. He filled his many posts to admiration. From his actions, now that Uncle Harry was dead, there was no appeal. Black Sheep had not been permitted to keep any self-respect at school: at home he was, of course, utterly discredited, and grateful for any pity that the servant girls – they changed frequently at Downe Lodge because they, too, were liars – might show. "You're just fit to row in the same boat with Black Sheep," was a sentiment that each new Jane or Eliza might expect to hear, before a month was over, from Aunty Rosa's lips; and Black Sheep was used to ask new girls whether they had yet been compared to him. Harry was "Master Harry" in their mouths; Judy was officially "Miss Judy"; but Black Sheep was never anything more than Black Sheep *tout court*.

As time went on and the memory of Papa and Mamma became wholly overlaid by the unpleasant task of writing them letters, under Aunty Rosa's eye, each Sunday, Black Sheep forgot what manner of life he had led in the beginning of things. Even Judy's appeals to "try and remember about Bombay" failed to quicken him.

"I can't remember," he said. "I know I used to give orders and Mamma kissed me."

"Aunty Rosa will kiss you if you are good," pleaded Judy.

"Ugh! I don't want to be kissed by Aunty Rosa. She'd say I was doing it to get something more to eat."

The weeks lengthened into months, and the holidays came; but just before the holidays Black Sheep fell into deadly sin.

Among the many boys whom Harry had incited to "punch Black Sheep's head because he daren't hit back," was one more aggravating than the rest, who, in an unlucky moment, fell upon Black Sheep when Harry was not near. The blows stung, and Black Sheep struck back at random with all the power at his command. The boy dropped and whimpered. Black Sheep was astounded at his own act, but, feeling the unresisting body under him, shook it with both his hands in blind fury and then began to throttle his enemy; meaning honestly to slay him. There was a scuffle, and Black Sheep was torn off the body by Harry and some colleagues, and cuffed home tingling but exultant. Aunty Rosa was out: pending her arrival, Harry set himself to lecture Black Sheep on the sin of murder – which he described as the offence of Cain.

"Why didn't you fight him fair? What did you hit him when he was down for, you little cur?"

Black Sheep looked up at Harry's throat and then at a knife on the dinner-table.

*Georgiana Burne-Jones, Kipling's maternal aunt, photographed in 1920. A blessed month each year was spent with her at The Grange, the Burne-Jones house in Chelsea. But he kept his misery a secret even from beloved Aunt Georgie: "badly-treated children have a clear notion of what they are likely to get if they betray the secrets of a prison-house before they are clear of it."*

"I don't understand," he said wearily. "You always set him on me and told me I was a coward when I blubbed. Will you leave me alone until Aunty Rosa comes in? She'll beat me if you tell her I ought to be beaten; so it's all right."

"It's all wrong," said Harry magisterially. "You nearly killed him, and I shouldn't wonder if he dies."

"Will he die?" said Black Sheep.

"I daresay," said Harry, "and then you'll be hanged, and go to Hell."

"All right," said Black Sheep, picking up the table-knife. "Then I'll kill *you* now. You say things and do things and – and *I* don't know how things happen, and you never leave me alone – and I don't care *what* happens!"

He ran at the boy with the knife, and Harry fled upstairs to his room, promising Black Sheep the finest thrashing in the world when Aunty Rosa returned. Black Sheep sat at the bottom of the stairs, the table-knife in his hand, and wept for that he had not killed Harry. The servant-girl came up from the kitchen, took the knife away, and consoled him. But Black Sheep was beyond consolation. He would be badly beaten by Aunty Rosa; then there would be another beating at Harry's hands; then Judy would not be allowed to speak to him; then the tale would be told at school, and then –

There was no one to help and no one to care, and the best way out of the business was by death. A knife would hurt, but Aunty Rosa had told him, a year ago, that if he sucked paint he would die. He went into the nursery, unearthed the now disused Noah's Ark, and sucked the paint off as many animals as remained. It tasted abominable, but he had licked Noah's Dove clean by the time Aunty Rosa and Judy returned. He went upstairs and greeted them with: "Please, Aunty Rosa, I believe I've nearly killed a boy at school, and I've tried to kill Harry, and when you've done all about God and Hell, will you beat me and get it over?"

The tale of the assault as told by Harry could only be explained on the ground of possession by the Devil. Wherefore Black Sheep was not only most excellently beaten, once by Aunty Rosa and once, when thoroughly cowed down, by Harry, but he was further prayed for at family prayers, together with Jane who had stolen a cold rissole from the pantry, and snuffled audibly as her sin was brought before the Throne of Grace. Black Sheep was sore and stiff but triumphant. He would die that very night and be rid of them all. No, he would ask for no forgiveness from Harry, and at bed-time would stand no questioning at Harry's hands, even though addressed as "Young Cain".

"I've been beaten," said he, "and I've done other things. I don't care what I do. If you speak to me to-night, Harry, I'll get out and try to kill you. Now you can kill me if you like."

Harry took his bed into the spare room, and Black Sheep lay down to die.

It may be that the makers of Noah's Arks know that their animals are likely to find their way into young mouths, and paint them accordingly. Certain it is that the common, weary next morning broke through the windows and found Black Sheep quite well and a good deal ashamed of himself, but richer by the knowledge that he could, in extremity, secure himself against Harry for the future.

When he descended to breakfast on the first day of the holidays, he was greeted with the news that Harry, Aunty Rosa, and Judy were going away to Brighton, while Black Sheep was to stay in the house with the servant. His latest outbreak suited Aunty Rosa's plans admirably. It gave her good excuse for leaving the extra boy behind. Papa in Bombay, who really seemed to know a young sinner's wants to the hour, sent, that week, a package of new books. And with these, and the society of Jane on board-wages, Black Sheep was left alone for a month.

The books lasted for ten days. They were eaten too quickly in long gulps of twelve hours at a time. Then came days of doing absolutely nothing, of dreaming dreams and marching imaginary armies up and downstairs, of counting the number of banisters, and of measuring the length and breadth of every room in handspans – fifty down the side, thirty across, and fifty back again. Jane made many friends, and, after receiving Black Sheep's assurance that he would not tell of her

*Kipling's uncle, the artist Edward Burne-Jones; a self-portrait on an envelope sent to Katie Lewis in 1883. Whether Rudyard and Trix were treated to such epistolary fun is not clear. Although Burne-Jones and William Morris – "Uncle Topsy" – were kind to the Kipling children, they were slightly remote figures. Of all the beautiful objects at The Grange, the young Rudyard was most impressed by the "open-work iron bell-pull" at the gate. "When I had a house of my own, and The Grange was emptied of meaning, I begged for and was given that bell-pull for my entrance, in the hope that other children might also feel happy when they rang it."*

absences, went out daily for long hours. Black Sheep would follow the rays of the sinking sun from the kitchen to the dining-room and thence upward to his own bedroom until all was grey dark, and he ran down to the kitchen fire and read by its light. He was happy in that he was left alone and could read as much as he pleased. But, later, he grew afraid of the shadows of window-curtains and the flapping of doors and the creaking of shutters. He went out into the garden, and the rustling of the laurel-bushes frightened him.

He was glad when they all returned – Aunty Rosa, Harry, and Judy – full of news, and Judy laden with gifts. Who could help loving loyal little Judy? In return for all her merry babblement, Black Sheep confided to her that the distance from the hall-door to the top of the first landing was exactly one hundred and eighty-four handspans. He had found it out himself.

Then the old life recommenced; but with a difference, and a new sin. To his other iniquities Black Sheep had now added a phenomenal clumsiness – he was as unfit to trust in action as he was in word. He himself could not account for spilling everything he touched, upsetting glasses as he put his hand out, and bumping his head against doors that were manifestly shut. There was a grey haze upon all his world, and it narrowed month by month, until at last it left Black Sheep almost alone with the flapping curtains that were so like ghosts, and the nameless terrors of broad daylight that were only coats on pegs after all.

Holidays came and holidays went, and Black Sheep was taken to see many people whose faces were all exactly alike; was beaten when occasion demanded, and tortured by Harry on all possible occasions; but defended by Judy through good and evil report, though she hereby drew upon herself the wrath of Aunty Rosa.

The weeks were interminable, and Papa and Mamma were clean forgotten. Harry had left school and was a clerk in a Banking-Office. Freed from his presence, Black Sheep resolved that he should no longer be deprived of his allowance of pleasure-reading. Consequently when he failed at school he reported that all was well, and conceived a large contempt for Aunty Rosa as he saw how easy it was to deceive her. "She says I'm a little liar when I don't tell lies, and now I do, she doesn't know," thought Black Sheep. Aunty Rosa had credited him in the past with petty cunning and stratagem that had never entered into his head. By the light of the sordid knowledge that she had revealed to him he paid her back full tale. In a household where the most innocent of his motives, his natural yearning for a little affection, had been interpreted into a desire for more bread and jam, or to ingratiate himself with strangers and so put Harry into the background, his work was easy. Aunty Rosa could penetrate certain kinds of hypocrisy, but not all. He set his child's wits against hers and was no more beaten. It grew monthly more and more of a trouble to read the school-books, and even the pages of the open-print storybooks danced and were dim. So Black Sheep brooded in the shadows that fell about him and cut him off from the world, inventing horrible punishments for "dear Harry", or plotting another line of the tangled web of deception that he wrapped round Aunty Rosa.

Then the crash came and the cobwebs were broken. It was impossible to foresee everything. Aunty Rosa made personal inquiries as to Black Sheep's progress and received information that startled her. Step by step, with a delight as keen as when she convicted an underfed housemaid of the theft of cold meats, she followed the trail of Black Sheep's delinquencies. For weeks and weeks, in order to escape banishment from the bookshelves, he had made a fool of Aunty Rosa, of Harry, of God, of all the world! Horrible, most horrible, and evidence of an utterly depraved mind.

Black Sheep counted the cost. "It will only be one big beating and then she'll put a card with 'Liar' on my back, same as she did before. Harry will whack me and pray for me, and she will pray for me at prayers and tell me I'm a Child of the Devil and give me hymns to learn. But I've done all my reading and she never knew. She'll say she knew all along. She's an old liar too," said he.

For three days Black Sheep was shut in his own bedroom – to prepare his heart. "That means two beatings. One at school and one here. *That* one will hurt most." And it fell even as he thought. He was thrashed at school before the Jews and the *hubshi* for the heinous crime of carrying home false reports of progress. He was thrashed at home by Aunty Rosa on the same count, and then the placard was produced. Aunty Rosa stitched it between his shoulders and bade him go for a walk with it upon him.

"If you make me do that," said Black Sheep very quietly, "I shall burn this house down, and perhaps I'll kill you. I don't know whether I *can* kill you – you're so bony – but I'll try."

No punishment followed this blasphemy, though Black Sheep held himself ready to work his way to Aunty Rosa's withered throat, and grip there till he was beaten off. Perhaps Aunty Rosa was afraid, for Black Sheep, having reached the Nadir of Sin, bore himself with a new recklessness.

In the midst of all the trouble there came a visitor from over the seas to Downe Lodge, who knew Papa and Mamma, and was commissioned to see Punch and Judy. Black Sheep was sent to the drawing-room and charged into a solid tea-table laden with china.

"Gently, gently, little man," said the visitor, turning Black Sheep's face to the light slowly. "What's that big bird on the palings?"

"What bird?" asked Black Sheep.

The visitor looked deep down into Black Sheep's eyes for half a minute, and then said suddenly: "Good God, the little chap's nearly blind!"

It was a most business-like visitor. He gave orders, on his own responsibility, that Black Sheep was not to go to school or open a

*"Punch", sketched by Kipling on the fair copy of this story given to Edmonia Hill, in whose home in Allahabad it was written. The incident of the "Liar" placard may possibly have been suggested by* David Copperfield, *though in later years both Rudyard and Trix remembered it in circumstantial detail.*

book until Mamma came home. "She'll be here in three weeks, as you know of course," said he, "and I'm Inverarity Sahib. I ushered you into this wicked world, young man, and a nice use you seem to have made of your time. You must do nothing whatever. Can you do that?"

"Yes," said Punch in a dazed way. He had known that Mamma was coming. There was a chance, then, of another beating. Thank Heaven, Papa wasn't coming too. Aunty Rosa had said of late that he ought to be beaten by a man.

For the next three weeks Black Sheep was strictly allowed to do nothing. He spent his time in the old nursery looking at the broken toys, for all of which account must be rendered to Mamma. Aunty Rosa hit him over the hands if even a wooden boat were broken. But that sin was of small importance compared to the other revelations, so darkly hinted at by Aunty Rosa. "When your Mother comes, and hears what I have to tell her, she may appreciate you properly," she said grimly, and mounted guard over Judy lest that small maiden should attempt to comfort her brother, to the peril of her soul.

And Mamma came – in a four-wheeler – fluttered with tender excitement. Such a Mamma! She was young, frivolously young, and beautiful, with delicately-flushed cheeks, eyes that shone like stars, and a voice that needed no appeal of outstretched arms to draw little ones to her heart. Judy ran straight to her, but Black Sheep hesitated. Could this wonder be "showing off"? She would not put out her arms when she knew of his crimes. Meantime was it possible that by fondling she wanted to get anything out of Black Sheep? Only all his love and all his confidence; but that Black Sheep did not know. Aunty Rosa withdrew and left Mamma, kneeling between her children, half laughing, half crying, in the very hall where Punch and Judy had wept five years before.

"Well, chicks, do you remember me?"

"No," said Judy frankly, "but I said, 'God bless Papa and Mamma' ev'vy night."

"A little," said Black Sheep. "Remember I wrote to you every week, anyhow. That isn't to show off, but 'cause of what comes afterwards."

"What comes after? What should come after, my darling boy?" And she drew him to her again. He came awkwardly, with many angles. "Not used to petting," said the quick Mother-soul. "The girl is."

"She's too little to hurt any one," thought Black Sheep, "and if I said I'd kill her, she'd be afraid. I wonder what Aunty Rosa will tell."

There was a constrained late dinner, at the end of which Mamma picked up Judy and put her to bed with endearments manifold. Faithless little Judy had shown her defection from Aunty Rosa already. And that lady resented it bitterly. Black Sheep rose to leave the room.

*Lockwood Kipling, "not only a mine of knowledge and help, but a humorous, tolerant, and expert fellow-craftsman". This story apart, Rudyard submitted most of his work to his father's judgement, accepting his advice, for instance, to abandon the Indian novel* Mother Maturin *from which he later quarried* Kim. *It was Lockwood who comforted Kipling after the reception of his precocious* Story of the Gadsbys, *with the words, "It wasn't all so dam' bad, Ruddy."*

"Come and say good-night," said Aunty Rosa, offering a withered cheek.

"Huh!" said Black Sheep. "I never kiss you, and I'm not going to show off. Tell that woman what I've done, and see what she says."

Black Sheep climbed into bed feeling that he had lost Heaven after a glimpse through the gates. In half an hour "that woman" was bending over him. Black Sheep flung up his right arm. It wasn't fair to come and hit him in the dark. Even Aunty Rosa never tried that. But no blow followed.

"Are you showing off? I won't tell you anything more than Aunty Rosa has, and *she* doesn't know everything," said Black Sheep as clearly as he could for the arms round his neck.

"Oh, my son – my little, little son! It was my fault – *my* fault, darling – and yet how could we help it? Forgive me, Punch." The voice died out in a broken whisper, and two hot tears fell on Black Sheep's forehead.

"Has she been making you cry too?" he asked. "You should see Jane cry. But you're nice, and Jane is a Born Liar – Aunty Rosa says so."

"Hush, Punch, hush! My boy, don't talk like that. Try to love me a little bit – a little bit. You don't know how I want it. Punch-*baba*, come back to me! I am your Mother – your own Mother – and never mind the rest. I know – yes, I know, dear. It doesn't matter now. Punch, won't you care for me a little?"

It is astonishing how much petting a big boy of ten can endure when he is quite sure that there is no one to laugh at him. Black Sheep had never been made much of before, and here was this beautiful woman treating him – Black Sheep, the Child of the Devil and the inheritor of undying flame – as though he were a small God.

"I care for you a great deal, Mother dear," he whispered at last, "and I'm glad you've come back; but are you sure Aunty Rosa told you everything?"

"Everything. What *does* it matter? But –" the voice broke with a sob that was also laughter – "Punch, my poor, dear, half-blind darling, don't you think it was a little foolish of you?"

"*No*. It saved a lickin'."

Mamma shuddered and slipped away in the darkness to write a long letter to Papa. Here is an extract:–

> ... Judy is a dear, plump little prig who adores the woman, and wears with as much gravity as her religious opinions – only eight, Jack! – a venerable horse-hair atrocity which she calls her Bustle! I have just burnt it, and the child is asleep in my bed as I write. She will come to me at once. Punch I cannot quite understand. He is well nourished, but seems to have been worried into a system of small deceptions which the woman magnifies into deadly sins. Don't you recollect our own upbringing, dear, when the Fear of the Lord was so often the beginning of falsehood? I shall win Punch to me before long. I am

*Alice Kipling, a gifted and witty woman who supplied Rudyard with several famous lines, including "What should they know of England, who only England know?" She justified her "shrivelling" criticism of his work with the words, "There's no Mother in Poetry, my dear."*

taking the children away into the country to get them to know me, and, on the whole, I am content, or shall be when you come home, dear boy, then, thank God, we shall be all under one roof again at last!

Three months later, Punch, no longer Black Sheep, has discovered that he is the veritable owner of a real, live, lovely Mamma, who is also a sister, comforter, and friend, and that he must protect her till the Father comes home. Deception does not suit the part of a protector, and, when one can do anything without question, where is the use of deception?

"Mother would be awfully cross if you walked through that ditch," says Judy, continuing a conversation.

"Mother's never angry," says Punch. "She'd just say, 'You're a little *pagal*'; and that's not nice, but I'll show."

Punch walks through the ditch and mires himself to the knees. "Mother, dear," he shouts, "I'm just as dirty as I can pos-*sib*-ly be!"

"Then change your clothes as quickly as you pos-*sib*-ly can!" Mother's clear voice rings out from the house. "And don't be a little *pagal*!"

"There! 'Told you so," says Punch. "It's all different now, and we are just as much Mother's as if she had never gone."

Not altogether, O Punch, for when young lips have drunk deep of the bitter waters of Hate, Suspicion, and Despair, all the Love in the world will not wholly take away that knowledge; though it may turn darkened eyes for a while to the light, and teach Faith where no Faith was.

**pagal:** fool

RIGHT: *Rudyard Kipling drawn by his father shortly after writing "Baa Baa, Black Sheep", and just before he left India for good. Kipling greatly liked this drawing.*

OPPOSITE: *Rudyard's sister Trix, Alice MacDonald Fleming, the "Judy" of this story.*

# Schooldays

At the age of twelve, after rescue from Southsea, Rudyard was sent to public school. The United Services College, Westward Ho!, near Bideford in North Devon, had been founded in 1874 to provide an inexpensive education which prepared boys for the army. The atmosphere was not military or jingoistic, but spartan and surprisingly unstuffy. The headmaster, Cormell Price, was a family friend, and encouraged Kipling's literary interests, giving him the free run of his extensive library, as did the English teacher Crofts. At first, Kipling was once again bullied and unhappy, but he came to enjoy and admire much in the school even while he and his friends George Beresford ("M'Turk") and Lionel Dunsterville ("Stalky") rebelled against its petty restrictions. Kipling used his school memories as the basis of *Stalky & Co.* in 1899. Subsequently, both Beresford and Dunsterville added their accounts to his. The Stalky stories are heightened reminiscence rather than strict autobiography. They reflect daydream life more closely than actual occurrences, but are perhaps not less accurate for that. Their realism, especially their cool acceptance of the boys' own ideas of morality, was a shocking revision of the accepted school story. The tinge of sadism has repelled some readers; others find the harsh edge refreshing. The stories are certainly full of verve, reflecting Kipling's fascination with the blurred edge between speech, chant and incantation. He describes, for instance, how *Uncle Remus* fever swept the school: "The book was amazing, and full of quotations that one could hurl like javelins." It was at school that Kipling, known as "Giglamps" or "Gigger" because of the glasses required by his damaged eyesight, made his first serious attempts at writing. Cormell Price established a school magazine for him to edit and fill with his work. Before writing *Stalky*, Kipling described Westward Ho! in his story "The Brushwood Boy", and in an essay of 1893, "An English School", from which the following prose extract is taken. The poem, a translation of Horace's ode "Donec gratus eram tibi" into Devonshire dialect, appeared in the tenth issue of the school magazine in 1882. It was conceived in a facetious spirit, to fend off punishment for ill-prepared work, but finished, surely, with the triumphant glee of a born writer who has at last understood the nature of his talent.

The institution that caused some more excitement was the School paper. Three of the boys, who had moved up the School side by side for four years and were allies in all things, started the notion as soon as they came to the dignity of a study of their own with a door that would lock. The other two told the third boy what to write, and held the staircase against invaders.

It was a real printed paper of eight pages, and at first the printer was more thoroughly ignorant of type-setting, and the Editor was more completely ignorant of proof-reading, than any printer and any Editor that ever was. It was printed off by a gas engine; and even the engine despised its work, for one day it fell through the floor of the shop, and crashed – still working furiously – into the cellar.

The paper came out at odd times and seasons, but every time it came out there was sure to be trouble, because the Editor was learning for the first time how sweet and good and profitable it is – and how nice it looks on the page – to make fun of people in actual print.

For instance, there was friction among the study-fags once, and the Editor wrote a descriptive account of the Lower School – the classes whence the fags were drawn – their manners and customs, their ways of cooking half-plucked sparrows and imperfectly cleaned blackbirds at the gas-jets on a rusty nib, and their fights over sloe-jam made in a gallipot. It was an absolutely truthful article, but the Lower School knew nothing about truth, and would not even consider it as literature.

It is less safe to write a study of an entire class than to discuss individuals one by one; but apart from the fact that boys throw books and inkpots with a straighter eye, there is very little difference between the behaviour of grown-up people and that of children.

In those days the Editor had not learned this; so when the study below the Editorial study threw coal at the Editorial legs and kicked in the panels of the door, because of personal paragraphs in the last number, the Editorial Staff – and there never was so loyal and hard-fighting a staff – fried fat bacon till there was half an inch of grease in the pan, and let the greasy chunks down at the end of a string to bob against and defile the lower study windows.

*"He saw himself already controlling* The Times*", a drawing by L. Raven Hill from the original publication of the Stalky stories in the* Windsor *magazine in 1899.*

*"The Head fantastically attired in old tweeds and a deer-stalker." By coincidence or not, Raven Hill's drawing looks very like Cormell Price in Beresford's schoolboy sketches. Price was a friend of Burne-Jones, and this family connection ensured his keen interest in Rudyard. In later years he and Kipling were close friends, and* Stalky & Co. *is dedicated to him. Kipling was grateful that "the dear fellow never gave me away".*

When that lower study – and there never was a public so low and unsympathetic as that lower study – looked out to see what was frosting their window-panes, the Editorial Staff emptied the hot fat on their heads, and it stayed in their hair for days and days, wearing shiny to the very last.

The boy who suggested this sort of warfare was then reading a sort of magazine, called *Fors Clavigera*, which he did not in the least understand – it was not exactly a boy's paper – and when the lower study had scraped some of the fat off their heads and were thundering with knobby pokers on the door-lock, this boy began to chant pieces of the *Fors* as a war-song, and to show that his mind was free from low distractions. He was an extraordinary person, and the only boy in the School who had a genuine contempt for his masters. There was no affectation in his quiet insolence. He honestly *did* despise them; and threats that made us all wince only caused him to put his head a little on one side and watch the master as a sort of natural curiosity.

The worst of this was that his allies had to take their share of his punishments, for they lived as communists and socialists hope to live one day, when everybody is good. They were bad, as bad as they dared to be, but their possessions were in common, absolutely. And when "the Study" was out of funds they took the most respectable clothes in possession of the Syndicate, and leaving the owner one Sunday and one weekday suit, sold the rest in Bideford town. Later, when there was another crisis, it was *not* the respectable one's watch that was taken by force for the good of the Study and pawned, and never redeemed.

Later still, money came into the Syndicate honestly, for a London paper that did not know with whom it was dealing, published and paid a whole guinea for some verses that one of the boys had written and sent up under a *nom de plume*, and the Study caroused on chocolate and condensed milk and pilchards and Devonshire cream, and voted poetry a much sounder business than it looks.

## Donec Gratus Eram

*He:* So long as 'twuz me alone
    An' there wasn't no other chaps,
    I was praoud as a King on 'is throne –
    Happier tu, per'aps.

*She:* So long as 'twuz only I
    An' there wasn't no other she
    Yeou cared for so much – surely
    I was glad as glad could be.

*He:* But now I'm in lovv with Jane Pritt –
    She can play the piano, she can;
    An' if dyin' 'ud 'elp 'er a bit
    I'd die laike a man.

*She:* Yeou'm like me. I'm in lovv with young Frye –
    Him as lives out tu Appledore Quay;
    An' if dyin' 'ud 'elp 'im I'd die –
    Twice ovver for he.

*He:* But s'posin' I threwed up Jane
    An' niver went walkin' with she –
    An' come back to yeou again –
    How 'ud that be?

*She:* Frye's sober. Yeou've allus done badly –
    An' yeou shifts like cut net-floats, yeou du:
    But – I'd throw that young Frye ovver gladly
    An' lovv 'ee right thru!

*Lockwood Kipling made this drawing of his son following a procession of great poets – Browning, Tennyson, Shelley, Shakespeare, Dante and Homer – as a frontispiece for the manuscript book in which Rudyard wrote the verses privately published by his mother as* Schoolboy Lyrics *in 1881. Kipling burnt the book, but salvaged his father's "scandalous sepia-sketch".*

# The City of Dreadful Night

James Thomson's poem "The City of Dreadful Night" was a favourite of Kipling's, and he used the title both for this flashily effective portrait of "the heat-tortured city of Lahore and seventy thousand men and women sleeping in the moonlight", and for a series of reports from Calcutta in 1888. The essay printed here was written in August 1885, when Kipling was not yet twenty. It was printed in *The Civil and Military Gazette*, on which Kipling served an exacting journalistic apprenticeship as sub-editor. His return to India in 1881 delighted Kipling. He discovered in his parents two loving friends who from then until their deaths were the first and most valued audience for his work. He discovered in journalism the discipline of working to a deadline. He discovered in the Anglo-Indian community a ready audience for his apprentice verses and stories. And he discovered in the polite intrigues of Simla, in the barracks of Mian Mir and in the back streets and low haunts of Lahore a rich vibrant world to people his imagination. When, in Kipling's expressive phrase, the night got into his head, "I would wander till dawn in all manner of odd places – liquor-shops, gambling- and opium-dens, which are not a bit mysterious, wayside entertainments such as puppet-shows, native dances; or in and about the narrow gullies under the Mosque of Wazir Khan for the sheer sake of looking."

The dense wet heat that hung over the face of land, like a blanket, prevented all hope of sleep in the first instance. The cicadas helped the heat, and the yelling jackals the cicadas. It was impossible to sit still in the dark, empty, echoing house and watch the punkah beat the dead air. So, at ten o'clock of the night, I set my walking-stick on end in the middle of the garden, and waited to see how it would fall. It pointed directly down the moonlit road that leads to the City of Dreadful Night. The sound of its fall disturbed a hare. She limped from her form and ran across to a disused Mahomedan burial-ground, where the jawless skulls and rough-butted shank-bones, heartlessly exposed by the July rains, glimmered like mother o' pearl on the rain-channelled soil. The heated air and the heavy earth had driven the very dead upward for coolness' sake. The hare limped on; snuffed curiously at a fragment of a smoke-stained lamp-shard, and died out, in the shadow of a clump of tamarisk trees.

The mat-weaver's hut under the lee of the Hindu temple was full of sleeping men who lay like sheeted corpses. Overhead blazed the unwinking eye of the Moon. Darkness gives at least a false impression of coolness. It was hard not to believe that the flood of light from above was warm. Not so hot as the Sun, but still sickly warm, and heating the heavy air beyond what was our due. Straight as a bar of polished steel ran the road to the City of Dreadful Night; and on either side of the road lay corpses disposed on beds in fantastic attitudes – one hundred and seventy bodies of men. Some shrouded all in white with bound-up mouths; some naked and black as ebony in the strong light; and one – that lay face upwards with dropped jaw, far away from the others – silvery white and ashen grey.

"A leper asleep; and the remainder wearied coolies, servants, small shopkeepers, and drivers from the hack-stand hard by. The scene – a main approach to Lahore city, and the night a warm one in August." This was all that there was to be seen; but by no means all that one could see. The witchery of the moonlight was everywhere; and the world was horribly changed. The long line of the naked dead, flanked by the rigid silver statue, was not pleasant to look upon. It was made up of men alone. Were the womenkind, then, forced to sleep in the shelter of the stifling mud-huts as best they might? The fretful wail of a child from a low mud-roof answered the question. Where the children are the mothers must be also to look after them. They need care on these sweltering nights. A black little bullet-head peeped over the coping, and a thin – a painfully thin – brown leg was slid over on to the gutter pipe. There was a sharp clink of glass bracelets; a woman's arm showed for an instant above the parapet, twined itself round the lean little neck, and the child was dragged back, protesting, to the shelter of the bedstead. His thin, high-pitched shriek died out in the thick air almost as soon as it was raised; for even the children of the soil found it too hot to weep.

More corpses; more stretches of moonlit, white road; a string of sleeping camels at rest by the wayside; a vision of scudding jackals; ekka-ponies asleep – the harness still on their backs, and the brass-studded country carts, winking in the moonlight – and again more corpses. Wherever a grain cart atilt, a tree trunk, a sawn log, a couple of bamboos and a few handfuls of thatch cast a shadow, the ground is covered with them. They lie – some face downwards, arms folded, in the dust; some with clasped hands flung up above their heads; some curled up dog-wise; some thrown like limp gunny-bags over the side of the grain carts; and some bowed with their brows on their knees in the full glare of the Moon. It would be a comfort if they were only given to snoring; but they are not, and the likeness to corpses is unbroken in all respects save one. The lean dogs snuff at them and turn away. Here and there a tiny child lies on his father's bedstead, and a protecting arm is thrown round it in every instance. But, for the most part, the children sleep with their mothers on the house-tops. Yellow-skinned white-toothed pariahs are not to be trusted within reach of brown bodies.

A stifling hot blast from the mouth of the Delhi Gate nearly ends my resolution of entering the City of Dreadful Night at this hour. It is a compound of all evil savours, animal and vegetable, that a walled city can brew in a day and a night. The temperature within the motionless groves of plantain and orange-trees outside the city walls seems chilly by comparison. Heaven help all sick persons and young children within the city to-night! The high house-walls are still

*A sketch by Lockwood Kipling.*

radiating heat savagely, and from obscure side gullies fetid breezes eddy that ought to poison a buffalo. But the buffaloes do not heed. A drove of them are parading the vacant main street; stopping now and then to lay their ponderous muzzles against the closed shutters of a grain-dealer's shop, and to blow thereon like grampuses.

Then silence follows – the silence that is full of the night noises of a great city. A stringed instrument of some kind is just, and only just audible. High overhead some one throws open a window, and the rattle of the woodwork echoes down the empty street. On one of the roofs a hookah is in full blast; and the men are talking softly as the pipe gutters. A little farther on the noise of conversation is more distinct. A slit of light shows itself between the sliding shutters of a shop. Inside, a stubble-bearded, weary-eyed trader is balancing his account-books among the bales of cotton prints that surround him. Three sheeted figures bear him company, and throw in a remark from time to time. First he makes an entry, then a remark; then passes the back of his hand across his streaming forehead. The heat in the built-in street is fearful. Inside the shops it must be almost unendurable. But the work goes on steadily; entry, guttural growl, and uplifted hand-stroke succeeding each other with the precision of clock-work.

A policeman – turbanless and fast asleep – lies across the road on the way to the Mosque of Wazir Khan. A bar of moonlight falls

*A watercolour drawing by Lockwood Kipling.*

OFT IN THE STILLY NIGHT.
MOORE.

PUNKA-WALA

N. INDIA.

across the forehead and eyes of the sleeper, but he never stirs. It is close upon midnight, and the heat seems to be increasing. The open square in front of the Mosque is crowded with corpses; and a man must pick his way carefully for fear of treading on them. The moonlight stripes the Mosque's high front of coloured enamel work in broad diagonal bands; and each separate dreaming pigeon in the niches and corners of the masonry throws a squab little shadow. Sheeted ghosts rise up wearily from their pallets, and flit into the dark depths of the building. Is it possible to climb to the top of the great Minars, and thence to look down on the city? At all events the attempt is worth making, and the chances are that the door of the staircase will be unlocked. Unlocked it is; but a deeply sleeping janitor lies across the threshold, face turned to the Moon. A rat dashes out of his turban at the sound of approaching footsteps. The man grunts, opens his eyes for a minute, turns round, and goes to sleep again. All the heat of a decade of fierce Indian summers is stored in the pitch-black, polished walls of the corkscrew staircase. Half-way up there is something alive, warm, and feathery; and it snores. Driven from step to step as it catches the sound of my advance, it flutters to the top and reveals itself as a yellow-eyed, angry kite. Dozens of kites are asleep on this and the other Minars, and on the

*The "growling, flaring, creed-drunk city" of Lahore, from the Mosque of Wazir Khan, Kipling's vantage point in this article. A photograph by Bourne and Shepherd of Calcutta.*

*"Kuppeleen Sahib": a confident Kipling pictured in Simla in 1886.*

domes below. There is the shadow of a cool, or at least a less sultry breeze at this height; and, refreshed thereby, turn to look on the City of Dreadful Night.

Doré might have drawn it! Zola could describe it – this spectacle of sleeping thousands in the moonlight and in the shadow of the Moon. The roof-tops are crammed with men, women, and children; and the air is full of undistinguishable noises. They are restless in the City of Dreadful Night; and small wonder. The marvel is that they can even breathe. If you gaze intently at the multitude you can see that they are almost as uneasy as a daylight crowd; but the tumult is subdued. Everywhere, in the strong light, you can watch the sleepers turning to and fro; shifting their beds and again resettling them. In the pit-like courtyards of the houses there is the same movement.

The pitiless Moon shows it all. Shows, too, the plains outside the city, and here and there a hand's-breadth of the Ravee without the walls. Shows lastly, a splash of glittering silver on a house-top almost directly below the mosque Minar. Some poor soul has risen to throw a jar of water over his fevered body; the tinkle of the falling water strikes faintly on the ear. Two or three other men, in far-off corners of the City of Dreadful Night, follow his example, and the water flashes like heliographic signals. A small cloud passes over the face of the Moon, and the city and its inhabitants – clear-drawn in black and white before – fade into masses of black and deeper black. Still the unrestful noise continues, the sigh of a great city overwhelmed with the heat, and of a people seeking in vain for rest. It is only the lower-class women who sleep on the house-tops. What must the torment be in the latticed zenanas, where a few lamps are still twinkling? There are footfalls in the court below. It is the *Muezzin* – faithful minister; but he ought to have been here an hour ago to tell the Faithful that prayer is better than sleep – the sleep that will not come to the city.

The *Muezzin* fumbles for a moment with the door of one of the Minars, disappears awhile, and a bull-like roar – a magnificent bass thunder – tells that he has reached the top of the Minar. They must hear the cry to the banks of the shrunken Ravee itself! Even across the courtyard it is almost overpowering. The cloud drifts by and shows him outlined in black against the sky, hands laid upon his ears, and broad chest heaving with the play of his lungs – "Allah ho Akbar"; then a pause while another *Muezzin* somewhere in the direction of the Golden Temple takes up the call – "Allah ho Akbar". Again and again; four times in all; and from the bedsteads a dozen men have risen up already – "I bear witness that there is no God but God." What a splendid cry it is, the proclamation of the creed that brings men out of their beds by scores at midnight! Once again he thunders through the same phrase, shaking with the vehemence of his own voice; and then, far and near, the night air rings with "Mahomed is the Prophet of God." It is as though he were flinging his defiance to the far-off horizon, where the summer lightning plays and leaps like a bared sword. Every *Muezzin* in the city is in full cry, and some men on the roof-tops are beginning to kneel. A long pause precedes the last cry, "La ilaha Illallah", and the silence closes up on it, as the ram on the head of a cotton-bale.

The *Muezzin* stumbles down the dark stairway grumbling in his beard. He passes the arch of the entrance and disappears. Then the stifling silence settles down over the City of Dreadful Night. The kites on the Minar sleep again, snoring more loudly, the hot breeze comes up in puffs and lazy eddies, and the Moon slides down towards the horizon. Seated with both elbows on the parapet of the tower, one can watch and wonder over that heat-tortured hive till the dawn. "How do they live down there? What do they think of? When will they awake?" More tinkling of sluiced water-pots; faint jarring of wooden bedsteads moved into or out of the shadows; uncouth music of stringed instruments softened by distance into a plaintive wail, and one low grumble of far-off thunder. In the courtyard of the mosque

*An unfinished architectural sketch by Lockwood Kipling.*

**ram:** main part of a power-press

51

the janitor, who lay across the threshold of the Minar when I came up, starts wildly in his sleep, throws his hands above his head, mutters something, and falls back again. Lulled by the snoring of the kites – they snore like over-gorged humans – I drop off into an uneasy doze, conscious that three o'clock has struck, and that there is a slight – a very slight – coolness in the atmosphere. The city is absolutely quiet now, but for some vagrant dog's love-song. Nothing save dead heavy sleep.

Several weeks of darkness pass after this. For the Moon has gone out. The very dogs are still, and I watch for the first light of the dawn before making my way homeward. Again the noise of shuffling feet. The morning call is about to begin, and my night watch is over. "Allah ho Akbar! Allah ho Akbar!" The east grows grey, and presently saffron; the dawn wind comes up as though the *Muezzin* had summoned it; and, as one man, the City of Dreadful Night rises from its bed and turns its face towards the dawning day. With return of life comes return of sound. First a low whisper, then a deep bass hum; for it must be remembered that the entire city is on the house-tops. My eyelids weighed down with the arrears of long deferred sleep, I escape from the Minar through the courtyard and out into the square beyond, where the sleepers have risen, stowed away the bedsteads, and are discussing the morning hookah. The minute's freshness of the air has gone, and it is as hot as at first.

"Will the Sahib, out of his kindness, make room?" What is it? Something borne on men's shoulders comes by in the half-light, and I stand back. A woman's corpse going down to the burning-*ghât*, and a bystander says, "She died at midnight from the heat." So the city was of Death as well as Night after all.

ABOVE: *Brownlow Fforde's cover design for the suppressed Indian Railway Library edition of Kipling's 1888 reports from Calcutta.*

RIGHT: *A drawing by Lockwood Kipling, 1894.*

# The Strange Ride of Morrowbie Jukes

"The Strange Ride of Morrowbie Jukes" was written in late 1884/early 1885, and first published in *Quartette*, a Christmas supplement to the *Civil and Military Gazette* written by Rudyard, Trix and their parents. When he reprinted the story in *The Phantom 'Rickshaw*, Kipling added the opening frame section, a device that was to be increasingly characteristic of his fiction. The influence of Edgar Allan Poe is strongly felt here, and in other macabre stories of this period, such as "The Phantom 'Rickshaw", which Kipling described as "my first serious attempt to think in another man's skin". But there is much that belongs to Kipling alone. "Morrowbie Jukes" is a terrifying fable of the reversal of power between rulers and ruled, conceived as a nightmare for an audience it could properly haunt. The setting is real enough, but the terrible sand-pit into which Jukes falls is Kipling's invention. It is a way of confronting extreme experience: the equivalent of Duncan Parrenness's fetch in "The Dream of Duncan Parrenness", Gabral Misquitta's opium in "The Gate of the Hundred Sorrows" or McIntosh Jellaludin's drink in "To be Filed for Reference". The success of all these stories depends entirely on Kipling's ability to maintain the patterns of speech and thought of his protagonist. With McIntosh, for instance, the real story lies not in what he says but in the cadences of his speech: "I *was* drunk – filthily drunk. I who am the son of a man with whom you have no concern – I who was once a Fellow of a College whose buttery-hatch you have not seen." So too Jukes's rather stolid and unimaginative character adds an extra depth to his bizarre narrative.

Alive or dead – there is no other way. *Native Proverb.*

There is no invention about this tale. Jukes by accident stumbled upon a village that is well known to exist, though he is the only Englishman who has been there. A somewhat similar institution used to flourish on the outskirts of Calcutta, and there is a story that if you go into the heart of Bikanir, which is in the heart of the Great Indian Desert, you shall come across, not a village, but a town where the Dead who did not die, but may not live, have established their headquarters. And, since it is perfectly true that in the same Desert is a wonderful city where all the rich money-lenders retreat after they have made their fortunes (fortunes so vast that the owners cannot trust even the strong hand of the Government to protect them, but take refuge in the waterless sands), and drive sumptuous C-spring barouches, and buy beautiful girls, and decorate their palaces with gold and ivory and Minton tiles and mother o' pearl, I do not see why Jukes's tale should not be true. He is a Civil Engineer, with a head for plans and distances and things of that kind, and he certainly would not take the trouble to invent imaginary traps. He could earn more by doing his legitimate work. He never varies the tale in the telling, and grows very hot and indignant when he thinks of the disrespectful treatment he received. He wrote this quite straightforwardly at first, but he has touched it up in places and introduced Moral Reflections, thus:–

In the beginning it all arose from a slight attack of fever. My work necessitated my being in camp for some months between Pakpattan and Mubarakpur – a desolate sandy stretch of country as every one who has had the misfortune to go there may know. My coolies were neither more nor less exasperating than other gangs, and my work demanded sufficient attention to keep me from moping, had I been inclined to so unmanly a weakness.

On the 23rd December 1884 I felt a little feverish. There was a full moon at the time, and, in consequence, every dog near my tent was baying it. The brutes assembled in twos and threes and drove me frantic. A few days previously I had shot one loud-mouthed singer and suspended his carcass *in terrorem* about fifty yards from my tent-door, but his friends fell upon, fought for, and ultimately devoured the body; and, as it seemed to me, sang their hymns of thanksgiving afterwards with renewed energy.

The light-headedness which accompanies fever acts differently on different men. My irritation gave way, after a short time, to a fixed determination to slaughter one huge black and white beast who had been foremost in song and first in flight throughout the evening. Thanks to a shaking hand and a giddy head I had already missed him twice with both barrels of my shotgun, when it struck me that my best plan would be to ride him down in the open and finish him off with a hog-spear. This, of course, was merely the semi-delirious notion of a fever-patient; but I remember that it struck me at the time as being eminently practical and feasible.

I therefore ordered my groom to saddle Pornic and bring him round quietly to the rear of my tent. When the pony was ready, I stood at his head prepared to mount and dash out as soon as the dog should again lift up his voice. Pornic, by the way, had not been out of his pickets for a couple of days; the night air was crisp and chilly; and I was armed with a specially long and sharp pair of persuaders with which I had been rousing a sluggish cob that afternoon. You will easily believe, then, that when he was let go he went quickly. In one moment, for the brute bolted as straight as a die, the tent was left far behind, and we were flying over the smooth sandy soil at racing speed. In another we had passed the wretched dog, and I had almost forgotten why it was that I had taken horse and hog-spear.

The delirium of fever and the excitement of rapid motion through the air must have taken away the remnant of my senses. I have a faint recollection of standing upright in my stirrups, and of brandishing my hog-spear at the great white moon that looked down so calmly on my mad gallop; and of shouting challenges to the camelthorn bushes as they whizzed past. Once or twice, I believe, I swayed forward on Pornic's neck, and literally hung on by my spurs – as the marks next morning showed.

*The covers for Kipling's early volumes of stories were designed at the Mayo School of Art in Lahore under the direction of Lockwood Kipling.*

The wretched beast went forward like a thing possessed, over what seemed to be a limitless expanse of moonlit sand. Next, I remember, the ground rose suddenly in front of us, and as we topped the ascent I saw the waters of the Sutlej shining like a silver bar below. Then Pornic blundered heavily on his nose, and we rolled together down some unseen slope.

I must have lost consciousness, for when I recovered I was lying on my stomach in a heap of soft white sand, and the dawn was beginning to break dimly over the edge of the slope down which I had fallen. As the light grew stronger I saw I was at the bottom of a horseshoe-shaped crater of sand, opening on one side directly on to the shoals of the Sutlej. My fever had altogether left me, and, with the exception of a slight dizziness in the head, I felt no bad effects from the fall overnight.

*An illustration by Dudley Cleaver for Kipling's poem "Giffen's Debt", 1898.*

Pornic, who was standing a few yards away, was naturally a good deal exhausted, but had not hurt himself in the least. His saddle, a favourite polo one, was much knocked about, and had been twisted under his belly. It took me some time to put him to rights, and in the meantime I had ample opportunities of observing the spot into which I had so foolishly dropped.

At the risk of being considered tedious, I must describe it at length; inasmuch as an accurate mental picture of its peculiarities will be of material assistance in enabling the reader to understand what follows.

Imagine then, as I have said before, a horseshoe-shaped crater of sand with steeply-graded sand walls about thirty-five feet high. (The slope, I fancy, must have been about sixty-five degrees.) This crater enclosed a level piece of ground about fifty yards long by thirty at its broadest part, with a rude well in the centre. Round the bottom of the crater, about three feet from the level of the ground proper, ran a series of eighty-three semicircular, ovoid, square, and multilateral holes, all about three feet at the mouth. Each hole on inspection showed that it was carefully shored internally with driftwood and bamboos, and over the mouth a wooden drip-board projected, like the peak of a jockey's cap, for two feet. No sign of life was visible in these tunnels, but a most sickening stench pervaded the entire amphitheatre – a stench fouler than any which my wanderings in Indian villages have introduced me to.

Having remounted Pornic, who was as anxious as I to get back to camp, I rode round the base of the horseshoe to find some place whence an exit would be practicable. The inhabitants, whoever they might be, had not thought fit to put in an appearance, so I was left to my own devices. My first attempt to "rush" Pornic up the steep sand-banks showed me that I had fallen into a trap exactly on the same model as that which the ant-lion sets for its prey. At each step the shifting sand poured down from above in tons, and rattled on the drip-boards of the holes like small shot. A couple of ineffectual charges sent us both rolling down to the bottom, half choked with the torrents of sand; and I was constrained to turn my attention to the river-bank.

Here everything seemed easy enough. The sand-hills ran down to the river edge, it is true, but there were plenty of shoals and shallows across which I could gallop Pornic, and find my way back to *terra firma* by turning sharply to the right or the left. As I led Pornic over the sands I was startled by the faint pop of a rifle across the river; and at the same moment a bullet dropped with a sharp "*whit*" close to Pornic's head.

There was no mistaking the nature of the missile – a regulation Martini-Henry "picket". About five hundred yards away a country-boat was anchored in mid-stream; and a jet of smoke drifting away from its bows in the still morning air showed me whence the delicate attention had come. Was ever a respectable gentleman in such an *impasse*? The treacherous sand-slope allowed no escape from a spot which I had visited most involuntarily, and a promenade on the river frontage was the signal for a bombardment from some insane native in a boat. I'm afraid that I lost my temper very much indeed.

Another bullet reminded me that I had better save my breath to cool my porridge; and I retreated hastily up the sands and back to the horseshoe, where I saw that the noise of the rifle had drawn sixty-five human beings from the badger-holes which I had up till that point supposed to be untenanted. I found myself in the midst of a crowd of spectators – about forty men, twenty women, and one child who could not have been more than five years old. They were all scantily clothed in that salmon-coloured cloth which one associates with Hindu mendicants, and, at first sight, gave me the impression of a band of loathsome *fakirs*. The filth and repulsiveness of the assembly were beyond all description, and I shuddered to think what their life in the badger-holes must be.

Even in these days, when local self-government has destroyed the greater part of a native's respect for a Sahib, I have been accustomed to a certain amount of civility from my inferiors, and on approaching the crowd naturally expected that there would be some recognition of my presence. As a matter of fact there was, but it was by no means what I had looked for.

The ragged crew actually laughed at me – such laughter I hope I may never hear again. They cackled, yelled, whistled, and howled as I walked into their midst; some of them literally throwing themselves down on the ground in convulsions of unholy mirth. In a moment I had let go Pornic's head, and, irritated beyond expression at the morning's adventure, commenced cuffing those nearest to me with all the force I could. The wretches dropped under my blows like ninepins, and the laughter gave place to wails for mercy; while those yet untouched clasped me round the knees, imploring me in all sorts of uncouth tongues to spare them.

In the tumult, and just when I was feeling very much ashamed of

*An Indian fakir, drawn by the Rev. W. Urwick, 1891.*

myself for having thus easily given way to my temper, a thin high voice murmured in English from behind my shoulder: "Sahib! Sahib! Do you not know me? Sahib, it is Gunga Dass, the telegraph-master."

I spun round quickly and faced the speaker.

Gunga Dass (I have, of course, no hesitation in mentioning the man's real name) I had known four years before as a Deccanee Brahmin lent by the Punjab Government to one of the Khalsia States. He was in charge of a branch telegraph-office there, and when I had last met him was a jovial, full-stomached, portly Government servant with a marvellous capacity for making bad puns in English – a peculiarity which made me remember him long after I had forgotten his services to me in his official capacity. It is seldom that a Hindu makes English puns.

Now, however, the man was changed beyond all recognition. Caste-mark, stomach, slate-coloured continuations, and unctuous speech were all gone. I looked at a withered skeleton, turbanless and almost naked, with long matted hair and deep-set codfish-eyes. But for a crescent-shaped scar on the left cheek – the result of an accident for which I was responsible – I should never have known him. But it was indubitably Gunga Dass, and – for this I was thankful – an English-speaking native who might at least tell me the meaning of all that I had gone through that day.

The crowd retreated to some distance as I turned towards the miserable figure, and ordered him to show me some method of escaping from the crater. He held a freshly-plucked crow in his hand, and in reply to my question climbed slowly to a platform of sand which ran in front of the holes, and commenced lighting a fire there in silence. Dried bents, sand-poppies, and driftwood burn quickly; and I derived much consolation from the fact that he lit them with an ordinary sulphur match. When they were in a bright glow and the crow was neatly spitted in front thereof, Gunga Dass began without a word of preamble: –

"There are only two kinds of men, Sar – the alive and the dead. When you are dead you are dead, but when you are alive you live." (Here the crow demanded his attention for an instant as it twirled before the fire in danger of being burnt to a cinder.) "If you die at home and do not die when you come to the *ghât* to be burnt you come here."

The nature of the reeking village was made plain now, and all that I had known or read of the grotesque and the horrible paled before the fact just communicated by the ex-Brahmin. Sixteen years ago, when I first landed in Bombay, I had been told by a wandering Armenian of the existence, somewhere in India, of a place to which such Hindus as had the misfortune to recover from trance or catalepsy were conveyed and kept, and I recollect laughing heartily at what I was then pleased to consider a traveller's tale. Sitting at the bottom of the sand-trap, the memory of Watson's Hotel, with its swinging punkahs, white-robed servants, and the sallow-faced Armenian, rose up in my mind as vividly as a photograph, and I burst into a loud fit of laughter. The contrast was too absurd!

Gunga Dass, as he bent over the unclean bird, watched me curiously. Hindus seldom laugh, and his surroundings were not such as to move him that way. He removed the crow solemnly from the wooden spit and as solemnly devoured it. Then he continued his story, which I give in his own words:—

"In epidemics of the cholera you are carried to be burnt almost before you are dead. When you come to the riverside the cold air, perhaps, makes you alive, and then, if you are only a little alive, mud is put on your nose and mouth and you die conclusively. If you are rather more alive, more mud is put; but if you are too lively they let you go and take you away. I was too lively, and made protestation with anger against the indignities that they endeavoured to press upon me. In those days I was Brahmin and proud man. Now I am dead man and eat" – here he eyed the well-gnawed breast-bone with the first sign of emotion that I had seen in him since we met – "crows, and – other things. They took me from my sheets when they saw that I was too lively and gave me medicines for one week, and I survived

*The burning-ghât, Benares, on the banks of the sacred Ganges; a photograph by Bourne and Shepherd of Calcutta. "From the burning-ghât rose lazily a welt of thick blue smoke, and an eddy of the air blew a wreath across the water".*

*"Once I was Brahmin & proud
man: & now I eat crows"*, a
terracotta bas-relief plaque made
in 1897 by Lockwood Kipling for
the Scribner's Works of Rudyard
Kipling. *Lockwood later illustrated*
Kim *in the same manner. Making
the plaques was a labour of love for
the perfectionist artist/craftsman,
but they were ill suited to
reproduction.*

successfully. Then they sent me by rail from my place to Okara
Station, with a man to take care of me; and at Okara Station we met
two other men, and they conducted we three on camels, in the night,
from Okara Station to this place, and they propelled me from the top
to the bottom, and the other two succeeded, and I have been here ever
since two and a half years. Once I was Brahmin and proud man, and
now I eat crows."

"There is no way of getting out?"

"None of what kind at all. When I first came I made experiments
frequently, and all the others also, but we have always succumbed to
the sand which is precipitated upon our heads."

"But surely," I broke in at this point, "the river-front is open, and
it is worth while dodging the bullets; while at night – "

I had already matured a rough plan of escape which a natural
instinct of selfishness forbade me sharing with Gunga Dass. He,
however, divined my unspoken thought almost as soon as it was
formed; and, to my intense astonishment, gave vent to a long low
chuckle of derision – the laughter, be it understood, of a superior or at
least of an equal.

"You will not" – he had dropped the Sir after his first sentence –
"make any escape that way. But you can try. I have tried. Once
only."

The sensation of nameless terror which I had in vain attempted to
strive against overmastered me completely. My long fast – it was now
close upon ten o'clock, and I had eaten nothing since tiffin on the
previous day – combined with the violent agitation of the ride had
exhausted me, and I verily believe that, for a few minutes, I acted as
one mad. I hurled myself against the sand-slope. I ran round the base
of the crater, blaspheming and praying by turns. I crawled out among
the sedges of the river-front, only to be driven back each time in an
agony of nervous dread by the rifle-bullets which cut up the sand
round me – for I dared not face the death of a mad dog among that

hideous crowd – and so fell, spent and raving, at the curb of the well. No one had taken the slightest notice of an exhibition which makes me blush hotly even when I think of it now.

Two or three men trod on my panting body as they drew water, but they were evidently used to this sort of thing, and had no time to waste upon me. Gunga Dass, indeed, when he had banked the embers of his fire with sand, was at some pains to throw half a cupful of fetid water over my head, an attention for which I could have fallen on my knees and thanked him, but he was laughing all the while in the same mirthless, wheezy key that greeted me on my first attempt to force the shoals. And so, in a half-fainting state, I lay till noon. Then, being only a man after all, I felt hungry, and said as much to Gunga Dass, whom I had begun to regard as my natural protector. Following the impulse of the outer world when dealing with natives, I put my hand into my pocket and drew out four annas. The absurdity of the gift struck me at once, and I was about to replace the money.

Gunga Dass, however, cried: "Give me the money, all you have, or I will get help, and we will kill you!"

A Briton's first impulse, I believe, is to guard the contents of his pockets; but a moment's thought showed me the folly of differing with the one man who had it in his power to make me comfortable; and with whose help it was possible that I might eventually escape from the crater. I gave him all the money in my possession, Rs.9–8–5 – nine rupees, eight annas, and five pie – for I always keep small change as *bakshish* when I am in camp. Gunga Dass clutched the coins, and hid them at once in his ragged loin-cloth, looking round to assure himself that no one had observed us.

"*Now* I will give you something to eat," said he.

What pleasure my money could have given him I am unable to say; but inasmuch as it did please him I was not sorry that I had parted with it so readily, for I had no doubt that he would have had me killed if I had refused. One does not protest against the doings of a den of wild beasts; and my companions were lower than any beasts. While I ate what Gunga Dass had provided, a coarse *chapatti* and a cupful of the foul well-water, the people showed not the faintest sign of curiosity – that curiosity which is so rampant, as a rule, in an Indian village.

I could even fancy that they despised me. At all events they treated me with the most chilling indifference, and Gunga Dass was nearly as bad. I plied him with questions about the terrible village, and received extremely unsatisfactory answers. So far as I could gather, it had been in existence from time immemorial – whence I concluded that it was at least a century old – and during that time no one had ever been known to escape from it. [I had to control myself here with both hands, lest the blind terror should lay hold of me a second time and drive me raving round the crater.] Gunga Dass took a malicious pleasure in emphasising this point and in watching me wince.

Nothing that I could do would induce him to tell me who the mysterious "They" were.

"It is so ordered," he would reply, "and I do not yet know any one who has disobeyed the orders."

"Only wait till my servants find that I am missing," I retorted, "and I promise you that this place shall be cleared off the face of the earth, and I'll give you a lesson in civility, too, my friend."

"Your servants would be torn in pieces before they came near this place; and, besides, you are dead, my dear friend. It is not your fault, of course, but nonetheless you are dead *and* buried."

At irregular intervals supplies of food, I was told, were dropped down from the land side into the amphitheatre, and the inhabitants fought for them like wild beasts. When a man felt his death coming on he retreated to his lair and died there. The body was sometimes dragged out of the hole and thrown on to the sand, or allowed to rot where it lay.

The phrase "thrown on to the sand" caught my attention, and I asked Gunga Dass whether this sort of thing was not likely to breed a pestilence.

"That," said he, with another of his wheezy chuckles, "you may see for yourself subsequently. You will have much time to make observations."

Whereat, to his great delight, I winced once more and hastily continued the conversation: "And how do you live here from day to day? What do you do?" The question elicited exactly the same answer as before – coupled with the information that "this place is like your European heaven; there is neither marrying nor giving in marriage."

Gunga Dass had been educated at a Mission School, and, as he himself admitted, had he only changed his religion "like a wise man", might have avoided the living grave which was now his portion. But as long as I was with him I fancy he was happy.

*A fakir, 1898.*

Here was a Sahib, a representative of the dominant race, helpless as a child and completely at the mercy of his native neighbours. In a deliberate lazy way he set himself to torture me as a schoolboy would devote a rapturous half-hour to watching the agonies of an impaled beetle, or as a ferret in a blind burrow might glue himself comfortably to the neck of a rabbit. The burden of his conversation was that there was no escape "of no kind whatever", and that I should stay here till I died and was "thrown on to the sand". If it were possible to forejudge the conversation of the Damned on the advent of a new soul in their abode, I should say that they would speak as Gunga Dass did to me throughout that long afternoon. I was powerless to protest or answer; all my energies being devoted to a struggle against the inexplicable terror that threatened to overwhelm me again and again. I can compare the feeling to nothing except the struggles of a man against the overpowering nausea of the Channel passage – only my agony was of the spirit and infinitely more terrible.

As the day wore on, the inhabitants began to appear in full strength to catch the rays of the afternoon sun, which were now sloping in at the mouth of the crater. They assembled by little knots, and talked among themselves without even throwing a glance in my direction. About four o'clock, so far as I could judge, Gunga Dass rose and dived into his lair for a moment, emerging with a live crow in his hands. The wretched bird was in a most draggled and deplorable condition, but seemed to be in no way afraid of its master. Advancing cautiously to the river-front, Gunga Dass stepped from tussock to tussock until he had reached a smooth patch of sand directly in the line of the boat's fire. The occupants of the boat took no notice. Here he stopped, and, with a couple of dexterous turns of the wrist, pegged the bird on its back with outstretched wings. As was only natural, the crow began to shriek at once and beat the air with its claws. In a few seconds the clamour had attracted the attention of a bevy of wild crows on a shoal a few hundred yards away, where they were discussing something that looked like a corpse. Half-a-dozen crows flew over at once to see what was going on, and also, as it proved, to attack the pinioned bird. Gunga Dass, who had lain down on a tussock, motioned to me to be quiet, though I fancy this was a needless precaution. In a moment, and before I could see how it happened, a wild crow, which had grappled with the shrieking and helpless bird, was entangled in the latter's claws, swiftly disengaged by Gunga Dass, and pegged down beside its companion in adversity. Curiosity, it seemed, overpowered the rest of the flock, and almost before Gunga Dass and I had time to withdraw to the tussock, two more captives were struggling in the upturned claws of the decoys. So the chase – if I can give it so dignified a name – continued until Gunga Dass had captured seven crows. Five of them he throttled at once, reserving two for further operations another day. I was a good deal impressed by this, to me, novel method of securing food, and complimented Gunga Dass on his skill.

"It is nothing to do," said he. "To-morrow you must do it for me. You are stronger than I am."

This calm assumption of superiority upset me not a little, and I answered peremptorily: "Indeed, you old ruffian? What do you think I have given you money for?"

"Very well," was the unmoved reply. "Perhaps not to-morrow, nor the day after, nor subsequently; but in the end, and for many years, you will catch crows and eat crows, and you will thank your European God that you have crows to catch and eat."

I could have cheerfully strangled him for this, but judged it best under the circumstances to smother my resentment. An hour later I was eating one of the crows; and, as Gunga Dass had said, thanking my God that I had a crow to eat. Never as long as I live shall I forget that evening meal. The whole population were squatting on the hard

"HE IS UNCLEAN, HE SHALL DWELL ALONE, WITHOUT THE CAMP SHALL HIS HABITATION BE."

*An outcast leper and a pariah dog; a sketch by Lockwood Kipling for an illustration in his* Beast and Man in India *(1891).*

sand platform opposite their dens, huddled over tiny fires of refuse and dried rushes. Death, having once laid his hand upon these men and forborne to strike, seemed to stand aloof from them now; for most of our company were old men, bent and worn and twisted with years, and women aged to all appearances as the Fates themselves. They sat together in knots and talked – God only knows what they found to discuss – in low equable tones, curiously in contrast to the strident babble with which natives are accustomed to make day hideous. Now and then an access of that sudden fury which had possessed me in the morning would lay hold on a man or woman; and with yells and imprecations the sufferer would attack the steep slope until, baffled and bleeding, he fell back on the platform incapable of moving a limb. The others would never even raise their eyes when this happened, as men too well aware of the futility of their fellows' attempts and wearied with their useless repetition. I saw four such outbursts in the course of that evening.

Gunga Dass took an eminently business-like view of my situation, and while we were dining – I can afford to laugh at the recollection now, but it was painful enough at the time – propounded the terms on which he would consent to "do" for me. My nine rupees eight annas, he argued, at the rate of three annas a day, would provide me with food for fifty-one days, or about seven weeks; that is to say, he would be willing to cater for me for that length of time. At the end of it I was to look after myself. For a further consideration – *videlicet* my boots – he would be willing to allow me to occupy the den next to his own, and would supply me with as much dried grass for bedding as he could spare.

"Very well, Gunga Dass," I replied; "to the first terms I cheerfully agree, but, as there is nothing on earth to prevent my killing you as you sit here and taking everything that you have," (I thought of the two invaluable crows at the time) "I flatly refuse to give you my boots and shall take whichever den I please."

The stroke was a bold one, and I was glad when I saw that it had succeeded. Gunga Dass changed his tone immediately, and disavowed all intention of asking for my boots. At the time it did not strike me as at all strange that I, a Civil Engineer, a man of thirteen years' standing in the Service, and, I trust, an average Englishman, should thus calmly threaten murder and violence against the man who had, for a consideration it is true, taken me under his wing. I had left the world, it seemed, for centuries. I was as certain then as I am now of my own existence, that in the accursed settlement there was no law save that of the strongest; that the living dead men had thrown behind them every canon of the world which had cast them out; and that I had to depend for my own life on my strength and vigilance alone. The crew of the ill-fated *Mignonette* are the only men who would understand my frame of mind. "At present," I argued to myself, "I am strong and a match for six of these wretches. It is

the crew of the Mignonette: shipwrecked cannibals

imperatively necessary that I should, for my own sake, keep both health and strength until the hour of my release comes – if it ever does."

Fortified with these resolutions, I ate and drank as much as I could, and made Gunga Dass understand that I intended to be his master, and that the least sign of insubordination on his part would be visited with the only punishment I had it in my power to inflict – sudden and violent death. Shortly after this I went to bed. That is to say, Gunga Dass gave me a double armful of dried bents which I thrust down the mouth of the lair to the right of his, and followed myself, feet foremost; the hole running about nine feet into the sand with a slight downward inclination, and being neatly shored with timbers. From my den, which faced the river-front, I was able to watch the waters of the Sutlej flowing past under the light of a young moon and compose myself to sleep as best I might.

The horrors of that night I shall never forget. My den was nearly as narrow as a coffin, and the sides had been worn smooth and greasy by the contact of innumerable naked bodies, added to which it smelt abominably. Sleep was altogether out of the question to one in my excited frame of mind. As the night wore on, it seemed that the entire amphitheatre was filled with legions of unclean devils that, trooping up from the shoals below, mocked the unfortunates in their lairs.

Personally I am not of an imaginative temperament – very few Engineers are – but on that occasion I was as completely prostrated with nervous terror as any woman. After half an hour or so, however, I was able once more to calmly review my chances of escape. Any exit by the steep sand walls was, of course, impracticable. I had been thoroughly convinced of this some time before. It was possible, just possible, that I might, in the uncertain moonlight, safely run the gauntlet of the rifle shots. The place was so full of terror for me that I was prepared to undergo any risk in leaving it. Imagine my delight, then, when after creeping stealthily to the river-front I found that the infernal boat was not there. My freedom lay before me in the next few steps!

By walking out to the first shallow pool that lay at the foot of the projecting left horn of the horseshoe, I could wade across, turn the flank of the crater, and make my way inland. Without a moment's hesitation I marched briskly past the tussocks where Gunga Dass had snared the crows, and out in the direction of the smooth white sand beyond. My first step from the tufts of dried grass showed me how utterly futile was any hope of escape; for, as I put my foot down, I felt an indescribable drawing, sucking motion of the sand below. Another moment and my leg was swallowed up nearly to the knee. In the moonlight the whole surface of the sand seemed to be shaken with devilish delight at my disappointmemt. I struggled clear, sweating with terror and exertion, back to the tussocks behind me and fell on my face.

My only means of escape from the semicircle was protected by a quicksand!

How long I lay I have not the faintest idea; but I was roused at last by the malevolent chuckle of Gunga Dass at my ear. "I would advise you, Protector of the Poor," (the ruffian was speaking English) "to return to your house. It is unhealthy to lie down here. Moreover, when the boat returns you will most certainly be rifled at." He stood over me in the dim light of the dawn, chuckling and laughing to himself. Suppressing my first impulse to catch the man by the neck and throw him on to the quicksand, I rose sullenly and followed him to the platform below the burrows.

Suddenly, and futilely as I thought while I spoke, I asked: "Gunga Dass, what is the good of the boat if I can't get out *anyhow*?" I recollect that even in my deepest trouble I had been speculating vaguely on the waste of ammunition in guarding an already well-protected foreshore.

Gunga Dass laughed again and made answer: "They have the boat only in daytime. It is for the reason that *there is a way*. I hope we shall have the pleasure of your company for much longer time. It is a pleasant spot when you have been here some years and eaten roast crow long enough."

I staggered, numbed and helpless, towards the fetid burrow allotted to me, and fell asleep. An hour or so later I was awakened by a piercing scream – the shrill, high-pitched scream of a horse in pain. Those who have once heard that will never forget the sound. I found some little difficulty in scrambling out of the burrow. When I was in the open, I saw Pornic, my poor old Pornic, lying dead on the sandy soil. How they had killed him I cannot guess. Gunga Dass explained that horse was better than crow, and "greatest good of greatest number is political maxim. We are now Republic, Mister Jukes, and you are entitled to a fair share of the beast. If you like, we will pass a vote of thanks. Shall I propose?"

Yes, we were a Republic indeed! A Republic of wild beasts penned at the bottom of a pit, to eat and fight and sleep till we died. I attempted no protest of any kind, but sat down and stared at the hideous sight in front of me. In less time almost than it takes me to write this, Pornic's body was divided, in some unclean way or other; the men and women had dragged the fragments on to the platform and were preparing their morning meal. Gunga Dass cooked mine. The almost irresistible impulse to fly at the sand walls until I was wearied laid hold of me afresh, and I had to struggle against it with all my might. Gunga Dass was offensively jocular till I told him that if he addressed another remark of any kind whatever to me I should strangle him where he sat. This silenced him till the silence became insupportable, and I bade him say something.

"You will live here till you die like the other Feringhi," he said coolly, watching me over the fragment of gristle that he was gnawing.

*At a burning-ghât, 1898.*

65

"What other Sahib, you swine? Speak at once, and don't stop to tell me a lie."

"He is over there," answered Gunga Dass, pointing to a burrow-mouth about four doors to the left of my own. "You can see for yourself. He died in the burrow as you will die, and I will die, and as all these men and women and the one child will also die."

"For pity's sake tell me all you know about him. Who was he? When did he come, and when did he die?"

This appeal was a weak step on my part. Gunga Dass only leered and replied: "I will not – unless you give me something first."

Then I recollected where I was, and struck the man between the eyes, partially stunning him. He stepped down from the platform at once, and, cringing and fawning and weeping and attempting to embrace my feet, led me round to the burrow which he had indicated.

"I know nothing whatever about the gentleman. Your God be my witness that I do not. He was as anxious to escape as you were, and he was shot from the boat, though we all did all things to prevent him from attempting. He was shot here." Gunga Dass laid his hand on his lean stomach and bowed to the earth.

"Well, and what then? Go on!"

*The "other Sahib", an etching by W. Strang, 1900.*

"And then – and then, Your Honour, we carried him into his house and gave him water, and put wet cloths on the wound, and he laid down in his house and gave up the ghost."

"In how long? In how long?"

"About half an hour after he received his wound. I call Vishnu to witness," yelled the wretched man, "that I did everything for him. Everything which was possible, that I did!"

He threw himself down on the ground and clasped my ankles. But I had my doubts about Gunga Dass's benevolence, and kicked him off as he lay protesting.

"I believe you robbed him of everything he had. But I can find out in a minute or two. How long was the Sahib here?"

"Nearly a year and a half. I think he must have gone mad. But hear me swear, Protector of the Poor! Won't Your Honour hear me swear that I never touched an article that belonged to him? What is Your Worship going to do?"

I had taken Gunga Dass by the waist and had hauled him on to the platform opposite the deserted burrow. As I did so I thought of my wretched fellow-prisoner's unspeakable misery among all these horrors for eighteen months, and the final agony of dying like a rat in a hole, with a bullet-wound in the stomach. Gunga Dass fancied I was going to kill him and howled pitifully. The rest of the population, in the plethora that follows a full flesh meal, watched us without stirring.

"Go inside, Gunga Dass," said I, "and fetch it out."

I was feeling sick and faint with horror now. Gunga Dass nearly rolled off the platform and howled aloud.

"But I am Brahmin, Sahib – a high-caste Brahmin. By your soul, by your father's soul, do not make me do this thing!"

"Brahmin or no Brahmin, by my soul and my father's soul, in you go!" I said, and, seizing him by the shoulders, I crammed his head into the mouth of the burrow, kicked the rest of him in, and, sitting down, covered my face with my hands.

At the end of a few minutes I heard a rustle and a creak; then Gunga Dass in a sobbing, choking whisper speaking to himself; then a soft thud – and I uncovered my eyes.

The dry sand had turned the corpse entrusted to its keeping into a yellow-brown mummy. I told Gunga Dass to stand off while I examined it. The body – clad in an olive-green hunting-suit much stained and worn, with leather pads on the shoulders – was that of a man between thirty and forty, above middle height, with light sandy hair, long moustache, and a rough unkempt beard. The left canine of the upper jaw was missing, and a portion of the lobe of the right ear was gone. On the second finger of the left hand was a ring – a shield-shaped bloodstone set in gold, with a monogram that might have been either 'B. K.'' or "B. L." On the third finger of the right hand was a silver ring in the shape of a coiled cobra, much worn and tarnished. Gunga Dass deposited a handful of trifles he had picked out of the burrow at my feet, and, covering the face of the body with my handkerchief, I turned to examine these. I give the full list in the hope that it may lead to the identification of the unfortunate man:—

1. Bowl of a briarwood pipe, serrated at the edge; much worn and blackened; bound with string at the screw.

2. Two patent-lever keys; wards of both broken.

3. Tortoise-shell-handled penknife, silver or nickel, name-plate marked with monogram "B. K."

4. Envelope, postmark undecipherable, bearing a Victorian stamp, addressed to "Miss Mon –" (rest illegible) – "ham" – "nt".

5. Imitation crocodile-skin notebook with pencil. First forty-five pages blank; four and a half illegible; fifteen others filled with private memoranda relating chiefly to three persons – a Mrs. L. Singleton, abbreviated several times to "Lot Single", "Mrs. S. May", and "Garmison", referred to in places as "Jerry" or "Jack".

6. Handle of small-sized hunting-knife. Blade snapped short. Buck's horn, diamond-cut, with swivel and ring on the butt; fragment of cotton cord attached.

It must not be supposed that I inventoried all these things on the spot as fully as I have here written them down. The notebook first attracted my attention, and I put it in my pocket with a view to studying it later on. The rest of the articles I conveyed to my burrow for safety's sake, and there, being a methodical man, I inventoried them. I then returned to the corpse and ordered Gunga Dass to help me to carry it out to the river-front. While we were engaged in this, the exploded shell of an old brown cartridge dropped out of one of the pockets and rolled at my feet. Gunga Dass had not seen it; and I fell to thinking that a man does not carry exploded cartridge-cases, especially "browns", which will not bear loading twice, about with him when shooting. In other words, that cartridge-case had been fired inside the crater. Consequently there must be a gun somewhere. I was on the verge of asking Gunga Dass, but checked myself, knowing that he would lie. We laid the body down on the edge of the quicksand by the tussocks. It was my intention to push it out and let it be swallowed up – the only possible mode of burial that I could think of. I ordered Gunga Dass to go away.

Then I gingerly put the corpse out on the quicksand. In doing so – it was lying face downward – I tore the frail and rotten khaki shooting-coat open, disclosing a hideous cavity in the back. I have already told you that the dry sand had, as it were, mummified the body. A moment's glance showed that the gaping hole had been caused by a gunshot wound; the gun must have been fired with the muzzle almost touching the back. The shooting-coat, being intact, had been drawn over the body after death, which must have been instantaneous. The secret of the poor wretch's death was plain to me in a flash. Some one of the crater, presumably Gunga Dass, must have shot him with his own gun – the gun that fitted the brown cartridges. He had never attempted to escape in the face of the rifle-fire from the boat.

I pushed the corpse out hastily, and saw it sink from sight literally in a few seconds. I shuddered as I watched. In a dazed, half-conscious way I turned to peruse the notebook. A stained and discoloured slip of paper had been inserted between the binding and the back, and dropped out as I opened the pages. This is what it contained: *"Four out from crow-clump; three left; nine out; two right; three back; two left; fourteen out; two left; seven out; one left; nine back; two right; six back; four right; seven back."* The paper had been burnt and charred at the edges. What it meant I could not understand. I sat down on the dried bents turning it over and over between my fingers, until I was aware of Gunga Dass standing immediately behind me with glowing eyes and outstretched hands.

"Have you got it?" he panted. "Will you not let me look at it also? I swear that I will return it."

"Got what? Return what?" I asked.

"That which you have in your hands. It will help us both." He stretched out his long bird-like talons, trembling with eagerness.

"I could never find it," he continued. "He had secreted it about his person. Therefore I shot him, but nevertheless I was unable to obtain it."

Gunga Dass had quite forgotten his little fiction about the rifle-bullet. I heard him calmly. Morality is blunted by consorting with the Dead who are alive.

"What on earth are you raving about? What is it you want me to give you?"

"The piece of paper in the notebook. It will help us both. Oh, you fool! You fool! Can you not see what it will do for us? We shall escape!"

His voice rose almost to a scream, and he danced with excitement before me. I own I was moved at the chance of getting away.

"Do you mean to say that this slip of paper will help us? What does it mean?"

"Read it aloud! Read it aloud! I beg and I pray to you to read it aloud."

I did so. Gunga Dass listened delightedly, and drew an irregular line in the sand with his fingers.

"See now! It was the length of his gun-barrels without the stock. I have those barrels. Four gun-barrels out from the place where I caught crows. Straight out; do you mind me? Then three left. Ah! Now well I remember how that man worked it out night after night. Then nine out, and so on. Out is always straight before you across the quicksand to the north. He told me so before I killed him."

"But if you knew all this why didn't you get out before?"

"I did *not* know it. He told me that he was working it out a year

*A Brahmin, drawn by the Rev. W. Urwick, 1891.*

and a half ago, and how he was working it out night after night when the boat had gone away, and he could get out near the quicksand safely. Then he said that we would get away together. But I was afraid that he would leave me behind one night when he had worked it all out, and so I shot him. Besides, it is not advisable that the men who once get in here should escape. Only I, and *I* am a Brahmin."

The hope of escape had brought Gunga Dass's caste back to him. He stood up, walked about, and gesticulated violently. Eventually I managed to make him talk soberly, and he told me how this Englishman had spent six months night after night in exploring, inch by inch, the passage across the quicksand; how he had declared it to be simplicity itself up to within about twenty yards of the river bank after turning the flank of the left horn of the horseshoe. This much he had evidently not completed when Gunga Dass shot him with his own gun.

In my frenzy of delight at the possibilities of escape I recollect shaking hands wildly with Gunga Dass, after we had decided that we were to make an attempt to get away that very night. It was weary work waiting throughout the afternoon.

About ten o'clock, as far as I could judge, when the moon had just risen above the lip of the crater, Gunga Dass made a move for his burrow to bring out the gun-barrels whereby to measure our path. All the other wretched inhabitants had retired to their lairs long ago. The guardian boat drifted down-stream some hours before, and we were utterly alone by the crow-clump. Gunga Dass, while carrying the gun-barrels, let slip the piece of paper which was to be our guide. I stooped down hastily to recover it, and, as I did so, I was aware that the creature was aiming a violent blow at the back of my head with the gun-barrels. It was too late to turn round. I must have received the blow somewhere on the nape of my neck, for I fell senseless at the edge of the quicksand.

When I recovered consciousness the moon was going down, and I was sensible of intolerable pain in the back of my head. Gunga Dass had disappeared and my mouth was full of blood. I lay down again and prayed that I might die without more ado. Then the unreasoning fury which I have before mentioned laid hold upon me, and I staggered inland towards the walls of the crater. It seemed that some one was calling to me in a whisper – "Sahib! Sahib! Sahib!" exactly as my bearer used to call me in the mornings. I fancied that I was delirious until a handful of sand fell at my feet. Then I looked up and saw a head peering down into the amphitheatre – the head of Dunnoo, my dog-boy, who attended to my collies. As soon as he had attracted my attention, he held up his hand and showed a rope. I motioned, staggering to and fro the while, that he should throw it down. It was a couple of leather punkah-ropes knotted together, with a loop at one end. I slipped the loop over my head and under my arms; heard Dunnoo urge something forward; was conscious that I was being dragged, face downward, up the steep sand-slope, and the next instant found myself choked and half-fainting on the sand-hills overlooking the crater. Dunnoo, with his face ashy grey in the moonlight, implored me not to stay, but to get back to my tent at once.

It seems that he had tracked Pornic's footprints fourteen miles across the sands to the crater; had returned and told my servants, who flatly refused to meddle with any one, white or black, once fallen into the hideous Village of the Dead; whereupon Dunnoo had taken one of my ponies and a couple of punkah-ropes, returned to the crater, and hauled me out as I have described.

*Rudyard Kipling, from a gravure print after the painting by John Collier, 1891. Hugh Walpole noted, "His body is nothing but his eyes terrific, lambent, kindly, gentle and exceedingly proud."*

# The Ballad of the King's Jest

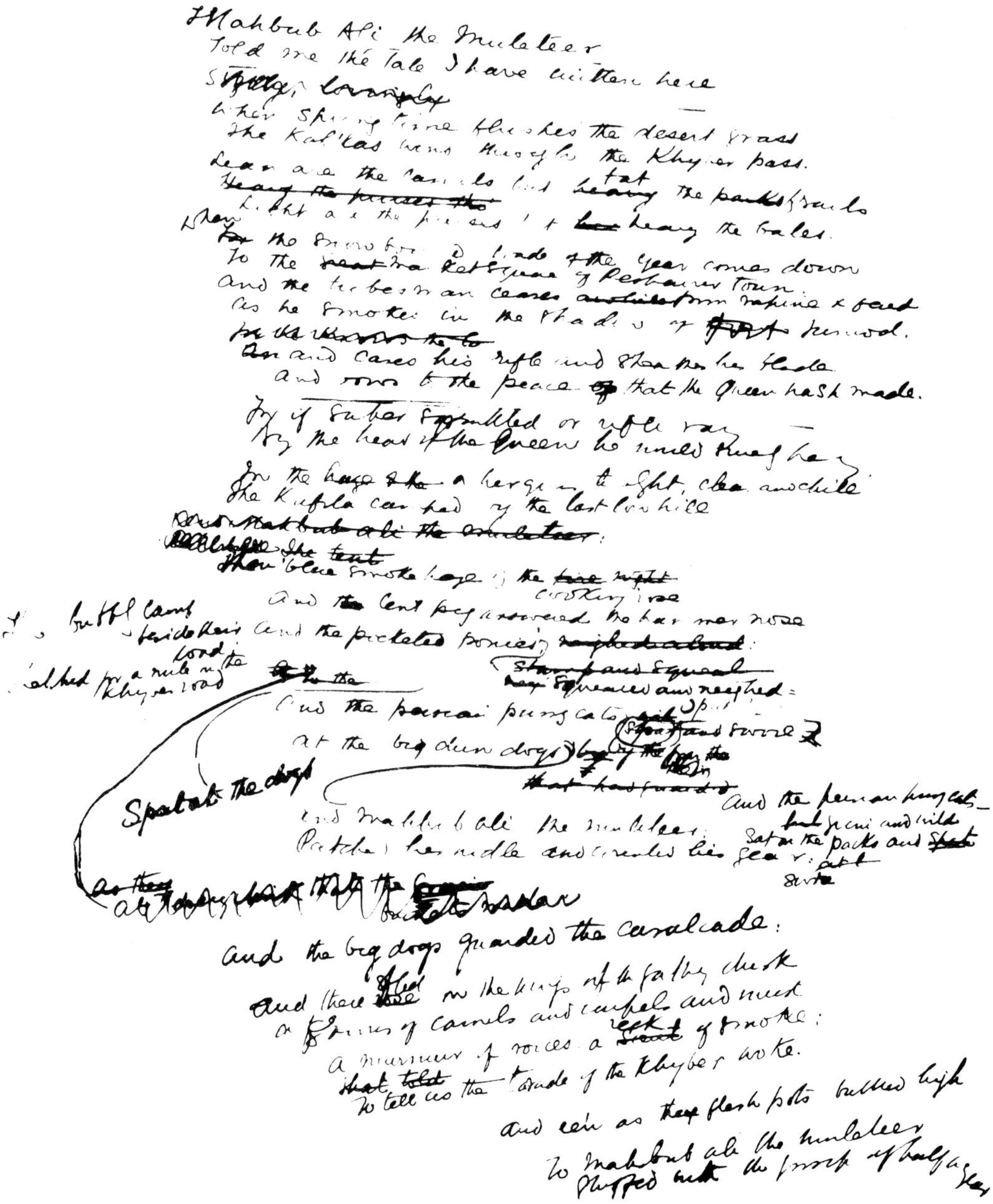

Mahbub Ali the Muleteer
Told me the Tale I have written here

When Spring time flushes the desert grass
The Kafilas wind through the Khyber pass.
Lean are the camels but heavy the packs & bales
Light are the purses & heavy the bales.

For the Minotaur's [?] the year comes down
To the Retinue of Peshawur town
And the tribesman ceases & [...] rapine & feud
As he smoke in the shadow of [...] renewd.

[...]
And cares his rifle and [...] his blade
And vows to the peace that the Queen hath made.

[...] if father [...] or rifle ran
[...] the heart of the Queen he [...]

In the [...] a bargain [...] lght, clear awchile
The Kaifla caravan [...] of the last low hill
[...] Mahbub ali the muleteer:

Thro' blue smoke haze; the tent
[...] crossing [?]
And the tent peg answered the [...] nose
[...] beside his and the picketed ponies [...]
[...] for a rule in the
Khyber road [...] Stamp and squeal
And the [...] pony cats up
at the big dun dogs [...]
Spat at the dogs
And Mahbub ali the muleteer,
Patted his mule and cursed his gear [...]

And the big dogs guarded the cavalcade:
And there [...] on the kings of the [...] dusk
of [...] of camels and [...] and musk
a murmur of voices a [...] of smoke:
To tell us the tide of the Khyber woke.
And even as the flesh pots bubbled high
To Mahbub ali the muleteer
Slipped with the [...] of half a [...]

When spring-time flushes the desert grass,
Our kafilas wind through the Khyber Pass.
Lean are the camels but fat the frails,
Light are the purses but heavy the bales,
As the snowbound trade of the North comes down
To the market-square of Peshawur town.

In a turquoise twilight, crisp and chill,
A kafila camped at the foot of the hill.
Then blue smoke-haze of the cooking rose,
And tent-peg answered to hammer-nose;
And the picketed ponies, shag and wild,
Strained at their ropes as the feed was piled;
And the bubbling camels beside the load
Sprawled for a furlong adown the road;
And the Persian pussy-cats, brought for sale,
Spat at the dogs from the camel-bale;
And the tribesmen bellowed to hasten the food;
And the camp-fires twinkled by Fort Jumrood;
And there fled on the wings of the gathering dusk
A savour of camels and carpets and musk,
A murmur of voices, a reek of smoke,
To tell us the trade of the Khyber woke.

The lid of the flesh-pot chattered high,
The knives were whetted and – then came I
To Mahbub Ali, the muleteer,
Patching his bridles and counting his gear,
Crammed with the gossip of half a year.
But Mahbub Ali the kindly said,
"Better is speech when the belly is fed."
So we plunged the hand to the mid-wrist deep
In a cinnamon stew of the fat-tailed sheep,
And he who never hath tasted the food,
By Allah! he knoweth not bad from good.
We cleansed our beards of the mutton-grease,
We lay on the mats and were filled with peace,
And the talk slid north, and the talk slid south,
With the sliding puffs from the hookah-mouth.

Four things greater than all things are –
Women and Horses and Power and War.
We spake of them all, but the last the most.
For I sought a word of a Russian post,
Of a shifty promise, an unsheathed sword,
And a grey-coat guard on the Helmund ford.
Then Mahbub Ali lowered his eyes

ABOVE: *A decorative letter "W" by Lockwood Kipling, 1891.*

OPPOSITE: *Kipling's manuscript draft of the opening of "The Ballad of the King's Jest". Kipling destroyed many manuscripts and letters, determined that "No one's going to make a monkey out of me after I die."*

In the fashion of one who is weaving lies.
Quoth he: "Of the Russians who can say?
When the night is gathering all is grey.
But we look that the gloom of the night shall die
In the morning flush of a blood-red sky.
Friend of my heart, is it meet or wise
To warn a King of his enemies?
We know what Heaven or Hell may bring,
But no man knoweth the mind of the King.
That unsought counsel is cursed of God
Attesteth the story of Wali Dad.

"His sire was leaky of tongue and pen,
His dam was a clucking Khattack hen;
And the colt bred close to the vice of each,
For he carried the curse of an unstaunched speech.
Therewith madness – so that he sought
The favour of kings at the Kabul Court;
And travelled, in hope of honour, far
To the line where the grey-coat squadrons are.
There have I journeyed too – but I
Saw naught, said naught, and – did not die!
*He* hearked to rumour, and snatched at a breath
Of 'this one knoweth', and 'that one saith' –
Legends that ran from mouth to mouth
Of a grey-coat coming, and sack of the South.
These have I also heard – they pass
With each new spring and the winter grass.

*From a lithograph, 1862. Kipling's editor on the* Civil and Military Gazette, *E. Kay Robinson, wrote: "I remember well one long-limbed Pathan, indescribably filthy, but with magnificent mien and features – Mahbub Ali, I think was his name – who regarded Kipling as a man apart from all other 'sahibs'. After each of his wanderings across the unexplored fringes of Afghanistan, where his restless spirit of adventure led him, Mahbub Ali always used to turn up travel-stained, dirtier and more majestic than ever, for confidential colloquy with 'Kuppeleen Sahib', his 'friend'."*

"Hot-foot southward, forgotten of God,
Back to the city ran Wali Dad,
Even to Kabul – in full durbar
The King held talk with his Chief in War.
Into the press of the crowd he broke,
And what he had heard of the coming spoke.
Then Gholam Hyder, the Red Chief, smiled,
As a mother might on a babbling child;
But those who would laugh restrained their breath,
When the face of the King showed dark as death.
Evil it is in full durbar
To cry to a ruler of gathering war!
Slowly he led to a peach-tree small,
That grew by a cleft of the city wall.
And he said to the boy: 'They shall praise thy zeal
So long as the red spurt follows the steel.
And the Russ is upon us even now?
Great is thy prudence – wait them, thou.
Watch from the tree. Thou art young and strong.
Surely the vigil is not for long.
The Russ is upon us, thy clamour ran?
Surely an hour shall bring their van.
Wait and watch. When the host is near,
Shout aloud that my men may hear.'

*"Halt of a caravan at Peshawur", a photograph by Bourne and Shepherd of Calcutta. Peshawur, at the southern entrance of the Khyber Pass, was where the rail network, and the authority of European civilisation, stopped. It was a clearing house of strange goods and strange news. Kipling visited Peshawur as a journalist in 1885: "The main road teems with magnificent scoundrels and handsome ruffians; all giving the on-looker the impression of wild beasts held back from murder and violence, and chafing against the restraint."*

"Friend of my heart, is it meet or wise
To warn a King of his enemies?
A guard was set that he might not flee –
A score of bayonets ringed the tree.
The peach-bloom fell in showers of snow,
When he shook at his death as he looked below.
By the power of God, Who alone is great,
Till the seventh day he fought with his fate.
Then madness took him, and men declare
He mowed in the branches as ape and bear,
And last as a sloth, ere his body failed,
And he hung like a bat in the forks, and wailed,
And sleep the cord of his hands untied,
And he fell, and was caught on the points and died.

"Heart of my heart, is it meet or wise
To warn a King of his enemies?
We know what Heaven or Hell may bring,
But no man knoweth the mind of the King.
Of the grey-coat coming who can say?
When the night is gathering all is grey.
Two things greater than all things are,
The first is Love, and the second War.
And since we know not how War may prove,
Heart of my heart, let us talk of Love!"

Kipling lived in India just seven years as an adult. In October 1889, after travels he described in *From Sea to Sea*, he returned to England, aged nearly 24. The combination of his unusual self-possession and the vigour and originality of his writing made a dramatic impact on the tired literary scene. Part of his attraction was his outlandish and romantic subject matter. Two poems published in *Macmillan's Magazine* under the pseudonym Yussuf, "The Ballad of the King's Mercy" and "The Ballad of East and West", opened up a strange world of wild, elemental justice. Kipling knew what he was writing about. As a journalist, he had access to many unorthodox sources of information. Notably, there was "the Serai where the horse-traders and the best of the blackguards of Central Asia live", and where Kipling met the original of Mahbub Ali. He describes it in "The Man who would be King": "The Kumharsen Serai is the great four-square sink of humanity where the strings of camels and horse from the North load and unload. All the nationalities of Central Asia may be found there, and most of the folk of India proper. Balkh and Bokhara there meet Bengal and Bombay, and try to draw eye-teeth. You can buy ponies, turquoises, Persian pussy-cats, saddle-bags, fat-tailed sheep and musk in the Kumharsen Serai, and get many strange things for nothing." The tales that filtered through such places provided, in the savagery of their "jests", a curious counterpart of the heartless practical joking of the Stalky days. This particular poem, "The Ballad of the King's Jest", is notable because it shows some of the seeds of *Kim*: the Russian intrigues, and also the character of Mahbub Ali, whom we can imagine in the ballad as he is described in the novel, "lying on a pair of silk carpet saddle-bags, pulling lazily at an immense silver hookah."

# Without Benefit of Clergy

"Without Benefit of Clergy" was written in 1890. Several stories in *Plain Tales from the Hills*, published two years earlier, had also explored its theme of inter-racial love, but never with such delicacy of touch. "Beyond the Pale", the best known of these, is a deliberate shocker, with a heavy-handed pseudo-moral, "Let the White go to the White and the Black to the Black." Kipling did believe in racial and cultural distinctions, but he was – surprisingly for his day – sympathetic to the despised mixed-race Eurasians. Kim, although Irish by origin, speaks in their "clipped uncertain sing-song". In "His Chance of Life" he writes: "One of these days, this people . . . will turn out a writer or a poet, and then we shall know how they live and what they feel." Nor was Kipling censorious about inter-racial marriages. In "Yoked with an Unbeliever", Phil "did what many planters have done before him – that is to say, he made up his mind to marry a Hill-girl and settle down . . . So he married Dunmaya by the forms of the English Church, and some fellow-planters said he was a fool, and some said he was a wise man." There are also a number of stories of native girls whose love is betrayed by trifling Europeans, such as Lispeth, heroine of the first story in *Plain Tales*, who reappears as the Woman of Shamlegh in *Kim*. Most moving of all is "Georgie Porgie", in which Georgie cold-bloodedly decides, "If he were so thoroughly comfortable at the Back of Beyond with this Burmese girl who smoked cheroots, how much more comfortable would he be with a sweet English maiden who would not smoke cheroots, and would play upon a piano instead of a banjo." In none of those stories, however, is there anything approaching the poignant reciprocal love between Holden and Ameera in "Without Benefit of Clergy".

Before my Spring I garnered Autumn's gain,
Out of her time my field was white with grain,
   The year gave up her secrets to my woe.
Forced and deflowered each sick season lay,
In mystery of increase and decay;
I saw the sunset ere men saw the day,
   Who am too wise in that I should not know.

*Bitter Waters.*

## I

"But if it be a girl?"

"Lord of my life, it cannot be. I have prayed for so many nights, and sent gifts to Sheikh Badl's shrine so often, that I know God will give us a son – a man-child that shall grow into a man. Think of this and be glad. My mother shall be his mother till I can take him again, and the mullah of the Pattan mosque shall cast his nativity – God send he be born in an auspicious hour! – and then, and then thou wilt never weary of me, thy slave."

"Since when hast thou been a slave, my queen?"

"Since the beginning – till this mercy came to me. How could I be sure of thy love when I knew that I had been bought with silver?"

"Nay, that was the dowry. I paid it to thy mother."

"And she has buried it, and sits upon it all day long like a hen. What talk is yours of dower! I was bought as though I had been a Lucknow dancing-girl instead of a child."

"Art thou sorry for the sale?"

"I have sorrowed; but to-day I am glad. Thou wilt never cease to love me now? – answer, my king."

"Never – never. No."

"Not even though the *mem-log* – the white women of thy own blood – love thee? And remember, I have watched them driving in the evening; they are very fair."

"I have seen fire-balloons by the hundred. I have seen the moon, and – then I saw no more fire-balloons."

Ameera clapped her hands and laughed. "Very good talk," she said. Then with an assumption of great stateliness, "It is enough. Thou hast my permission to depart – if thou wilt."

The man did not move. He was sitting on a low red-lacquered couch in a room furnished only with a blue and white floor-cloth, some rugs, and a very complete collection of native cushions. At his feet sat a woman of sixteen, and she was all but all the world in his eyes. By every rule and law she should have been otherwise, for he was an Englishman, and she a Mussulman's daughter bought two years before from her mother, who, being left without money, would have sold Ameera shrieking to the Prince of Darkness if the price had been sufficient.

It was a contract entered into with a light heart; but even before the girl had reached her bloom she came to fill the greater portion of John Holden's life. For her, and the withered hag her mother, he had taken a little house overlooking the great red-walled city, and found – when the marigolds had sprung up by the well in the courtyard, and Ameera had established herself according to her own ideas of comfort, and her mother had ceased grumbling at the inadequacy of the cooking-places, the distance from the daily market, and at matters of house-keeping in general – that the house was to him his home. Any one could enter his bachelor's bungalow by day or night, and the life that he led there was an unlovely one. In the house in the city his feet only could pass beyond the outer courtyard to the women's rooms; and when the big wooden gate was bolted behind him he was king in his own territory, with Ameera for queen. And there was going to be added to this kingdom a third person whose arrival Holden felt inclined to resent. It interfered with his perfect happiness. It disarranged the orderly peace of the house that was his own. But Ameera was wild with delight at the thought of it, and her mother not less so. The love of a man, and particularly a white man, was at the best an inconstant affair, but it might, both women argued, be held fast by a baby's hands. "And then," Ameera would always say, "then he will never care for the white *mem-log*. I hate them all – I hate them all."

"He will go back to his own people in time," said the mother; "but by the blessing of God that time is yet afar off."

Holden sat silent on the couch thinking of the future, and his thoughts were not pleasant. The drawbacks of a double life are manifold. The Government, with singular care, had ordered him out of the station for a fortnight on special duty in the place of a man who was watching by the bedside of a sick wife. The verbal notification of the transfer had been edged by a cheerful remark that Holden ought to think himself lucky in being a bachelor and a free man. He came to break the news to Ameera.

"It is not good," she said slowly, "but it is not all bad. There is my mother here, and no harm will come to me – unless indeed I die of pure joy. Go thou to thy work and think no troublesome thoughts. When the days are done I believe . . . nay, I am sure. And – and then I shall lay *him* in thy arms, and thou wilt love me for ever. The train goes to-night, at midnight is it not? Go now, and do not let thy heart be heavy by cause of me. But thou wilt not delay in returning? Thou wilt not stay on the road to talk to the bold white *mem-log*. Come back to me swiftly, my life."

As he left the courtyard to reach his horse that was tethered to the gate-post, Holden spoke to the white-haired old watchman who guarded the house, and bade him under certain contingencies despatch the filled-up telegraph-form that Holden gave him. It was all that could be done, and with the sensations of a man who has attended his own funeral Holden went away by the night mail to his exile. Every hour of the day he dreaded the arrival of the telegram, and every hour of the night he pictured to himself the death of Ameera. In consequence his work for the State was not of first-rate quality, nor was his temper towards his colleagues of the most amiable. The fortnight ended without a sign from his home, and, torn to pieces by his anxieties, Holden returned to be swallowed up for two precious hours by a dinner at the club, wherein he heard, as a man hears in a swoon, voices telling him how execrably he had performed the other man's duties, and how he had endeared himself to all his associates. Then he fled on horseback through the night with his heart in his mouth. There was no answer at first to his blows on the gate, and he had just wheeled his horse round to kick it in when Pir Khan appeared with a lantern and held his stirrup.

"Has aught occurred?" said Holden.

"The news does not come from my mouth, Protector of the Poor, but –" He held out his shaking hand as befitted the bearer of good news who is entitled to a reward.

Holden hurried through the courtyard. A light burned in the upper room. His horse neighed in the gateway, and he heard a shrill little wail that sent all the blood into the apple of his throat. It was a new voice, but it did not prove that Ameera was alive.

"Who is there?" he called up the narrow brick staircase.

*"The white-haired old watchman", a drawing by J. Pedder, 1898.*

79

There was a cry of delight from Ameera, and then the voice of the mother, tremulous with old age and pride – "We be two women and – the – man – thy – son."

On the threshold of the room Holden stepped on a naked dagger, that was laid there to avert ill-luck, and it broke at the hilt under his impatient heel.

"God is great!" cooed Ameera in the half-light. "Thou hast taken his misfortunes on thy head."

"Ay, but how is it with thee, life of my life? Old woman, how is it with her?"

"She has forgotten her sufferings for joy that the child is born. There is no harm; but speak softly," said the mother.

"It only needed thy presence to make me all well," said Ameera. "My king, thou hast been very long away. What gifts hast thou for me? Ah, ah! It is I that bring gifts this time. Look, my life, look. Was there ever such a babe? Nay, I am too weak even to clear my arm from him."

"Rest then, and do not talk. I am here, *bachari*."

bachari: little woman
heel-rope: *peecharee*

ya-illah: my God!

"Well said, for there is a bond and a heel-rope between us now that nothing can break. Look – canst thou see in this light? He is without spot or blemish. Never was such a man-child. *Ya illah!* he shall be a pundit – no, a trooper of the Queen. And, my life, dost thou love me as well as ever, though I am faint and sick and worn? Answer truly."

"Yea. I love as I have loved, with all my soul. Lie still, pearl, and rest."

"Then do not go. Sit by my side here – so. Mother, the lord of this house needs a cushion. Bring it." There was an almost imperceptible movement on the part of the new life that lay in the hollow of Ameera's arm. "Aho!" she said, her voice breaking with love. "The babe is a champion from his birth. He is kicking me in the side with mighty kicks. Was there ever such a babe! And he is ours to us – thine and mine. Put thy hand on his head, but carefully, for he is very young, and men are unskilled in such matters."

Very cautiously Holden touched with the tips of his fingers the downy head.

"He is of the Faith," said Ameera; "for lying here in the night-watches I whispered the call to prayer and the profession of faith into his ears. And it is most marvellous that he was born upon a Friday, as I was born. Be careful of him, my life; but he can almost grip with his hands."

Holden found one helpless little hand that closed feebly on his finger. And the clutch ran through his body till it settled about his heart. Till then his sole thought had been for Ameera. He began to realise that there was some one else in the world, but he could not feel that it was a veritable son with a soul. He sat down to think, and Ameera dozed lightly.

"Get hence, *sahib*," said her mother under her breath. "It is not

*A Muslim domestic sacrifice in honour of a new-born son, drawn by Lockwood Kipling, 1891.*

good that she should find you here on waking. She must be still."

"I go," said Holden submissively. "Here be rupees. See that my *baba* gets fat and finds all that he needs."

The chink of the silver roused Ameera. "I am his mother, and no hireling," she said weakly. "Shall I look to him more or less for the sake of money? Mother, give it back. I have borne my lord a son."

The deep sleep of weakness came upon her almost before the sentence was completed. Holden went down to the courtyard very softly with his heart at ease. Pir Khan, the old watchman, was chuckling with delight. "This house is now complete," he said, and without further comment thrust into Holden's hands the hilt of a sabre worn many years ago when he, Pir Khan, served the Queen in the police. The bleat of a tethered goat came from the well-kerb.

"There be two," said Pir Khan, "two goats of the best. I bought them, and they cost much money; and since there is no birth-party assembled their flesh will be all mine. Strike craftily, *sahib*! 'Tis an ill-balanced sabre at the best. Wait till they raise their heads from cropping the marigolds."

"And why?" said Holden, bewildered.

"For the birth-sacrifice. What else? Otherwise the child being unguarded from fate may die. The Protector of the Poor knows the fitting words to be said."

Holden had learned them once with little thought that he would ever speak them in earnest. The touch of the cold sabre-hilt in his palm turned suddenly to the clinging grip of the child upstairs – the child that was his own son – and a dread of loss filled him.

"Strike!" said Pir Khan. "Never life came into the world but life was paid for it. See, the goats have raised their heads. Now! With a drawing cut!"

Hardly knowing what he did, Holden cut twice as he muttered the Mahomedan prayer that runs: "Almighty! In place of this my son I offer life for life, blood for blood, head for head, bone for bone, hair for hair, skin for skin." The waiting horse snorted and bounded in his pickets at the smell of the raw blood that spurted over Holden's riding-boots.

"Well smitten!" said Pir Khan, wiping the sabre. "A swordsman was lost in thee. Go with a light heart, Heaven-born. I am thy servant, and the servant of thy son. May the Presence live a thousand years and ... the flesh of the goats is all mine?" Pir Khan drew back richer by a month's pay. Holden swung himself into the saddle and rode off through the low-hanging wood-smoke of the evening. He was full of riotous exultation, alternating with a vast vague tenderness directed towards no particular object, that made him choke as he bent over the neck of his uneasy horse. "I never felt like this in my life," he thought. "I'll go to the club and pull myself together."

A game of pool was beginning, and the room was full of men. Holden entered, eager to get to the light and the company of his fellows, singing at the top of his voice –

> In Baltimore a-walking, a lady I did meet!

"Did you?" said the club-secretary from his corner. "Did she happen to tell you that your boots were wringing wet? Great goodness, man, it's blood!"

"Bosh!" said Holden, picking his cue from the rack. "May I cut in? It's dew. I've been riding through high crops. My faith! my boots are in a mess though!

> And if it be a girl she shall wear a wedding-ring,
> And if it be a boy he shall fight for his king,
> With his dirk, and his cap, and his little jacket blue,
> He shall walk the quarter-deck –"

"Yellow on blue – green next player," said the marker monotonously.

"*He shall walk the quarter-deck* – Am I green, marker? *He shall walk the quarter-deck* – eh! that's a bad shot – *As his daddy used to do!*"

"I don't see that you have anything to crow about," said a zealous junior civilian acidly. "The Government is not exactly pleased with your work when you relieved Sanders."

"Does that mean a wigging from headquarters?" said Holden with an abstracted smile. "I think I can stand it."

The talk beat up round the ever-fresh subject of each man's work, and steadied Holden till it was time to go to his dark empty bungalow, where his butler received him as one who knew all his affairs. Holden remained awake for the greater part of the night, and his dreams were pleasant ones.

## II

"How old is he now?"

"*Ya illah!* What a man's question! He is all but six weeks old; and on this night I go up to the house-top with thee, my life, to count the stars. For that is auspicious. And he was born on a Friday under the sign of the Sun, and it has been told to me that he will outlive us both and get wealth. Can we wish for aught better, beloved?"

"There is nothing better. Let us go up to the roof, and thou shalt count the stars – but a few only, for the sky is heavy with cloud."

"The winter rains are late, and maybe they come out of season. Come, before all the stars are hid. I have put on my richest jewels."

"Thou hast forgotten the best of all."

"*Ai!* Ours. He comes also. He has never yet seen the skies."

Ameera climbed the narrow staircase that led to the flat roof. The child, placid and unwinking, lay in the hollow of her right arm, gorgeous in silver-fringed muslin with a small skull-cap on his head. Ameera wore all that she valued most. The diamond nose-stud that takes the place of the Western patch in drawing attention to the curve of the nostril, the gold ornament in the centre of the forehead studded with tallow-drop emeralds and flawed rubies, the heavy circlet of beaten gold that was fastened round her neck by the softness of the pure metal, and the chinking curb-patterned silver anklets hanging low over the rosy ankle-bone. She was dressed in jade-green muslin as befitted a daughter of the Faith, and from shoulder to elbow and elbow to wrist ran bracelets of silver tied with floss silk, frail glass bangles slipped over the wrist in proof of the slenderness of the hand, and certain heavy gold bracelets that had no part in her country's ornaments, but, since they were Holden's gift and fastened with a cunning European snap, delighted her immensely.

They sat down by the low white parapet of the roof, overlooking the city and its lights.

"They are happy down there," said Ameera. "But I do not think that they are as happy as we. Nor do I think the white *mem-log* are as happy. And thou?"

"I know they are not."

"How dost thou know?"

"They give their children over to the nurses."

"I have never seen that," said Ameera with a sigh, "nor do I wish to see. *Ahi!*" – she dropped her head on Holden's shoulder – "I have

*A drawing by Lockwood Kipling, 1891.*

counted forty stars, and I am tired. Look at the child, love of my life, he is counting too."

The baby was staring with round eyes at the dark of the heavens. Ameera placed him in Holden's arms, and he lay there without a cry.

"What shall we call him among ourselves?" she said. "Look! Art thou ever tired of looking? He carries thy very eyes. But the mouth – "

"Is thine, most dear. Who should know better than I?"

" 'Tis such a feeble mouth. Oh, so small! And yet it holds my heart between its lips. Give him to me now. He has been too long away."

"Nay, let him lie; he has not yet begun to cry."

"When he cries thou wilt give him back – eh? What a man of mankind thou art! If he cried he were only the dearer to me. But, my life, what little name shall we give him?"

The small body lay close to Holden's heart. It was utterly helpless and very soft. He scarcely dared to breathe for fear of crushing it. The caged green parrot that is regarded as a sort of guardian-spirit in most native households moved on its perch and fluttered a drowsy wing.

"There is the answer," said Holden. "Mian Mittu has spoken. He shall be the parrot. When he is ready he will talk mightily and run about. Mian Mittu is the parrot in thy – in the Mussulman tongue, is it not?"

"Why put me so far off?" said Ameera fretfully. "Let it be like unto some English name – but not wholly. For he is mine.'

"Then call him Tota, for that is likest English."

"Ay, Tota, and that is still the parrot. Forgive me, my lord, for a minute ago, but in truth he is too little to wear all the weight of Mian Mittu for name. He shall be Tota – our Tota to us. Hearest thou, oh, small one? Littlest, thou art Tota." She touched the child's cheek, and he waking wailed, and it was necessary to return him to his mother, who soothed him with the wonderful rhyme of *Aré koko, Jaré koko!* which says –

> Oh crow! Go crow! Baby's sleeping sound,
> And the wild plums grow in the jungle, only a penny a pound.
> Only a penny a pound, *baba*, only a penny a pound.

Reassured many times as to the price of those plums, Tota cuddled himself down to sleep. The two sleek, white well-bullocks in the courtyard were steadily chewing the cud of their evening meal; old Pir Khan squatted at the head of Holden's horse, his police sabre across his knees, pulling drowsily at a big water-pipe that croaked like a bull-frog in a pond. Ameera's mother sat spinning in the lower verandah, and the wooden gate was shut and barred. The music of a marriage-procession came to the roof above the gentle hum of the city, and a string of flying-foxes crossed the face of the low moon.

"I have prayed," said Ameera after a long pause, "I have prayed for two things. First, that I may die in thy stead if thy death is demanded, and in the second, that I may die in the place of the child. I have

*"The parrot's cage", a drawing by Lockwood Kipling, 1891. Lockwood's translation of Ameera's lullaby goes:*

> *Crow, crow! silence keep,*
> *Plums are ripe in jungle deep;*
> *Fetch a bushel fresh and cheap*
> *For a babe who wants to sleep.*

> *Crow, crow! the peacock cries,*
> *In the wood a thief there lies,*
> *Would steal my baby from my eyes.*

**Beebee Miriam:** the Virgin Mary

prayed to the Prophet and to Beebee Miriam. Thinkest thou either will hear?"

"From thy lips who would not hear the lightest word?"

"I asked for straight talk, and thou hast given me sweet talk. Will my prayers be heard?"

"How can I say? God is very good."

"Of that I am not sure. Listen now. When I die, or the child dies, what is thy fate? Living, thou wilt return to the bold white *mem-log*, for kind calls to kind."

"Not always."

"With a woman, no; with a man it is otherwise. Thou wilt in this life, later on, go back to thine own folk. That I could almost endure, for I should be dead. But in thy very death thou wilt be taken away to a strange place and a paradise that I do not know."

"Will it be paradise?"

"Surely, for who would harm thee? But we two – I and the child – shall be elsewhere, and we cannot come to thee, nor canst thou come to us. In the old days, before the child was born, I did not think of these things; but now I think of them always. It is very hard talk."

"It will fall as it will fall. To-morrow we do not know, but to-day and love we know well. Surely we are happy now."

"So happy that it were well to make our happiness assured. And thy Beebee Miriam should listen to me; for she is also a woman. But then she would envy me! It is not seemly for men to worship a woman."

Holden laughed aloud at Ameera's little spasm of jealousy.

"Is it not seemly? Why didst thou not turn me from worship of thee, then?"

"Thou a worshipper! And of me? My king, for all thy sweet words, well I know that I am thy servant and thy slave, and the dust under thy feet. And I would not have it otherwise. See!"

Before Holden could prevent her she stooped forward and touched his feet; recovering herself with a little laugh she hugged Tota closer to her bosom. Then, almost savagely –

"Is it true that the bold white *mem-log* live for three times the length of my life? Is it true that they make their marriages not before they are old women?"

"They marry as do others – when they are women."

"That I know, but they wed when they are twenty-five. Is that true?"

"That is true."

"*Ya illah!* At twenty-five! Who would of his own will take a wife even of eighteen? She is a woman – ageing every hour. Twenty-five! I shall be an old woman at that age, and – Those *mem-log* remain young for ever. How I hate them!"

"What have they to do with us?"

"I cannot tell. I know only that there may now be alive on this earth a woman ten years older than I who may come to thee and take thy love ten years after I am an old woman, grey-headed, and the nurse of Tota's son. That is unjust and evil. They should die too."

"Now, for all thy years thou art a child, and shalt be picked up and carried down the staircase."

"Tota! Have a care for Tota, my lord! Thou at least art as foolish as any babe!" Ameera tucked Tota out of harm's way in the hollow of her neck, and was carried downstairs laughing in Holden's arms, while Tota opened his eyes and smiled after the manner of the lesser angels.

He was a silent infant, and, almost before Holden could realise that he was in the world, developed into a small gold-coloured little god and unquestioned despot of the house overlooking the city. Those were months of absolute happiness to Holden and Ameera – happiness withdrawn from the world, shut in behind the wooden gate that Pir Khan guarded. By day Holden did his work with an immense pity for such as were not so fortunate as himself, and a sympathy for small children that amazed and amused many mothers at the little station-gatherings. At nightfall he returned to Ameera – Ameera, full of the wondrous doings of Tota; how he had been seen to clap his hands together and move his fingers with intention and purpose – which was manifestly a miracle – how later, he had of his own initiative crawled out of his bedstead on to the floor and swayed on both feet for the space of three breaths.

"And they were long breaths, for my heart stood still with delight," said Ameera.

Then Tota took the beasts into his councils – the well-bullocks, the little grey squirrels, the mongoose that lived in a hole near the well, and especially Mian Mittu, the parrot, whose tail he grievously pulled, and Mian Mittu screamed till Ameera and Holden arrived.

"Oh villain! Child of strength! This to thy brother on the house-top! *Tobah, tobah!* Fie! Fie! But I know a charm to make him wise as Suleiman and Aflatoun. Now look," said Ameera. She drew from an embroidered bag a handful of almonds. "See! we count seven. In the name of God!"

**Suleiman and Aflatoun:** Solomon and Plato

She placed Mian Mittu, very angry and rumpled, on the top of his cage, and seating herself between the babe and the bird she cracked and peeled an almond less white than her teeth. "This is a true charm, my life, and do not laugh. See! I give the parrot one-half and Tota the other." Mian Mittu with careful beak took his share from between Ameera's lips, and she kissed the other half into the mouth of the child, who ate it slowly with wondering eyes. "This I will do each day of seven, and without doubt he who is ours will be a bold speaker and wise. Eh, Tota, what wilt thou be when thou art a man and I am grey-headed?" Tota tucked his fat legs into adorable creases. He could crawl, but he was not going to waste the spring of his youth in idle speech. He wanted Mian Mittu's tail to tweak.

When he was advanced to the dignity of a silver belt – which, with a magic square engraved on silver and hung round his neck, made up the greater part of his clothing – he staggered on a perilous journey down the garden to Pir Khan, and proffered him all his jewels in exchange for one little ride on Holden's horse, having seen his mother's mother chaffering with pedlars in the verandah. Pir Khan wept and set the untried feet on his own grey head in sign of fealty, and brought the bold adventurer to his mother's arms, vowing that Tota would be a leader of men ere his beard was grown.

*A mother and child, sketched by Lockwood Kipling, about 1894.*

One hot evening, while he sat on the roof between his father and
mother watching the never-ending warfare of the kites that the city
boys flew, he demanded a kite of his own with Pir Khan to fly it,
because he had a fear of dealing with anything larger than himself,
and when Holden called him a "spark", he rose to his feet and
answered slowly in defence of his new-found individuality,
*"Hum'park nahin hai. Hum admi hai."*

**Hum'park . . .:** I am no spark, but a man

The protest made Holden choke and devote himself very seriously
to a consideration of Tota's future. He need hardly have taken the
trouble. The delight of that life was too perfect to endure. Therefore
it was taken away as many things are taken away in India – suddenly
and without warning. The little lord of the house, as Pir Khan called
him, grew sorrowful and complained of pains who had never known
the meaning of pain. Ameera, wild with terror, watched him through
the night, and in the dawning of the second day the life was shaken
out of him by fever – the seasonal autumn fever. It seemed altogether
impossible that he could die, and neither Ameera nor Holden at first
believed the evidence of the little body on the bedstead. Then Ameera
beat her head against the wall and would have flung herself down the
well in the garden had Holden not restrained her by main force.

One mercy only was granted to Holden. He rode to his office in
broad daylight and found waiting for him an unusually heavy mail
that demanded concentrated attention and hard work. He was not,
however, alive to this kindness of the gods.

### III

The first shock of a bullet is no more than a brisk pinch. The wrecked
body does not send in its protest to the soul till ten or fifteen seconds
later. Holden realised his pain slowly, exactly as he had realised his
happiness, and with the same imperious necessity for hiding all trace
of it. In the beginning he only felt that there had been a loss, and that
Ameera needed comforting, where she sat with her head on her knees
shivering as Mian Mittu from the house-top called, *Tota! Tota! Tota!*
Later all his world and the daily life of it rose up to hurt him. It was an
outrage that any one of the children at the band-stand in the evening
should be alive and clamorous, when his own child lay dead. It was
more than mere pain when one of them touched him, and stories told
by over-fond fathers of their children's latest performances cut him
to the quick. He could not declare his pain. He had neither help,
comfort, nor sympathy; and Ameera at the end of each weary day
would lead him through the hell of self-questioning reproach which
is reserved for those who have lost a child, and believe that with a
little – just a little more care – it might have been saved.

"Perhaps," Ameera would say, "I did not take sufficient heed. Did
I, or did I not? The sun on the roof that day when he played so long
alone and I was – *ahi!* braiding my hair – it may be that the sun then
bred the fever. If I had warned him from the sun he might have lived.

But, oh my life, say that I am guiltless! Thou knowest that I loved him as I love thee. Say that there is no blame on me, or I shall die – I shall die!"

"There is no blame – before God, none. It was written, and how could we do aught to save? What has been, has been. Let it go, beloved."

"He was all my heart to me. How can I let the thought go when my arm tells me every night that he is not here? *Ahi! Ahi!* Oh, Tota, come back to me – come back again, and let us be all together as it was before!"

"Peace, peace! For thine own sake, and for mine also, if thou lovest me – rest."

"By this I know thou dost not care; and how shouldst thou? The white men have hearts of stone and souls of iron. Oh, that I had married a man of mine own people – though he beat me – and had never eaten the bread of an alien!"

"Am I an alien – mother of my son?"

"What else – *Sahib*? . . . Oh, forgive me – forgive! The death has driven me mad. Thou art the life of my heart, and the light of my eyes, and the breath of my life, and – and I have put thee from me, though it was but for a moment. If thou goest away, to whom shall I look for help? Do not be angry. Indeed, it was the pain that spoke and not thy slave."

"I know, I know. We be two who were three. The greater need therefore that we should be one."

They were sitting on the roof as of custom. The night was a warm one in early spring, and sheet-lightning was dancing on the horizon to a broken tune played by far-off thunder. Ameera settled herself in Holden's arms.

"The dry earth is lowing like a cow for the rain, and I – I am afraid. It was not like this when we counted the stars. But thou lovest me as much as before, though a bond is taken away? Answer!"

"I love more because a new bond has come out of the sorrow that we have eaten together, and that thou knowest."

"Yea, I knew," said Ameera in a very small whisper. "But it is good to hear thee say so, my life, who art so strong to help. I will be a child no more, but a woman and an aid to thee. Listen! Give me my *sitar* and I will sing bravely."

She took the light silver-studded *sitar* and began a song of the great hero Rajah Rasalu. The hand failed on the strings, the tune halted, checked, and at a low note turned off to the poor little nursery-rhyme about the wicked crow –

And the wild plums grow in the jungle, only a penny a pound.
Only a penny a pound, *baba* – only . . .

Then came the tears, and the piteous rebellion against fate till she slept, moaning a little in her sleep, with the right arm thrown clear of

*An Indian woman with a sitar, 1898.*

89

*A sketch by Lockwood Kipling,
almost certainly showing Ameera.
Holden, asleep in the background,
is drawn with the lightest of pencils.*

the body as though it protected something that was not there. It was after this night that life became a little easier for Holden. The ever-present pain of loss drove him into his work, and the work repaid him by filling up his mind for nine or ten hours a day. Ameera sat alone in the house and brooded, but grew happier when she understood that Holden was more at ease, according to the custom of women. They touched happiness again, but this time with caution.

"It was because we loved Tota that he died. The jealousy of God was upon us," said Ameera. "I have hung up a large black jar before our window to turn the evil eye from us, and we must make no protestations of delight, but go softly underneath the stars, lest God find us out. Is that not good talk, worthless one?"

She had shifted the accent on the word that means "beloved", in proof of the sincerity of her purpose. But the kiss that followed the new christening was a thing that any deity might have envied. They went about henceforward saying, "It is naught, it is naught"; and hoping that all the Powers heard.

The Powers were busy on other things. They had allowed thirty million people four years of plenty, wherein men fed well and the crops were certain, and the birth-rate rose year by year; the districts reported a purely agricultural population varying from nine hundred to two thousand to the square mile of the overburdened earth; and the Member for Lower Tooting, wandering about India in top-hat and frock-coat, talked largely of the benefits of British rule, and suggested as the one thing needful the establishment of a duly qualified electoral system and a general bestowal of the franchise. His long-suffering hosts smiled and made him welcome, and when he paused to admire, with pretty picked words, the blossom of the blood-red *dhak*-tree that had flowered untimely for a sign of what was coming, they smiled more than ever.

It was the Deputy Commissioner of Kot-Kumharsen, staying at the club for a day, who lightly told a tale that made Holden's blood run cold as he overheard the end.

"He won't bother any one any more. Never saw a man so astonished in my life. By Jove, I thought he meant to ask a question in the House about it. Fellow-passenger in his ship – dined next him – bowled over by cholera and died in eighteen hours. You needn't laugh, you fellows. The Member for Lower Tooting is awfully angry about it; but he's more scared. I think he's going to take his enlightened self out of India."

"I'd give a good deal if he were knocked over. It might keep a few vestrymen of his kidney to their own parish. But what's this about cholera? It's full early for anything of that kind," said the warden of an unprofitable salt-lick.

"Don't know," said the Deputy Commissioner reflectively. "We've got locusts with us. There's sporadic cholera all along the north – at least we're calling it sporadic for decency's sake. The spring crops are short in five districts, and nobody seems to know where the rains are. It's nearly March now. I don't want to scare anybody, but it seems to me that Nature's going to audit her accounts with a big red pencil this summer."

"Just when I wanted to take leave, too!" said a voice across the room.

"There won't be much leave this year, but there ought to be a great deal of promotion. I've come in to persuade the Government to put my pet canal on the list of famine-relief works. It's an ill wind that blows no good. I shall get that canal finished at last."

"Is it the old programme then," said Holden; "famine, fever, and cholera?"

"Oh no. Only local scarcity and an unusual prevalence of seasonal sickness. You'll find it all in the reports if you live till next year. You're a lucky chap. *You* haven't got a wife to send out of harm's way. The hill-stations ought to be full of women this year."

"I think you're inclined to exaggerate the talk in the *bazars*," said a young civilian in the Secretariat. "Now I have observed –"

"I daresay you have," said the Deputy Commissioner, "but you've a great deal more to observe, my son. In the meantime, I wish to observe to you –" and he drew him aside to discuss the construction of the canal that was so dear to his heart. Holden went to his bungalow and began to understand that he was not alone in the world, and also that he was afraid for the sake of another – which is the most soul-satisfying fear known to man.

Two months later, as the Deputy had foretold, Nature began to audit her accounts with a red pencil. On the heels of the spring-reapings came a cry for bread, and the Government, which had decreed that no man should die of want, sent wheat. Then came the cholera from all four quarters of the compass. It struck a pilgrim-gathering of half a million at a sacred shrine. Many died at the feet of their god; the others broke and ran over the face of the land carrying the pestilence with them. It smote a walled city and killed two hundred a day. The people crowded the trains, hanging on to the footboards and squatting on the roofs of the carriages, and the cholera followed them, for at each station they dragged out the dead and the dying. They died by the roadside, and the horses of the Englishmen shied at the corpses in the grass. The rains did not come, and the earth turned to iron lest man should escape death by hiding in her. The English sent their wives away to the hills and went about their work, coming forward as they were bidden to fill the gaps in the fighting-line. Holden, sick with fear of losing his chiefest treasure on earth, had done his best to persuade Ameera to go away with her mother to the Himalayas.

"Why should I go?" said she one evening on the roof.

"There is sickness, and people are dying, and all the white *mem-log* have gone."

"All of them?"

"All – unless perhaps there remain some old scald-head who vexes her husband's heart by running risk of death."

"Nay; who stays is my sister, and thou must not abuse her, for I will be a scald-head too. I am glad all the bold *mem-log* are gone."

"Do I speak to a woman or a babe? Go to the hills, and I will see to it that thou goest like a queen's daughter. Think, child. In a red-lacquered bullock cart, veiled and curtained, with brass peacocks upon the pole and red cloth hangings. I will send two orderlies for guard and – "

"Peace! Thou art the babe in speaking thus. What use are those toys to me? *He* would have patted the bullocks and played with the housings. For his sake, perhaps – thou hast made me very English – I might have gone. Now, I will not. Let the *mem-log* run."

"Their husbands are sending them, beloved."

"Very good talk. Since when hast thou been my husband to tell me what to do? I have but borne thee a son. Thou art only all the desire of my soul to me. How shall I depart when I know that if evil befall thee by the breadth of so much as my littlest finger-nail – is that not small? – I should be aware of it though I were in paradise. And here, this summer thou mayest die – *ai, janee*, die! and in dying they might call to tend thee a white woman, and she would rob me in the last of thy love!"

"But love is not born in a moment or on a death-bed!"

"What dost thou know of love, stoneheart? She would take thy thanks at least and, by God and the Prophet and Beebee Miriam the mother of thy Prophet, that I will never endure. My lord and my love, let there be no more foolish talk of going away. Where thou art,

I am. It is enough." She put an arm round his neck and a hand on his mouth.

There are not many happinesses so complete as those that are snatched under the shadow of the sword. They sat together and laughed, calling each other openly by every pet name that could move the wrath of the gods. The city below them was locked up in its own torments. Sulphur fires blazed in the streets; the conches in the Hindu temples screamed and bellowed, for the gods were inattentive in those days. There was a service in the great Mahomedan shrine, and the call to prayer from the minarets was almost unceasing. They heard the wailing in the houses of the dead, and once the shriek of a mother who had lost a child and was calling for its return. In the grey dawn they saw the dead borne out through the city gates, each litter with its own little knot of mourners. Wherefore they kissed each other and shivered.

It was a red and heavy audit, for the land was very sick and needed a little breathing-space ere the torrent of cheap life should flood it anew. The children of immature fathers and undeveloped mothers made no resistance. They were cowed and sat still, waiting till the

*The lower bazaar, Simla; a photograph by Bourne and Shepherd of Calcutta. The English retreated from the intense summer heat to Simla, on the slopes of the Himalayas, the setting of some of the brittle social vignettes in Kipling's early stories. "Simla was another new world. There the Hierarchy lived, and one saw and heard the machinery of administration stripped bare."*

sword should be sheathed in November if it were so willed. There were gaps among the English, but the gaps were filled. The work of superintending famine-relief, cholera-sheds, medicine-distribution, and what little sanitation was possible, went forward because it was so ordered.

Holden had been told to keep himself in readiness to move to replace the next man who should fall. There were twelve hours in each day when he could not see Ameera, and she might die in three. He was considering what his pain would be if he could not see her for three months, or if she died out of his sight. He was absolutely certain that her death would be demanded – so certain, that when he looked up from the telegram and saw Pir Khan breathless in the doorway, he laughed aloud. "And?" said he –

"When there is a cry in the night and the spirit flutters into the throat, who has a charm that will restore? Come swiftly, Heaven-born! It is the black cholera."

Holden galloped to his home. The sky was heavy with clouds, for the long-deferred rains were near and the heat was stifling. Ameera's mother met him in the courtyard, whimpering, "She is dying. She is nursing herself into death. She is all but dead. What shall I do, *sahib*?"

Ameera was lying in the room in which Tota had been born. She made no sign when Holden entered, because the human soul is a very lonely thing and, when it is getting ready to go away, hides itself in a misty borderland where the living may not follow. The black cholera does its work quietly and without explanation. Ameera was being thrust out of life as though the Angel of Death had himself put his hand upon her. The quick breathing seemed to show that she was either afraid or in pain, but neither eyes nor mouth gave any answer to Holden's kisses. There was nothing to be said or done. Holden could only wait and suffer. The first drops of the rain began to fall on the roof and he could hear shouts of joy in the parched city.

The soul came back a little and the lips moved. Holden bent down to listen. "Keep nothing of mine," said Ameera. "Take no hair from my head. *She* would make thee burn it later on. That flame I should feel. Lower! Stoop lower! Remember only that I was thine and bore thee a son. Though thou wed a white woman to-morrow, the pleasure of receiving in thy arms thy first son is taken from thee for ever. Remember me when thy son is born – the one that shall carry thy name before all men. His misfortunes be on my head. I bear witness – I bear witness" – the lips were forming the words on his ear – "that there is no God but – thee, beloved!"

Then she died. Holden sat still, and all thought was taken from him – till he heard Ameera's mother lift the curtain.

"Is she dead, *sahib*?"

"She is dead."

"Then I will mourn, and afterwards take an inventory of the furniture in this house. For that will be mine. The *sahib* does not mean to resume it? It is so little, so very little, *sahib*, and I am an old woman. I would like to lie softly."

"For the mercy of God be silent a while. Go out and mourn where I cannot hear."

"*Sahib*, she will be buried in four hours."

"I know the custom. I shall go ere she is taken away. That matter is in thy hands. Look to it, that the bed on which – on which she lies –"

"Aha! That beautiful red-lacquered bed. I have long desired –"

"That the bed is left here untouched for my disposal. All else in the house is thine. Hire a cart, take everything, go hence, and before sunrise let there be nothing in this house but that which I have ordered thee to respect."

"I am an old woman. I would stay at least for the days of mourning, and the rains have just broken. Whither shall I go?"

"What is that to me? My order is that there is a going. The house-gear is worth a thousand rupees and my orderly shall bring thee a hundred rupees to-night."

"That is very little. Think of the cart-hire."

"It shall be nothing unless thou goest, and with speed. O woman, get hence and leave me with my dead!"

The mother shuffled down the staircase, and in her anxiety to take stock of the house-fittings forgot to mourn. Holden stayed by Ameera's side and the rain roared on the roof. He could not think connectedly by reason of the noise, though he made many attempts to do so. Then four sheeted ghosts glided dripping into the room and stared at him through their veils. They were the washers of the dead. Holden left the room and went out to his horse. He had come in a dead, stifling calm through ankle-deep dust. He found the courtyard a rain-lashed pond alive with frogs; a torrent of yellow water ran under the gate, and a roaring wind drove the bolts of the rain like buckshot against the mud-walls. Pir Khan was shivering in his little hut by the gate, and the horse was stamping uneasily in the water.

"I have been told the *sahib*'s order," said Pir Khan. "It is well. This house is now desolate. I go also, for my monkey-face would be a reminder of that which has been. Concerning the bed, I will bring that to thy house yonder in the morning; but remember, *sahib*, it will be to thee a knife turning in a green wound. I go upon a pilgrimage, and I will take no money. I have grown fat in the protection of the Presence whose sorrow is my sorrow. For the last time I hold his stirrup."

*A drawing by Lockwood Kipling, 1891.*

He touched Holden's foot with both hands and the horse sprang out into the road, where the creaking bamboos were whipping the sky and all the frogs were chuckling. Holden could not see for the rain in his face. He put his hands before his eyes and muttered –

"Oh you brute! You utter brute!"

The news of his trouble was already in his bungalow. He read the knowledge in his butler's eyes when Ahmed Khan brought in food,

*A drawing by Lockwood Kipling, 1894.*

and for the first and last time in his life laid a hand upon his master's shoulder, saying, "Eat, *sahib*, eat. Meat is good against sorrow. I also have known. Moreover the shadows come and go, *sahib*; the shadows come and go. These be curried eggs."

Holden could neither eat nor sleep. The heavens sent down eight inches of rain in that night and washed the earth clean. The waters tore down walls, broke roads, and scoured open the shallow graves on the Mahomedan burying-ground. All next day it rained, and Holden sat still in his house considering his sorrow. On the morning of the third day he received a telegram which said only, "Ricketts, Myndonie. Dying. Holden relieve. Immediate." Then he thought that before he departed he would look at the house wherein he had been master and lord. There was a break in the weather, and the rank earth steamed with vapour.

He found that the rains had torn down the mud pillars of the gateway, and the heavy wooden gate that had guarded his life hung lazily from one hinge. There was grass three inches high in the courtyard; Pir Khan's lodge was empty, and the sodden thatch sagged between the beams. A grey squirrel was in possession of the verandah, as if the house had been untenanted for thirty years instead of three days. Ameera's mother had removed everything except some mildewed matting. The *tick-tick* of the little scorpions as they hurried across the floor was the only sound in the house. Ameera's room and the other one where Tota had lived were heavy with mildew; and the narrow staircase leading to the roof was streaked and stained with rain-borne mud. Holden saw all these things, and came out again to meet in the road Durga Dass, his landlord – portly, affable, clothed in white muslin, and driving a C-spring buggy. He was overlooking his property to see how the roofs stood the stress of the first rains.

"I have heard," said he, "you will not take this place any more, *sahib*?"

"What are you going to do with it?"

"Perhaps I shall let it again."

"Then I will keep it on while I am away."

Durga Dass was silent for some time. "You shall not take it on, *sahib*," he said. "When I was a young man, I also –, but to-day I am a member of the Municipality. Ho! Ho! No. When the birds have gone what need to keep the nest? I will have it pulled down – the timber will sell for something always. It shall be pulled down, and the Municipality shall make a road across, as they desire, from the burning-*ghât* to the city wall, so that no man may say where this house stood."

# The Miracle of Purun Bhagat

"The Miracle of Purun Baghat" has always seemed uncomfortably placed in *The Second Jungle Book*. Written in May 1894, its affinities are not with the Mowgli stories but with *Kim*, which in many ways it anticipates. In Lahore, Kipling associated most closely with Muslims, and when first he moved to Allahabad in 1887 he found Hindu ways strange. This story expresses the admiration he came to feel for Hinduism, as *Kim* does for Buddhism. Strickland in *Kim* affects the ordinary Englishman's contempt for what Kipling termed elsewhere "the wandering mendicants, charm-sellers, and holy vagabonds" of India; entering the train carriage in which Kim, the Lama and the Saddhu are, he observes, "Nothing here but a parcel of holy-bolies." Again, Kipling is unrepresentative of his time. The preface to *Life's Handicap* (1891) describes his friendship with Gobind, a holy man who sat in a decaying monastery telling stories as he waited to die. "The people brought him food and little clumps of marigold flowers, and he gave his blessing in return." The important thing about Purun Baghat for Kipling is that he has competed on equal terms with the English without losing his identity. In an earlier story, "On the City Wall", Kipling describes a young Muslim, Wali Dad, who has been educated out of his faith. Wali Dad prophesies, "There will never be any more great men in India. They will all, when they are young, go whoring after strange gods, and they will become citizens – 'fellow-citizens' – 'illustrious fellow-citizens'. What is it the native papers call them?" Kipling's verdict in 1930 was that "Gandhi is just a paste-board front": but by then he was old and tired and increasingly out of touch with his own experience. As a young man, he might have passed a more interesting verdict.

There was once a man in India who was Prime Minister of one of the semi-independent native States in the north-western part of the country. He was a Brahmin, so high-caste that caste ceased to have any particular meaning for him; and his father had been an important official in the gay-coloured tag-rag and bobtail of an old-fashioned Hindu Court. But as Purun Dass grew up he felt that the old order of things was changing, and that if any one wished to get on in the world he must stand well with the English, and imitate all that the English believed to be good. At the same time a native official must keep his own master's favour. This was a difficult game, but the quiet, close-mouthed young Brahmin, helped by a good English education at a Bombay University, played it coolly, and rose, step by step, to be Prime Minister of the kingdom. That is to say, he held more real power than his master the Maharajah.

When the old king – who was suspicious of the English, their railways and telegraphs – died, Purun Dass stood high with his young successor, who had been tutored by an Englishman; and between them, though he always took care that his master should have the credit, they established schools for little girls, made roads, and started State dispensaries and shows of agricultural implements, and

*A Hindu student, 1898.*

published a yearly blue-book on the "Moral and Material Progress of the State", and the Foreign Office and the Government of India were delighted. Very few native States take up English progress altogether, for they will not believe, as Purun Dass showed he did, that what was good for the Englishman must be twice as good for the Asiatic. The Prime Minister became the honoured friend of Viceroys, and Governors, and Lieutenant-Governors, and medical missionaries, and common missionaries, and hard-riding English officers who came to shoot in the State preserves, as well as of whole hosts of tourists who travelled up and down India in the cold weather, showing how things ought to be managed. In his spare time he would endow scholarships for the study of medicine and manufactures on strictly English lines, and write letters to the *Pioneer*, the greatest Indian daily paper, explaining his master's aims and objects.

At last he went to England on a visit, and had to pay enormous sums to the priests when he came back; for even so high-caste a Brahmin as Purun Dass lost caste by crossing the black sea. In London he met and talked with every one worth knowing – men whose names go all over the world – and saw a great deal more than he said. He was given honorary degrees by learned universities, and he made speeches and talked of Hindu social reform to English ladies in evening dress, till all London cried, "This is the most fascinating man we have ever met at dinner since cloths were first laid."

When he returned to India there was a blaze of glory, for the Viceroy himself made a special visit to confer upon the Maharajah the Grand Cross of the Star of India – all diamonds and ribbons and enamel; and at the same ceremony, while the cannon boomed, Purun Dass was made a Knight Commander of the Order of the Indian Empire; so that his name stood Sir Purun Dass, K.C.I.E.

That evening, at dinner in the big Viceregal tent, he stood up with the badge and the collar of the Order on his breast, and replying to the toast of his master's health, made a speech few Englishmen could have bettered.

Next month, when the city had returned to its sun-baked quiet, he did a thing no Englishman would have dreamed of doing; for, so far as the world's affairs went, he died. The jewelled order of his knighthood went back to the Indian Government, and a new Prime Minister was appointed to the charge of affairs, and a great game of General Post began in all the subordinate appointments. The priests knew what had happened, and the people guessed; but India is the one place in the world where a man can do as he pleases and nobody asks why; and the fact that Dewan Sir Purun Dass, K.C.I.E., had resigned position, palace, and power, and taken up the begging-bowl and ochre-coloured dress of a Sunnyasi, or holy man, was considered nothing extraordinary. He had been, as the Old Law recommends, twenty years a youth, twenty years a fighter – though he had never carried a weapon in his life – and twenty years head of a household.

*A religious mendicant, drawn by the Rev. W. Urwick, 1891.*

*Mohamad Ali Khan, G.C.I.E., the Nawab of Tonk, photographed in 1866, the year he was deposed for complicity in his uncle's murder. The semi-independent native states were hotbeds of intrigue; the best scenes of* The Naulahka *show Kipling's easy familiarity with such palace politics.*

He had used his wealth and his power for what he knew both to be worth; he had taken honour when it came his way; he had seen men and cities far and near, and men and cities had stood up and honoured him. Now he would let those things go, as a man drops the cloak he no longer needs.

Behind him, as he walked through the city gates, an antelope skin and brass-handled crutch under his arm, and a begging-bowl of polished brown *coco-de-mer* in his hand, barefoot, alone, with eyes cast on the ground – behind him they were firing salutes from the bastions in honour of his happy successor. Purun Dass nodded. All that life was ended; and he bore it no more ill-will or good-will than a man bears to a colourless dream of the night. He was a Sunnyasi – a houseless, wandering mendicant, depending on his neighbours for his daily bread; and so long as there is a morsel to divide in India, neither priest nor beggar starves. He had never in his life tasted meat, and very seldom eaten even fish. A five-pound note would have covered his personal expenses for food through any one of the many years in which he had been absolute master of millions of money. Even when he was being lionised in London he had held before him his dream of peace and quiet – the long, white, dusty Indian road, printed all over with bare feet, the incessant, slow-moving traffic, and the sharp-smelling wood smoke curling up under the fig-trees in the twilight, where the wayfarers sit at their evening meal.

When the time came to make that dream true the Prime Minister took the proper steps, and in three days you might more easily have found a bubble in the trough of the long Atlantic seas than Purun Dass among the roving, gathering, separating millions of India.

At night his antelope skin was spread where the darkness overtook him – sometimes in a Sunnyasi monastery by the roadside; sometimes by a mud-pillar shrine of Kala Pir, where the Jogis, who are another misty division of holy men, would receive him as they do those who know what castes and divisions are worth; sometimes on the outskirts of a little Hindu village, where the children would steal up with the food their parents had prepared; and sometimes on the pitch of the bare grazing-grounds, where the flame of his stick fire waked the drowsy camels. It was all one to Purun Dass – or Purun Bhagat, as he called himself now. Earth, people, and food were all one. But unconsciously his feet drew him away northward and eastward; from the south to Rohtak; from Rohtak to Kurnool; from Kurnool to ruined Samanah, and then up-stream along the dried bed of the Gugger river that fills only when the rain falls in the hills, till one day he saw the far line of the great Himalayas.

Then Purun Bhagat smiled, for he remembered that his mother was of Rajput Brahmin birth, from Kulu way – a Hill-woman, always home-sick for the snows – and that the least touch of Hill blood draws a man in the end back to where he belongs.

"Yonder," said Purun Bhagat, breasting the lower slopes of the Sewaliks, where the cacti stand up like seven-branched candlesticks – "yonder I shall sit down and get knowledge"; and the cool wind of the Himalayas whistled about his ears as he trod the road that led to Simla.

The last time he had come that way it had been in state, with a clattering cavalry escort, to visit the gentlest and most affable of

*A Himalayan hill girl, drawn by the Rev. W. Urwick, 1891. Kipling wrote: "When a Hill-girl grows lovely, she is worth travelling fifty miles over bad ground to look upon."*

Viceroys; and the two had talked for an hour together about mutual friends in London, and what the Indian common folk really thought of things. This time Purun Bhagat paid no calls, but leaned on the rail of the Mall, watching that glorious view of the Plains spread out forty miles below, till a native Mahomedan policeman told him he was obstructing traffic; and Purun Bhagat salaamed reverently to the Law, because he knew the value of it, and was seeking for a Law of his own. Then he moved on, and slept that night in an empty hut at Chota Simla, which looks like the very last end of the earth, but it was only the beginning of his journey.

He followed the Himalaya–Tibet road, the little ten-foot track that is blasted out of solid rock, or strutted out on timbers over gulfs a thousand feet deep; that dips into warm, wet, shut-in valleys, and climbs out across bare, grassy hill-shoulders where the sun strikes like a burning-glass; or turns through dripping, dark forests where the tree-ferns dress the trunks from head to heel, and the pheasant calls to his mate. And he met Tibetan herdsmen with their dogs and flocks of sheep, each sheep with a little bag of borax on his back, and wandering wood-cutters, and cloaked and blanketed Lamas from Tibet, coming into India on pilgrimage, and envoys of little solitary Hill-states, posting furiously on ring-streaked and piebald ponies, or the cavalcade of a Rajah paying a visit; or else for a long, clear day he would see nothing more than a black bear grunting and rooting below in the valley. When he first started, the roar of the world he had left still rang in his ears, as the roar of a tunnel rings long after the train has passed through; but when he had put the Mutteeanee Pass behind him that was all done, and Purun Bhagat was alone with himself, walking, wondering, and thinking, his eyes on the ground, and his thoughts with the clouds.

One evening he crossed the highest pass he had met till then – it had been a two-days' climb – and came out on a line of snow-peaks that banded all the horizon – mountains from fifteen to twenty thousand feet high, looking almost near enough to hit with a stone, though they were fifty or sixty miles away. The pass was crowned with dense, dark forest – deodar, walnut, wild cherry, wild olive, and wild pear, but mostly deodar, which is the Himalayan cedar; and under the shadow of the deodars stood a deserted shrine to Kali – who is Durga, who is Sitala, who is sometimes worshipped against the smallpox.

Purun Dass swept the stone floor clean, smiled at the grinning statue, made himself a little mud fireplace at the back of the shrine, spread his antelope skin on a bed of fresh pine-needles, tucked his *bairagi* – his brass-handled crutch – under his armpit, and sat down to rest.

Immediately below him the hillside fell away, clean and cleared for fifteen hundred feet, where a little village of stone-walled houses, with roofs of beaten earth, clung to the steep tilt. All round it the tiny terraced fields lay out like aprons of patchwork on the knees of the

*The Himalaya–Tibet road, drawn by the Rev. W. Urwick, 1891.*

101

mountain, and cows no bigger than beetles grazed between the smooth stone circles of the threshing-floors. Looking across the valley, the eye was deceived by the size of things, and could not at first realise that what seemed to be low scrub, on the opposite mountain-flank, was in truth a forest of hundred-foot pines. Purun Bhagat saw an eagle swoop across the gigantic hollow, but the great bird dwindled to a dot ere it was half-way over. A few bands of scattered clouds strung up and down the valley, catching on a shoulder of the hills, or rising up and dying out when they were level with the head of the pass. And "Here shall I find peace," said Purun Bhagat.

Now, a Hill-man makes nothing of a few hundred feet up or down, and as soon as the villagers saw the smoke in the deserted shrine, the village priest climbed up the terraced hillside to welcome the stranger.

When he met Purun Bhagat's eyes – the eyes of a man used to control thousands – he bowed to the earth, took the begging-bowl without a word, and returned to the village, saying, "We have at last a holy man. Never have I seen such a man. He is of the Plains – but pale-coloured – a Brahmin of the Brahmins." Then all the house-wives of the village said, "Think you he will stay with us?" and each did her best to cook the most savoury meal for the Bhagat. Hill-food is very simple, but with buckwheat and Indian corn, and rice and red pepper, and little fish out of the stream in the valley, and honey from the flue-like hives built in the stone walls, and dried apricots, and turmeric, and wild ginger, and bannocks of flour, a devout woman can make good things, and it was a full bowl that the priest carried to the Bhagat. Was he going to stay? asked the priest. Would he need a *chela* – a disciple – to beg for him? Had he a blanket against the cold weather? Was the food good?

Purun Bhagat ate, and thanked the giver. It was in his mind to stay. That was sufficient, said the priest. Let the begging-bowl be placed outside the shrine, in the hollow made by those two twisted roots, and daily should the Bhagat be fed; for the village felt honoured that such a man – he looked timidly into the Bhagat's face – should tarry among them.

That day saw the end of Purun Bhagat's wanderings. He had come to the place appointed for him – the silence and the space. After this, time stopped, and he, sitting at the mouth of the shrine, could not tell whether he were alive or dead; a man with control of his limbs, or a part of the hills, and the clouds, and the shifting rain and sunlight. He would repeat a Name softly to himself a hundred hundred times, till, at each repetition, he seemed to move more and more out of his body, sweeping up to the doors of some tremendous discovery; but, just as the door was opening, his body would drag him back, and, with grief, he felt he was locked up again in the flesh and bones of Purun Bhagat.

Every morning the filled begging-bowl was laid silently in the

OPPOSITE: *Purun Baghat, an etching by W. Strang, 1900.*

102

crutch of the roots outside the shrine. Sometimes the priest brought it; sometimes a Ladakhi trader, lodging in the village, and anxious to get merit, trudged up the path; but, more often, it was the woman who had cooked the meal overnight; and she would murmur, hardly above her breath: "Speak for me before the gods, Bhagat. Speak for such a one, the wife of so-and-so!" Now and then some bold child would be allowed the honour, and Purun Bhagat would hear him drop the bowl and run as fast as his little legs could carry him, but the Bhagat never came down to the village. It was laid out like a map at his feet. He could see the evening gatherings, held on the circle of the threshing-floors, because that was the only level ground; could see the wonderful unnamed green of the young rice, the indigo blues of the Indian corn, the dock-like patches of buckwheat, and, in its season, the red bloom of the amaranth, whose tiny seeds, being neither grain nor pulse, make a food that can be lawfully eaten by Hindus in time of fasts.

When the year turned, the roofs of the huts were all little squares of purest gold, for it was on the roofs that they laid out their cobs of the corn to dry. Hiving and harvest, rice-sowing and husking, passed before his eyes, all embroidered down there on the many-sided plots of fields, and he thought of them all, and wondered what they all led to at the long last.

Even in populated India a man cannot a day sit still before the wild things run over him as though he were a rock; and in that wilderness very soon the wild things, who knew Kali's Shrine well, came back to look at the intruder. The *langurs*, the big grey-whiskered monkeys of the Himalayas, were, naturally, the first, for they are alive with curiosity; and when they had upset the begging-bowl, and rolled it round the floor, and tried their teeth on the brass-handled crutch, and made faces at the antelope skin, they decided that the human being who sat so still was harmless. At evening, they would leap down from the pines, and beg with their hands for things to eat, and then swing off in graceful curves. They liked the warmth of the fire, too, and huddled round it till Purun Bhagat had to push them aside to throw on more fuel; and in the morning, as often as not, he would find a furry ape sharing his blanket. All day long, one or other of the tribe would sit by his side, staring out at the snows, crooning and looking unspeakably wise and sorrowful.

RIGHT: *A headpiece for this story, drawn by Lockwood Kipling for the* Second Jungle Book *in 1895.*

OPPOSITE: *From a sketch by Lockwood Kipling for this illustration.*

After the monkeys came the *barasingh*, that big deer which is like our red deer, but stronger. He wished to rub off the velvet of his horns against the cold stones of Kali's statue, and stamped his feet when he saw the man at the shrine. But Purun Bhagat never moved, and, little by little, the royal stag edged up and nuzzled his shoulder. Purun Bhagat slid one cool hand along the hot antlers, and the touch soothed the fretted beast, who bowed his head, and Purun Bhagat very softly rubbed and ravelled off the velvet. Afterward, the *barasingh* brought his doe and fawn – gentle things that mumbled on the holy man's blanket – or would come alone at night, his eyes green in the fire-flicker, to take his share of fresh walnuts. At last, the musk-deer, the shyest and almost the smallest of the deerlets, came, too, her big rabbity ears erect; even brindled, silent *mushick-nabha* must needs find out what the light in the shrine meant, and drop out her moose-like nose into Purun Bhagat's lap, coming and going with the shadows of the fire. Purun Bhagat called them all "my brothers", and his low call of *"Bhai! Bhai!"* would draw them from the forest at noon if they were within earshot. The Himalayan black bear, moody and suspicious – Sona, who has the V-shaped white mark under his chin – passed that way more than once; and since the Bhagat showed no fear, Sona showed no anger, but watched him, and came closer, and begged a share of the caresses, and a dole of bread or wild berries. Often, in the still dawns, when the Bhagat would climb to the very crest of the pass to watch the red day walking along the peaks of the snows, he would find Sona shuffling and grunting at his heels, thrusting a curious fore-paw under fallen trunks, and bringing it away with a *whoof* of impatience; or his early steps would wake Sona where he lay curled up, and the great brute, rising erect, would think to fight, till he heard the Bhagat's voice and knew his best friend.

Nearly all hermits and holy men who live apart from the big cities have the reputation of being able to work miracles with the wild things, but all the miracle lies in keeping still, in never making a hasty movement, and, for a long time, at least, in never looking directly at a visitor. The villagers saw the outline of the *barasingh* stalking like a shadow through the dark forest behind the shrine; saw the *minaul*, the Himalayan pheasant, blazing in her best colours before Kali's statue; and the *langurs* on their haunches, inside, playing with the walnut shells. Some of the children, too, had heard Sona singing to himself, bear-fashion, behind the fallen rocks, and the Bhagat's reputation as miracle-worker stood firm.

Yet nothing was farther from his mind than miracles. He believed that all things were one big Miracle, and when a man knows that much he knows something to go upon. He knew for a certainty that there was nothing great and nothing little in this world: and day and night he strove to think out his way into the heart of things, back to the place whence his soul had come.

So thinking, his untrimmed hair fell down about his shoulders, the

stone slab at the side of the antelope skin was dented into a little hole by the foot of his brass-handled crutch, and the place between the tree-trunks, where the begging-bowl rested day after day, sunk and wore into a hollow almost as smooth as the brown shell itself; and each beast knew his exact place at the fire. The fields changed their colours with the seasons; the threshing-floors filled and emptied, and filled again and again; and again and again, when winter came, the *langurs* frisked among the branches feathered with light snow, till the mother-monkeys brought their sad-eyed little babies up from the warmer valleys with the spring. There were few changes in the village. The priest was older, and many of the little children who used to come with the begging-dish sent their own children now; and when you asked of the villagers how long their holy man had lived in Kali's Shrine at the head of the pass, they answered, "Always."

Then came such summer rains as had not been known in the Hills for many seasons. Through three good months the valley was wrapped in cloud and soaking mist – steady, unrelenting downfall, breaking off into thunder-shower after thunder-shower. Kali's Shrine stood above the clouds, for the most part, and there was a whole month in which the Bhagat never caught a glimpse of his village. It was packed away under a white floor of cloud that swayed and shifted and rolled on itself and bulged upward, but never broke from its piers – the streaming flanks of the valley.

All that time he heard nothing but the sound of a million little waters, overhead from the trees, and underfoot along the ground, soaking through the pine-needles, dripping from the tongues of draggled fern, and spouting in newly-torn muddy channels down the slopes. Then the sun came out, and drew forth the good incense of the deodars and the rhododendrons, and that far-off, clean smell which the Hill people call "the smell of the snows". The hot sunshine lasted for a week, and then the rains gathered together for their last downpour, and the water fell in sheets that flayed off the skin of the ground and leaped back in mud. Purun Bhagat heaped his fire high that night, for he was sure his brothers would need warmth; but never a beast came to the shrine, though he called and called till he dropped asleep, wondering what had happened in the woods.

It was in the black heart of the night, the rain drumming like a thousand drums, that he was roused by a plucking at his blanket, and, stretching out, felt the little hand of a *langur*. "It is better here than in the trees," he said sleepily, loosening a fold of blanket; "take it and be warm." The monkey caught his hand and pulled hard. "Is it food, then?" said Purun Bhagat. "Wait awhile, and I will prepare some." As he kneeled to throw fuel on the fire the *langur* ran to the door of the shrine, crooned and ran back again, plucking at the man's knee.

"What is it? What is thy trouble, Brother?" said Purun Bhagat, for the *langur*'s eyes were full of things that he could not tell. "Unless one of thy caste be in a trap – and none set traps here – I will not go

ABOVE *and* OPPOSITE: *Langurs, from a sketch by Lockwood Kipling for the* Second Jungle Book.

into that weather. Look, Brother, even the *barasingh* comes for shelter!"

The deer's antlers clashed as he strode into the shrine, clashed against the grinning statue of Kali. He lowered them in Purun Bhagat's direction and stamped uneasily, hissing through his half-shut nostrils.

"Hai! Hai! Hai!" said the Bhagat, snapping his fingers, "Is *this* payment for a night's lodging?" But the deer pushed him toward the door, and as he did so Purun Bhagat heard the sound of something opening with a sigh, and saw two slabs of the floor draw away from each other, while the sticky earth below smacked its lips.

"Now I see," said Purun Bhagat. "No blame to my brothers that they did not sit by the fire to-night. The mountain is falling. And yet – why should I go?" His eye fell on the empty begging-bowl, and his face changed. "They have given me good food daily since – since I came, and, if I am not swift, to-morrow there will not be one mouth in the valley. Indeed, I must go and warn them below. Back there, Brother! Let me get to the fire."

The *barasingh* backed unwillingly as Purun Bhagat drove a pine torch deep into the flame, twirling it till it was well lit. "Ah! ye came to warn me," he said, rising. "Better than that we shall do; better than that. Out, now, and lend me thy neck, Brother, for I have but two feet."

He clutched the bristling withers of the *barasingh* with his right hand, held the torch away with his left, and stepped out of the shrine into the desperate night. There was no breath of wind, but the rain nearly drowned the flare as the great deer hurried down the slope, sliding on his haunches. As soon as they were clear of the forest more of the Bhagat's brothers joined them. He heard, though he could not see, the *langurs* pressing about him, and behind them the *uhh! uhh!* of Sona. The rain matted his long white hair into ropes; the water splashed beneath his bare feet, and his yellow robe clung to his frail old body, but he stepped down steadily, leaning against the *barasingh*. He was no longer a holy man, but Sir Purun Dass, K.C.I.E., Prime Minister of no small State, a man accustomed to command, going out to save life. Down the steep, plashy path they poured all together, the Bhagat and his brothers, down and down till the deer's feet clicked and stumbled on the wall of a threshing-floor, and he snorted because he smelt Man. Now they were at the head of the one crooked village street, and the Bhagat beat with his crutch on the barred windows of the blacksmith's house, as his torch blazed up in the shelter of the eaves. "Up and out!" cried Purun Bhagat; and he did not know his own voice, for it was years since he had spoken aloud to a man. "The hill falls! The hill is falling! Up and out, oh, you within!"

"It is our Bhagat," said the blacksmith's wife. "He stands among his beasts. Gather the little ones and give the call."

*An Indian village scene, a watercolour drawing by Lockwood Kipling, almost certainly illustrating this story.*

It ran from house to house, while the beasts, cramped in the narrow way, surged and huddled round the Bhagat, and Sona puffed impatiently.

The people hurried into the street – they were no more than seventy souls all told – and in the glare of the torches they saw their Bhagat holding back the terrified *barasingh*, while the monkeys plucked piteously at his skirts, and Sona sat on his haunches and roared.

"Across the valley and up the next hill!" shouted Purun Bhagat. "Leave none behind! We follow!"

Then the people ran as only Hill folk can run, for they knew that in a landslip you must climb for the highest ground across the valley. They fled, splashing through the little river at the bottom, and panted up the terraced fields on the far side, while the Bhagat and his brethren followed. Up and up the opposite mountain they climbed, calling to each other by name – the roll-call of the village – and at their heels toiled the big *barasingh*, weighted by the failing strength of Purun Bhagat. At last the deer stopped in the shadow of a deep pinewood, five hundred feet up the hillside. His instinct, that had warned him of the coming slide, told him he would be safe here.

Purun Bhagat dropped fainting by his side, for the chill of the rain and that fierce climb were killing him; but first he called to the scattered torches ahead, "Stay and count your numbers"; then, whispering to the deer as he saw the lights gather in a cluster: "Stay with me, Brother. Stay – till – I – go!"

There was a sigh in the air that grew to a mutter, and a mutter that grew to a roar, and a roar that passed all sense of hearing, and the hillside on which the villagers stood was hit in the darkness, and rocked to the blow. Then a note as steady, deep, and true as the deep C of the organ drowned everything for perhaps five minutes, while the very roots of the pines quivered to it. It died away, and the sound of the rain falling on miles of hard ground and grass changed to the muffled drum of water on soft earth. That told its own tale.

Never a villager – not even the priest – was bold enough to speak to the Bhagat who had saved their lives. They crouched under the pines and waited till the day. When it came they looked across the valley and saw that what had been forest, and terraced field, and track-threaded grazing-ground was one raw, red, fan-shaped smear, with a few trees flung head-down on the scarp. That red ran high up the hill of their refuge, damming back the little river, which had begun to spread into a brick-coloured lake. Of the village, of the road to the shrine, of the shrine itself, and the forest behind, there was no trace. For one mile in width and two thousand feet in sheer depth the mountainside had come away bodily, planed clean from head to heel.

And the villagers, one by one, crept through the wood to pray before their Bhagat. They saw the *barasingh* standing over him, who fled when they came near, and they heard the *langurs* wailing in the branches, and Sona moaning up the hill; but their Bhagat was dead, sitting cross-legged, his back against a tree, his crutch under his armpit, and his face turned to the north-east.

The priest said: "Behold a miracle after a miracle, for in this very attitude must all Sunnyasis be buried! Therefore where he now is we will build the temple to our holy man."

They built the temple before a year was ended – a little stone-and-earth shrine – and they called the hill the Bhagat's hill, and they worship there with lights and flowers and offerings to this day. But they do not know that the saint of their worship is the late Sir Purun Dass, K.C.I.E., D.C.L., Ph.D., etc., once Prime Minister of the progressive and enlightened State of Mohiniwala, and honorary or corresponding member of more learned and scientific societies than will ever do any good in this world or the next.

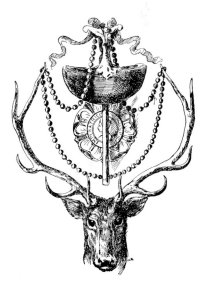

*Lockwood Kipling's tailpiece for this story in the* Second Jungle Book.

# Danny Deever

This was the first of the "Barrack-Room Ballads" which Kipling produced in London in the astonishingly fertile year of 1890. The ballads were published by W. E. Henley in his ultra-Tory, imperialist *Scots Observer*. When "Danny Deever" appeared on 22 February 1890, the Milton scholar Professor Masson is supposed to have waved the paper at his students, crying, "Here's Literature! Here's Literature at last!" The impetus for the ballads was Kipling's love of the London music-halls, which are vividly evoked in his story "My Great and Only". In *Something of Myself*, Kipling recalled: "the smoke, the roar, and the good-fellowship at Gatti's 'set' the scheme for a certain sort of song. The Private Soldier in India I thought I knew fairly well. His English brother (in the Guards mostly) sat and sang at my elbow any night I chose; and, for Greek chorus, I had the comments of my barmaid – deeply and dispassionately versed in all knowledge of evil as she had watched it across the zinc she was always swabbing off ... The outcome was the first of some verses called *Barrack-Room Ballads*."

"What are the bugles blowin' for?" said Files-on-Parade.
"To turn you out, to turn you out," the Colour-Sergeant said.
"What makes you look so white, so white?" said
  Files-on-Parade.
"I'm dreadin' what I've got to watch," the Colour-Sergeant said.
    For they're hangin' Danny Deever, you can hear the Dead
      March play,
    The regiment's in 'ollow square – they're hangin' him
      to-day;
    They've taken of his buttons off an' cut his stripes away,
    An' they're hangin' Danny Deever in the mornin'.

"What makes the rear-rank breathe so 'ard?" said
  Files-on-Parade.
"It's bitter cold, it's bitter cold," the Colour-Sergeant said.
"What makes that front-rank man fall down?" says
  Files-on-Parade.
"A touch o' sun, a touch o' sun," the Colour-Sergeant said.
    They are hangin' Danny Deever, they are marchin' of 'im
      round,
    They 'ave 'alted Danny Deever by 'is coffin on the ground;
    An' 'e'll swing in 'arf a minute for a sneakin' shootin'
      hound –
    O they're hangin' Danny Deever in the mornin'!

"'Is cot was right-'and cot to mine," said Files-on-Parade.
"'E's sleepin' out an' far to-night," the Colour-Sergeant said.
"I've drunk 'is beer a score o' times," said Files-on-Parade.
"'E's drinkin' bitter beer alone," the Colour-Sergeant said.
    They are hangin' Danny Deever, you must mark 'im to 'is
      place,
    For 'e shot a comrade sleepin' – you must look 'im in the
      face;
    Nine 'undred of 'is county an' the regiment's disgrace,
    While they're hangin' Danny Deever in the mornin'.

"What's that so black agin the sun?" said Files-on-Parade.
"It's Danny fightin' 'ard for life," the Colour-Sergeant said.
"What's that that whimpers over'ead?" said Files-on-Parade.
"It's Danny's soul that's passin' now," the Colour-Sergeant said.
    For they're done with Danny Deever, you can 'ear the
      quickstep play,
    The regiment's in column, an' they're marchin' us away;
    Ho! the young recruits are shakin', an' they'll want their
      beer to-day,
    After hangin' Danny Deever in the mornin'.

ABOVE: *Lockwood Kipling's
idealised version of the English
soldier.*

OPPOSITE: *The raw material of the
British Army, 1897: recruits outside
St. George's Barracks in London.*

# Cells

"Cells" is only one of many extraordinarily strong and original verses which followed hard on the heels of "Danny Deever". Kipling had already made a name for his unsentimental and unheroic stories of army life, many of them featuring the "Soldiers Three" trio of Learoyd, Ortheris and Mulvaney. While he was writing these verses he was also writing the best of his stories in this vein, "On Greenhow Hill" and "The Courting of Dinah Shadd". Many readers have objected to the phonetic dialect of the soldiers' speech, and particularly the "synthetic" Cockney of Ortheris and the "Barrack-Room Ballads"; Kipling's own comment on early mutterings in literary clubs was, "Seeing that not one of these critters has been within earshot of a barrack, I am naturally wrath."

*"Military Life on Board a Troopship": crime and punishment from the* Graphic, *July 1879.*

I've a head like a concertina: I've a tongue like a button-stick:
I've a mouth like an old potato, and I'm more than a little sick,
But I've had my fun o' the Corp'ral's Guard: I've made the
  cinders fly,
And I'm here in the Clink for a thundering drink and blacking
  the Corporal's eye.

   With a second-hand overcoat under my head,
     And a beautiful view of the yard,
   O it's pack-drill for me and a fortnight's C.B.
     For "drunk and resisting the Guard"!
   Mad drunk and resisting the Guard –
   'Strewth, but I socked it them hard!
   So it's pack-drill for me and a fortnight's C.B.
     For "drunk and resisting the Guard".

I started o' canteen porter, I finished o' canteen beer,
But a dose o' gin that a mate slipped in, it was that that brought
  me here.
'Twas that and an extry double Guard that rubbed my nose in
  the dirt;
But I fell away with the Corp'ral's stock and the best of the
  Corp'ral's shirt.

I left my cap in a public-house, my boots in the public road,
And Lord knows where, and I don't care, my belt and my tunic
  goed;
They'll stop my pay, they'll cut away the stripes I used to wear,
But I left my mark on the Corp'ral's face, and I think he'll keep
  it there!

My wife she cries on the barrack-gate, my kid in the
  barrack-yard,
It ain't that I mind the Ord'ly room – it's *that* that cuts so hard.
I'll take my oath before them both that I will sure abstain,
But as soon as I'm in with a mate and gin, I know I'll do it
  again!

   With a second-hand overcoat under my head,
     And a beautiful view of the yard,
   Yes, it's pack-drill for me and a fortnight's C.B.
     For "drunk and resisting the Guard"!
   Mad drunk and resisting the Guard –
   'Strewth, but I socked it them hard!
   So it's pack-drill for me and a fortnight's C.B.
     For "drunk and resisting the Guard".

*The outskirts of the barracks at
Meerut. This is where the Indian
Mutiny began in 1857.*

**C.B.:** confined to barracks

# Mandalay

Kipling visited Burma in 1889, recording his trip in the essays collected in *From Sea to Sea*. Of his visit to Moulmein, he writes, "I should better remember what that pagoda was like had I not fallen deeply and irrevocably in love with a Burmese girl at the foot of the first flight of steps. Only the fact of the steamer starting next noon prevented me from staying at Moulmein forever and owning a pair of elephants." In "Mandalay", written the following year, a mixture of memories from this trip is set in the mouth of a soldier yearning for the East.

By the old Moulmein Pagoda, lookin' eastward to the sea,
There's a Burma girl a-settin', and I know she thinks o' me;
For the wind is in the palm-trees, and the temple-bells they say:
"Come you back, you British soldier; come you back to
    Mandalay!"
      Come you back to Mandalay,
      Where the old Flotilla lay:
      Can't you 'ear their paddles chunkin' from Rangoon to
        Mandalay?
      On the road to Mandalay,
      Where the flyin'-fishes play,
      An' the dawn comes up like thunder outer China 'crost the
        Bay!

'Er petticoat was yaller an' 'er little cap was green,
An' 'er name was Supi-yaw-lat – jes' the same as Theebaw's
    Queen,
An' I seed her first a-smokin' of a whackin' white cheroot,
An' a-wastin' Christian kisses on an 'eathen idol's foot:
      Bloomin' idol made o' mud –
      Wot they called the Great Gawd Budd –
      Plucky lot she cared for idols when I kissed 'er where she
        stud!
      On the road to Mandalay . . .

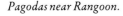

*Pagodas near Rangoon.*

When the mist was on the rice-fields an' the sun was droppin'
      slow,
She'd git 'er little banjo an' she'd sing *"Kulla-lo-lo!"*
With 'er arm upon my shoulder an' 'er cheek agin my cheek
We useter watch the steamers an' the *hathis* pilin' teak.
    Elephints a-pilin' teak
    In the sludgy, squdgy creek,
    Where the silence 'ung that 'eavy you was 'arf afraid to
      speak!
    On the road to Mandalay...

But that's all shove be'ind me – long ago an' fur away,
An' there ain't no 'buses runnin' from the Bank to Mandalay;
An' I'm learnin' 'ere in London what the ten-year soldier tells:
"If you've 'eard the East a-callin', you won't never 'eed naught
      else."
    No! you won't 'eed nothin' else
    But them spicy garlic smells,
    An' the sunshine an' the palm-trees an' the tinkly
      temple-bells;
    On the road to Mandalay...

I am sick o' wastin' leather on these gritty pavin'-stones,
An' the blasted Henglish drizzle wakes the fever in my bones;
Tho' I walks with fifty 'ousemaids outer Chelsea to the Strand,
An' they talks a lot o' lovin', but wot do they understand?
    Beefy face an' grubby 'and –
    Law! wot do they understand?
    I've a neater, sweeter maiden in a cleaner, greener land!
    On the road to Mandalay...

Ship me somewheres east of Suez, where the best is like the
      worst,
Where there aren't no Ten Commandments an' a man can raise a
      thirst;
For the temple-bells are callin' an' it's there that I would be –
By the old Moulmein Pagoda, looking lazy at the sea;
    On the road to Mandalay,
    Where the old Flotilla lay,
    With our sick beneath the awnings when we went to
      Mandalay!
    O the road to Mandalay,
    Where the flyin'-fishes play,
    An' the dawn comes up like thunder outer China 'crost the
      Bay!

*A Burmese girl with a cheroot. This studio photograph of 1898 probably refers directly to Kipling's poem which, set to a waltz tune, was a hugely popular song.*

# Winter in Vermont

Kipling lived at Brattleboro in Vermont from 1892 to 1896, and during that period sent reports from America to *The Times*. "Leaves from a Winter Notebook", though written in 1895, was not published until 1900 and not collected with its fellows until 1920. It describes the landscape in which he lived, and it also hints at the reason he had to leave: "the deep, instriking hate between neighbours, that is born of a hundred little things". Brattleboro was the home of the Balestier family, and on 18 January 1892, in a private ceremony, Kipling had married Carrie Balestier, the strong-minded sister of his dear friend, publisher Wolcott Balestier. During the previous year, Rudyard and Wolcott had collaborated on an adventure novel, *The Naulahka*, and Wolcott's untimely death from typhoid in December 1891 devastated him: "He died so suddenly and so far away; we had so much to say to each other, and now I have got to wait so long before I can say it." At first the Kiplings were happy in Vermont, and it was there that Rudyard wrote the Mowgli stories and his American novel *Captains Courageous*. Their daughter Josephine was born in December 1892, delighting her parents and stirring a new level of Kipling's creative imagination. But a devastating family quarrel erupted between the Kiplings and Carrie's happy-go-lucky, ne'er-do-well brother Beatty, culminating in a humiliating court case in which Rudyard, who accused Beatty of threatening his life, was exposed to public ridicule. Kipling's cherished privacy was destroyed: it was time to move on.

*"The roadside growth all dead from frost", one of the specially commissioned photographs by Arthur R. Dugmore which accompanied this essay on its first publication in* Harper's Magazine, *May 1900.*

We had walked abreast of the year from the very beginning, and that was when the first blood-root came up between the patches of April snow, while yet the big drift at the bottom of the meadow held fast. In the shadow of the woods and under the blown pine-needles, clots of snow lay till far into May, but neither the season nor the flowers took any note of them, and, before we were well sure Winter had gone, the lackeys of my Lord Baltimore in their new liveries came to tell us that Summer was in the valley, and please might they nest at the bottom of the garden?

Followed, Summer, angry, fidgety, and nervous, with the corn and tobacco to ripen in five short months, the pastures to reclothe, and the fallen leaves to hide away under new carpets. Suddenly, in the middle of her work, on a stuffy-still July day, she called a wind out of the North-west, a wind blown under an arch of steel-bellied clouds, a wicked bitter wind with a lacing of hail to it, a wind that came and was gone in less than ten minutes, but blocked the roads with fallen trees, toppled over a barn, and – blew potatoes out of the ground! When that was done, a white cloud shaped like a dumb-bell whirled down the valley across the evening blue, roaring and twisting and twisting and roaring all alone by itself. A West Indian hurricane could not have been quicker on its feet than our little cyclone, and when the house rose a-tiptoe, like a cockerel in act to crow, and a sixty-foot elm went by the board, and that which had been a dusty road became a roaring torrent all in three minutes, we felt that the New England summer had creole blood in her veins. She went away, red-faced and angry to the last, slamming all the doors of the hills behind her, and Autumn, who is a lady, took charge.

No pen can describe the turning of the leaves – the insurrection of the tree-people against the waning year. A little maple began it, flaming blood-red of a sudden where he stood against the dark green of a pine-belt. Next morning there was an answering signal from the swamp where the sumacs grow. Three days later, the hill-sides as far as the eye could range were afire, and the roads paved, with crimson and gold. Then a wet wind blew, and ruined all the uniforms of that gorgeous army; and the oaks, who had held themselves in reserve, buckled on their dull and bronzed cuirasses and stood it out stiffly to the last blown leaf, till nothing remained but pencil-shading of bare boughs, and one could see into the most private heart of the woods....

Men, who are of one blood with sheep, have followed their friends and the railway along the river valleys where the towns are. Across the hills the inhabitants are few, and, outside their State, little known. They withdraw from society in November if they live on the uplands,

*"The man with the ploughshare", another photograph by Arthur Dugmore.*

coming down in May as the snow gives leave. Not much more than a generation ago these farms made their own clothes, soap, and candles, and killed their own meat thrice a year, beef, veal, and pig, and sat still between-times. Now they buy shop-made clothes, patent soaps, and kerosene; and it is among their tents that the huge red and gilt Biographies of Presidents, and the twenty-pound family Bibles, with illuminated marriage-registers, mourning-cards, baptismal certificates, and hundreds of genuine steel-engravings, sell best. Here, too, off the main-travelled roads, the wandering quack – Patent Electric Pills, nerve cures, etc. – divides the field with the seed and fruit man and the seller of cattle-boluses. They dose themselves a good deal, I fancy, for it is a poor family that does not know all about nervous prostration. So the quack drives a pair of horses and a gaily-painted waggon with a hood, and sometimes takes his wife with him. Once only have I met a pedlar afoot. He was an old man, shaken with palsy, and he pushed a thing exactly like a pauper's burial-cart, selling pins, tape, scents, and flavourings. You helped yourself, for his hands had no direction, and he told a long tale in which the deeding away of a farm to one of his family was mixed up with pride at the distances he still could cover daily. As much as six miles sometimes. He was no Lear, as the gift of the farm might suggest, but sealed of the tribe of the Wandering Jew – a tremulous old giddy-gaddy. There are many such rovers, gelders of colts and the like, who work a long beat, south to Virginia almost, and north to the frontier, paying with talk and gossip for their entertainment.

Yet tramps are few, and that is well, for the American article answers almost exactly to the vagrant and criminal tribes of India, being a predatory ruffian who knows too much to work. Bad place to beg in after dark – on a farm – very – is Vermont. . . .

Winter has chased all these really interesting people south, and in a few weeks, if we have anything of a snow, the back farms will be unvisited save by the doctor's hooded sleigh. It is no child's play to hold a practice here through the winter months, when the drifts are really formed, and a pair can drop in up to their saddle-pads. Four horses a day some of them use, and use up – for they are good men.

Now in the big silence of the snow is born, perhaps, not a little of that New England conscience which her children write about. There is much time to think, and thinking is a highly dangerous business. Conscience, fear, undigested reading, and, it may be, not too well cooked food, have full swing. A man, and more particularly a woman, can easily hear strange voices – the Word of the Lord rolling between the dead hills; may see visions and dream dreams; get revelations and an outpouring of the spirit, and end (such things have been) lamentably enough in those big houses by the Connecticut River which have been tenderly christened The Retreat. Hate breeds as well as religion – the deep, instriking hate between neighbours, that is born of a hundred little things added up, brooded over, and

*Caroline Balestier, later Carrie Kipling, photographed as a young woman, probably at home in Brattleboro, Vermont.*

hatched by the stove when two or three talk together in the long evenings. . . . No one who has been through even so modified a blizzard as New England can produce talks lightly of the snow. Imagine eight-and-forty hours of roaring wind, the thermometer well down towards zero, scooping and gouging across a hundred miles of newly fallen snow. The air is full of stinging shot, and at ten yards the trees are invisible. The foot slides on a reef, polished and black as obsidian, where the wind has skinned an exposed corner of road down to the dirt ice of early winter. The next step ends hip-deep and over, for here an unseen wall is banking back the rush of the singing drifts. A scarped slope rises sheer across the road. The wind shifts a point or two, and all sinks down, like sand in the hour-glass, leaving a pot-hole of whirling whiteness. There is a lull, and you can see the surface of the fields settling furiously in one direction – a tide that spurts from between the tree-boles. The hollows of the pasture fill while you watch; empty, fill, and discharge anew. The rock-ledges show the bare flank of a storm-chased liner for a moment, and whitening, duck under. Irresponsible snow-devils dance by the lee of a barn where three gusts meet, or stagger out into the open till they are cut down by the main wind. At the worst of the storm there is neither Heaven nor Earth, but only a swizzle into which a man may be brewed. Distances grow to nightmare scale, and that which in the summer was no more than a minute's bare-headed run, is half an hour's gasping struggle, each foot won between the lulls. Then do the heavy-timbered barns talk like ships in a cross-sea, beam working against beam. The winter's hay is ribbed over with long lines of snow dust blown between the boards, and far below in the byre the oxen clash their horns and moan uneasily. . . .

In January or February come the great ice-storms, when every branch, blade, and trunk is coated with frozen rain, so that you can touch nothing truly. The spikes of the pines are sunk into pear-shaped crystals, and each fence-post is miraculously hilted with diamonds. If you bend a twig, the icing cracks like varnish, and a half-inch branch snaps off at the lightest tap. If wind and sun open the day together, the eye cannot look steadily at the splendour of this jewellery. The woods are full of the clatter of arms; the ringing of bucks' horns in flight; the stampede of mailed feet up and down the glades; and a great dust of battle is puffed out into the open, till the last of the ice is beaten away and the cleared branches take up their regular chant.

Again the mercury drops twenty and more below zero, and the very trees swoon. The snow turns to French chalk, squeaking under the heel, and their breath cloaks the oxen in rime. At night a tree's heart will break in him with a groan. According to the books, the frost has split something, but it is a fearful sound, this grunt as of a man stunned.

*Rudyard Kipling, probably photographed in Vermont.*

# Recessional

God of our fathers, known of old,
 Lord of our far-flung battle-line,
Beneath whose awful Hand we hold
 Dominion over palm and pine –
Lord God of Hosts, be with us yet,
Lest we forget – lest we forget!

The tumult and the shouting dies;
 The Captains and the Kings depart:
Still stands Thine ancient sacrifice,
 An humble and a contrite heart.
Lord God of Hosts, be with us yet,
Lest we forget – lest we forget!

*The review of the fleet at Spithead, 26 June 1897, about the time that Kipling took the first of the two trips with the Channel Squadron described in* A Fleet in Being. *"I've been around with the Channel Fleet for a fortnight and any other breed of white man, with such a weapon to their hand, would have been exploiting the round earth in their own interests long ago."*

120

Far-called, our navies melt away;
  On dune and headland sinks the fire:
Lo, all our pomp of yesterday
  Is one with Nineveh and Tyre!
Judge of the Nations, spare us yet,
Lest we forget – lest we forget!

If, drunk with sight of power, we loose
  Wild tongues that have not Thee in awe,
Such boastings as the Gentiles use,
  Or lesser breeds without the Law –
Lord God of Hosts, be with us yet,
Lest we forget – lest we forget!

For heathen heart that puts her trust
  In reeking tube and iron shard,
All valiant dust that builds on dust,
  And guarding, calls not Thee to guard,
For frantic boast and foolish word –
Thy mercy on Thy People, Lord!

"Recessional", a warning hymn for Queen Victoria's sixtieth Jubilee, was painstakingly composed at the Kiplings' new home in Rottingdean, Sussex, and published in *The Times* on 17 July 1897. Among the many who wrote in congratulation was the pacifist J. W. Mackail. Kipling, anxious not to be misinterpreted as supine, wrote back: "The big smash is coming one of these days, sure enough but I think we shall pull through not without credit. It will be common people – the 3rd class carriages – that'll save us."

# Cities and Thrones and Powers

From *Puck of Pook's Hill* (1906), this sets the tone for Kipling's marvellously alert and subtle apprehension of the nature of Roman rule in Britain. These stories were meant, he wrote, "to be a sort of balance to, as well as a seal upon, some aspects of my 'Imperialistic' output in the past". In essence, Kipling's imperialism was a Roman imperialism – an Empire of administrators such as he celebrates in his Indian stories, rather than a loot-and-grab Empire of conquest and domination. Even when, under the sway of Rhodes and Jameson, Kipling nurtured a vision of a white-owned, English-ruled South Africa, a South Africa in which the native inhabitants had no part to play, he was comparing Rhodes to "the Roman Emperor he so much resembled". Kipling believed that all things must pass, and also, paradoxically, that nothing ever really changed: "Remember always that, except for the appliances we make, the rates at which we move ourselves and our possessions through space, and the words which we use, nothing in life changes. The utmost any generation can do is to rebaptise each spiritual or emotional rebirth in its own tongue. Then it goes to its grave hot and bothered, because no new birth has been vouchsafed for its salvation, or even its relief."

Cities and Thrones and Powers
   Stand in Time's eye,
Almost as long as flowers,
   Which daily die:
But, as new buds put forth
   To glad new men,
Out of the spent and unconsidered Earth
   The Cities rise again.

This season's Daffodil,
   She never hears
What change, what chance, what chill,
   Cut down last year's;
But with bold countenance,
   And knowledge small,
Esteems her seven days' continuance
   To be perpetual.

So Time that is o'er-kind
   To all that be,
Ordains us e'en as blind,
   As bold as she:
That in our very death,
   And burial sure,
Shadow to shadow, well persuaded, saith,
   "See how our works endure!"

OPPOSITE: *Victoria, the Queen-Empress, in her state robes, 1887. The earliest poem of Kipling's to survive into his* Collected Poems, *"Ave Imperatrix", was a hymn of thanks for Victoria's escape from a would-be assassin, but his poems for the 1887 and 1897 Jubilees are concerned with wider issues: Victoria survives in his work only as the soldiers' employer, the sardonically styled "Widow at Windsor".*

122

# The Burial

C. J. Rhodes
buried in the Matoppos
10 April 1902

ABOVE: *Cecil Rhodes. "He was as inarticulate as a school-boy of fifteen . . . He said to me apropos of nothing in particular: 'What's your dream?' I answered that he was part of it."*

OPPOSITE: *Cape Town market, with Table Mountain in the background capped by cloud, 1897. "Behind all tiered the flank of Table Mountain and its copses of silver-trees, flanking scarred ravines."*

When that great Kings return to clay,
 Or Emperors in their pride,
Grief of a day shall fill a day,
 Because its creature died.
But we – we reckon not with those
 Whom the mere Fates ordain,
This Power that wrought on us and goes
 Back to the Power again.

Dreamer devout, by vision led
 Beyond our guess or reach,
The travail of his spirit bred
 Cities in place of speech.
So huge the all-mastering thought that drove –
 So brief the term allowed –
Nations, not words, he linked to prove
 His faith before the crowd.

It is his will that he look forth
 Across the world he won –
The granite of the ancient North –
 Great spaces washed with sun.
There shall he patient take his seat
 (As when the Death he dared),
And there await a people's feet
 In the paths that he prepared.

There, till the vision he foresaw
 Splendid and whole arise,
And unimagined Empires draw
 To council 'neath his skies,
The immense and brooding Spirit still
 Shall quicken and control.
Living he was the land, and dead,
 His soul shall be her soul!

Kipling struck up a friendship with Cecil Rhodes in 1897 and through him came to love South Africa, which he had visited in 1891 but now adopted as a second home. Rhodes built the Kiplings a cottage in the idyllic grounds of his house Groote Schuur, and from 1900 to 1908 they spent half of each year there. Kipling wrote, "My use to him was largely as a purveyor of words: for he was largely inarticulate. After the idea had been presented – and one had to know his code for it – he would say: 'What am I trying to express? Say it, *say* it!'" Rhodes's death – "so little done, so much to do" – was a terrible blow to Kipling's imperial dream, for he revered the would-be architect of a united British Africa to the point of hero-worship. Rhodes seemed the embodiment of the qualities Kipling had hymned in his great "Song of the English":

> We were dreamers, dreaming greatly, in the man-stifled town;
> We yearned beyond the sky-line where the strange roads go down.
> Came the Whisper, came the Vision, came the Power with the Need,
> Till the Soul that is not man's soul was lent us to lead.

Rhodes was not yet fifty when he died. He was buried in the granite of the Matoppos mountains on 10 April 1902, at a spot he had chosen during his negotiations with the Matabele in 1896. Kipling's elegy was read over the grave.

# The Elephant's Child

Kipling composed the first *Just So Stories* as a sleep-making charm for his "Best Beloved" daughter Josephine. Introducing them in *St. Nicholas* in December 1897, he wrote that, unlike daytime stories which could be altered as one pleased, these "were stories meant to put Effie to sleep, and you were not allowed to alter those by one single word. They had to be told just so, or Effie would wake up and put back the missing sentence. So at last they came to be like charms..." The novelist Angela Thirkell, daughter of J. W. Mackail, was of an age with Josephine, and recalled hearing the stories told: "The *Just So Stories* are a poor thing in print compared with the fun of hearing them told in Cousin Ruddy's deep unhesitating voice. There was a ritual about them, each phrase having its special intonation which had to be exactly the same each time and without which the stories are dried husks. There was an inimitable cadence, an emphasis of certain words, an exaggeration of certain phrases, a kind of intoning here and there which made his telling unforgettable." The earliest stories were written in Vermont, but Kipling continued to work on "Just So" stories in England and South Africa. "The Elephant's Child" was written in October 1899, its topography inspired by a journey through Rhodesia arranged for Kipling by Rhodes in 1898. His raucous Boer War verses, "The Absent-Minded Beggar", were written the same week.

In the High and Far-Off Times the Elephant, O Best Beloved, had no trunk. He had only a blackish, bulgy nose, as big as a boot, that he could wriggle about from side to side; but he couldn't pick up things with it. But there was one Elephant – a new Elephant – an Elephant's Child – who was full of 'satiable curtiosity, and that means he asked ever so many questions. *And* he lived in Africa, and he filled all Africa with his 'satiable curtiosities. He asked his tall aunt, the Ostrich, why her tail-feathers grew just so, and his tall aunt the Ostrich spanked him with her hard, hard claw. He asked his tall uncle, the Giraffe, what made his skin spotty, and his tall uncle, the Giraffe, spanked him with his hard, hard hoof. And still he was full of 'satiable curtiosity! He asked his broad aunt, the Hippopotamus, why her eyes were red, and his broad aunt, the Hippopotamus, spanked him with her broad, broad hoof; and he asked his hairy uncle, the Baboon, why melons tasted just so, and his hairy uncle, the Baboon, spanked him with his hairy, hairy paw. And *still* he was full of 'satiable curtiosity! He asked questions about everything that he saw, or heard, or felt, or smelt, or touched, and all his uncles and his aunts spanked him. And still he was full of 'satiable curtiosity!

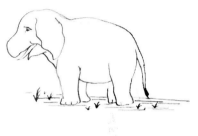

One fine morning in the middle of the Precession of the Equinoxes this 'satiable Elephant's Child asked a new fine question that he had never asked before. He asked, "What does the Crocodile have for dinner?" Then everybody said, "Hush!" in a loud and dretful tone, and they spanked him immediately and directly, without stopping, for a long time.

By and by, when that was finished, he came upon Kolokolo Bird sitting in the middle of a wait-a-bit thorn-bush, and he said, "My father has spanked me, and my mother has spanked me; all my aunts and uncles have spanked me for my 'satiable curtiosity; and *still* I want to know what the Crocodile has for dinner!"

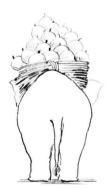

Then Kolokolo Bird said, with a mournful cry, "Go to the banks of the great grey-green, greasy Limpopo River, all set about with fever-trees, and find out."

That very next morning, when there was nothing left of the Equinoxes, because the Precession had preceded according to precedent, this 'satiable Elephant's Child took a hundred pounds of bananas (the little short red kind), and a hundred pounds of sugar-cane (the long purple kind), and seventeen melons (the greeny-crackly kind), and said to all his dear families, "Good-bye. I am going to the great grey-green, greasy Limpopo River, all set about with fever-trees, to find out what the Crocodile has for dinner." And they all spanked him once more for luck, though he asked them most politely to stop.

Then he went away, a little warm, but not at all astonished, eating melons, and throwing the rind about, because he could not pick it up.

He went from Graham's Town to Kimberley, and from Kimberley to Khama's Country, and from Khama's Country he went east by

ABOVE: *The Elephant's Child and the Kolokolo Bird, sketched by Rudyard Kipling.*

OPPOSITE: *Elsie, John and Josephine Kipling, photographed in 1898.*

*Ganesha, the Hindu God of good luck, drawn by Lockwood Kipling, 1891. Rudyard took Ganesha as his personal totem, and most editions feature the elephant's head on the title page or cover, with Ganesha's swastika symbol – which Kipling dropped when its meaning became perverted in the 1930s.*

north, eating melons all the time, till at last he came to the banks of the great grey-green, greasy Limpopo River, all set about with fever-trees, precisely as Kolokolo Bird had said.

Now you must know and understand, O Best Beloved, that till that very week, and day, and hour, and minute, this 'satiable Elephant's Child had never seen a Crocodile, and did not know what one was like. It was all his 'satiable curtiosity.

The first thing that he found was a Bi-Coloured-Python-Rock-Snake curled round a rock.

"'Scuse me," said the Elephant's Child most politely, "but have you seen such a thing as a Crocodile in these promiscuous parts?"

"*Have* I seen a Crocodile?" said the Bi-Coloured-Python-Rock-Snake, in a voice of dretful scorn. "What will you ask me next?"

"'Scuse me," said the Elephant's Child, "but could you kindly tell me what he has for dinner?"

Then the Bi-Coloured-Python-Rock-Snake uncoiled himself very quickly from the rock, and spanked the Elephant's Child with his scalesome, flailsome tail.

"That is odd," said the Elephant's Child, "because my father and my mother, and my uncle and my aunt, not to mention my other aunt, the Hippopotamus, and my other uncle, the Baboon, have all spanked me for my 'satiable curtiosity – and I suppose this is the same thing."

So he said good-bye very politely to the Bi-Coloured-Python-Rock-Snake, and helped to coil him up on the rock again, and went on, a little warm, but not at all astonished, eating melons, and throwing the rind about, because he could not pick it up, till he trod on what he thought was a log of wood at the very edge of the great grey-green, greasy Limpopo River, all set about with fever-trees.

But it was really the Crocodile, O Best Beloved, and the Crocodile winked one eye – like this!

"'Scuse me," said the Elephant's Child most politely, "but do you happen to have seen a Crocodile in these promiscuous parts?"

Then the Crocodile winked the other eye, and lifted half his tail out of the mud; and the Elephant's Child stepped back most politely, because he did not wish to be spanked again.

"Come hither, Little One," said the Crocodile. "Why do you ask such things?"

"'Scuse me," said the Elephant's Child most politely, "but my father has spanked me, my mother has spanked me, not to mention my tall aunt, the Ostrich, and my tall uncle, the Giraffe, who can kick ever so hard, as well as my broad aunt, the Hippopotamus, and my hairy uncle, the Baboon, *and* including the Bi-Coloured-Python-Rock-Snake, with the scalesome, flailsome tail, just up the bank, who spanks harder than any of them; and *so*, if it's quite all the same to you, I don't want to be spanked any more."

"Come hither, Little One," said the Crocodile, "for I am the

Crocodile," and he wept crocodile-tears to show it was quite true.

Then the Elephant's Child grew all breathless, and panted, and kneeled down on the bank and said, "You are the very person I have been looking for all these long days. Will you please tell me what you have for dinner?"

"Come hither, Little One," said the Crocodile, "and I'll whisper."

Then the Elephant's Child put his head down close to the Crocodile's musky, tusky mouth, and the Crocodile caught him by his little nose, which up to that very week, day, hour, and minute, had been no bigger than a boot, though much more useful.

"I think," said the Crocodile – and he said it between his teeth, like this – "I think today I will begin with Elephant's Child!"

At this, O Best Beloved, the Elephant's Child was much annoyed, and he said, speaking through his nose, like this, "Led go! You are hurtig be!"

Then the Bi-Coloured-Python-Rock-Snake scuffled down from the bank and said, "My young friend, if you do not now, immediately and instantly, pull as hard as ever you can, it is my opinion that your acquaintance in the large-pattern leather ulster" (and by this he meant the Crocodile) "will jerk you into yonder limpid stream before you can say Jack Robinson."

This is the way Bi-Coloured-Python-Rock-Snakes always talk.

Then the Elephant's Child sat back on his little haunches, and

ABOVE: *A sketch by Rudyard Kipling. Kipling took great trouble with his illustrations to the* Just So Stories *and would brook no criticism of them. They are crowded, quirky pictures executed in Indian ink, full of coded messages. The ark, for instance, is a cryptic signature,* "RK".

LEFT: *A drawing by Rudyard Kipling.* "This is the Elephant's Child having his nose pulled by the Crocodile. He is much surprised and astonished and hurt, and he is talking through his nose and saying, 'Led go! You are hurtig be!' He is pulling very hard, and so is the Crocodile; but the Bi-Coloured-Python-Rock-Snake is hurrying through the water to help the Elephant's Child. All that black stuff is the banks of the great grey-green, greasy Limpopo River (but I am not allowed to paint these pictures), and the bottly-tree with the twisty roots and the eight leaves is one of the fever-trees that grow there.

"Underneath the truly picture are the shadows of African animals walking into an African ark. There are two lions, two ostriches, two oxen, two camels, two sheep, and two other things that look like rats, but I think they are rock-rabbits. They don't mean anything. I put them in because I thought they looked pretty. They would look very fine if I were allowed to paint them."

*"The Bi-Coloured-Python-Rock-Snake pulled, and the Elephant's Child pulled, and the Crocodile pulled", an illustration by Frank Ver Beck from the first publication of "The Elephant's Child" in the* Windsor Magazine, *February 1902.*

pulled, and pulled, and pulled, and his nose began to stretch. And the Crocodile floundered into the water, making it all creamy with great sweeps of his tail, and *he* pulled, and pulled, and pulled.

And the Elephant's Child's nose kept on stretching; and the Elephant's Child spread all his little four legs and pulled, and pulled, and pulled, and his nose kept on stretching; and the Crocodile threshed his tail like an oar, and *he* pulled, and pulled, and pulled, and at each pull the Elephant's Child's nose grew longer and longer – and it hurt him hijjus!

Then the Elephant's Child felt his legs slipping, and he said through his nose, which was now nearly five feet long, "This is too butch for be!"

Then the Bi-Coloured-Python-Rock-Snake came down from the bank, and knotted himself in a double-clove-hitch round the Elephant's Child's hind-legs, and said, "Rash and inexperienced traveller, we will now seriously devote ourselves to a little high tension, because if we do not, it is my impression that yonder self-propelling man-of-war with the armour-plated upper deck" (and by this, O Best Beloved, he meant the Crocodile) "will permanently vitiate your future career."

That is the way all Bi-Coloured-Python-Rock-Snakes always talk.

So he pulled, and the Elephant's Child pulled, and the Crocodile pulled; but the Elephant's Child and the Bi-Coloured-Python-Rock-Snake pulled hardest; and at last the Crocodile let go of the Elephant's Child's nose with a plop that you could hear all up and down the Limpopo.

Then the Elephant's Child sat down most hard and sudden; but first he was careful to say "Thank you" to the Bi-Coloured-Python-Rock-Snake; and next he was kind to his poor pulled nose, and wrapped it all up in cool banana leaves, and hung it in the great grey-green, greasy Limpopo to cool.

"What are you doing that for?" said the Bi-Coloured-Python-Rock Snake.

" 'Scuse me," said the Elephant's Child, "but my nose is badly out of shape, and I am waiting for it to shrink."

"Then you will have to wait a long time," said the Bi-Coloured-Python-Rock-Snake. "Some people do not know what is good for them."

The Elephant's Child sat there for three days waiting for his nose to shrink. But it never grew any shorter, and, besides, it made him squint. For, O Best Beloved, you will see and understand that the Crocodile had pulled it out into a really truly trunk same as all Elephants have today.

At the end of the third day a fly came and stung him on the shoulder, and before he knew what he was doing he lifted up his trunk and hit that fly dead with the end of it.

"'Vantage number one!" said the Bi-Coloured-Python-Rock-Snake. "You couldn't have done that with a mere-smear nose. Try and eat a little now."

Before he thought what he was doing the Elephant's Child put out his trunk and plucked a large bundle of grass, dusted it clean against his fore-legs, and stuffed it into his own mouth.

"'Vantage number two!" said the Bi-Coloured-Python-Rock-Snake. "You couldn't have done that with a mere-smear nose. Don't you think the sun is very hot here?"

"It is," said the Elephant's Child, and before he thought what he was doing he schlooped up a schloop of mud from the banks of the great grey-green, greasy Limpopo, and slapped it on his head, where it made a cool schloopy-sloshy mud-cap all trickly behind his ears.

"'Vantage number three!" said the Bi-Coloured-Python-Rock-Snake. "You couldn't have done that with a mere-smear nose. Now how do you feel about being spanked again?"

"'Scuse me," said the Elephant's Child, "but I should not like it at all."

"How would you like to spank somebody?" said the Bi-Coloured-Python-Rock-Snake.

"I should like it very much indeed," said the Elephant's Child.

"Well," said the Bi-Coloured-Python-Rock-Snake, "you will find that new nose of yours very useful to spank people with."

"Thank you," said the Elephant's Child, "I'll remember that; and now I think I'll go home to all my dear families and try."

So the Elephant's Child went home across Africa frisking and whisking his trunk. When he wanted fruit to eat he pulled fruit down from a tree, instead of waiting for it to fall as he used to do. When he wanted grass he plucked grass up from the ground, instead of going on his knees as he used to do. When the flies bit him he broke off the branch of a tree and used it as a fly-whisk; and he made himself a new, cool, slushy-squshy mud-cap whenever the sun was hot. When he felt lonely walking through Africa he sang to himself down his trunk, and the noise was louder than several brass bands. He went specially out of his way to find a broad Hippopotamus (she was no relation of his), and he spanked her very hard, to make sure that the Bi-Coloured-Python-Rock-Snake had spoken the truth about his new trunk. The rest of the time he picked up the melon-rinds that he had dropped on his way to the Limpopo – for he was a Tidy Pachyderm.

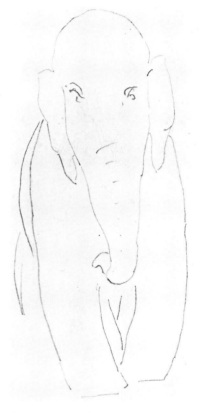

*It is uncertain whether this sketch is by Rudyard or Lockwood.*

*A drawing by Rudyard Kipling. "This is just a picture of the Elephant's Child going to pull bananas off a banana-tree after he had got his fine new long trunk. I don't think it is a very nice picture; but I couldn't make it any better, because elephants and bananas are hard to draw. The streaky things behind the Elephant's Child mean squoggy marshy country somewhere in Africa. The Elephant's Child made most of his mud-cakes out of the mud that he found there. I think it would look better if you painted the banana-tree green and the Elephant's Child red."*

One dark evening he came back to all his dear families, and he coiled up his trunk and said, "How do you do?" They were very glad to see him, and immediately said, "Come here and be spanked for your 'satiable curtiosity."

"Pooh," said the Elephant's Child. "I don't think you peoples know anything about spanking; but *I* do, and I'll show you."

Then he uncurled his trunk and knocked two of his dear brothers head over heels.

"O Bananas!" said they, "where did you learn that trick, and what have you done to your nose?"

"I got a new one from the Crocodile on the banks of the great grey-green, greasy Limpopo River," said the Elephant's Child. "I asked him what he had for dinner, and he gave me this to keep."

"It looks very ugly," said his hairy uncle, the Baboon.

"It does," said the Elephant's Child. "But it's very useful," and he picked up his hairy uncle, the Baboon, by one hairy leg, and hove him into a hornets' nest.

Then that bad Elephant's Child spanked all his dear families for a long time, till they were very warm and greatly astonished. He pulled out his tall Ostrich aunt's tail-feathers; and he caught his tall uncle, the Giraffe, by the hind-leg, and dragged him through a thorn-bush; and he shouted at his broad aunt, the Hippopotamus, and blew bubbles into her ear when she was sleeping in the water after meals; but he never let any one touch Kolokolo Bird.

At last things grew so exciting that his dear families went off one by one in a hurry to the banks of the great grey-green, greasy Limpopo River, all set about with fever-trees, to borrow new noses from the Crocodile. When they came back nobody spanked anybody any more; and ever since that day, O Best Beloved, all the Elephants you will ever see, besides all those that you won't, have trunks precisely like the trunk of the 'satiable Elephant's Child.

*Kipling telling stories on the way to the Cape in 1902. His avuncular tone enthralled many, irritated some. Punch responded with a "Very Nearly Story", "How the Ruddykip got his Great Big Side":*

*"Wherefore and 'cordingly, oh, Best-Beloved, the most-and-altogether-beyond-record-'defatigable Ruddykip took his little pen, and he wrote. Then they took the writing of the 'defatigable Ruddykip and put it in beautiful, big black print. For they knew, oh, Approximately Invaluable, that this is the kind of talk you like, and that you would thank the Ruddykip ever so much for tales written just in this way!*

*"'Chuck it!' said the Modern Child as he rose and fled."*

# Merrow Down

Kipling's children were a source of tender delight to him; he spent endless time playing with them and telling them stories. He had a special depth of love for the first-born, Josephine.

> Let's – oh, *anything*, daddy, so long as it's you and me,
> And going truly exploring, and not being in till tea!

He portrayed her as "Taffy" in three "Just So" stories, "How the Alphabet was Made", "How the First Letter was Written" and "The Tabu Tale". In February 1899, both Rudyard and Josephine fell desperately ill with pneumonia. Rudyard recovered, but six-year-old Josephine did not. This poignant lyric, hung on the two Taffy adventures collected in the *Just So Stories* in 1902, captures something of his aching sense of loss.

I

There runs a road by Merrow Down –
　A grassy track to-day it is –
An hour out of Guildford town,
　Above the river Wey it is.

Here, when they heard the horse-bells ring,
　The ancient Britons dressed and rode
To watch the dark Phœnicians bring
　Their goods along the Western Road.

Yes, here, or hereabouts, they met
　To hold their racial talks and such –
To barter beads for Whitby jet,
　And tin for gay shell torques and such.

But long and long before that time
　(When bison used to roam on it)
Did Taffy and her Daddy climb
　That Down, and had their home on it.

Then beavers built in Broadstonebrook
　And made a swamp where Bramley stands;
And bears from Shere would come and look
　For Taffimai where Shamley stands.

The Wey, that Taffy called Wagai,
　Was more than six times bigger then;
And all the Tribe of Tegumai
　They cut a noble figure then!

*Rudyard Kipling's illustration to "How the First Letter was Written". Part of the runic inscription reads: "the reason why I spell so queerly is because there are not enough letters in the runic alphabet for all the words I want to use to you oh beloved."*

## II

Of all the Tribe of Tegumai
    Who cut that figure, none remain –
On Merrow Down the cuckoos cry –
    The silence and the sun remain.

But as the faithful years return
    And hearts unwounded sing again,
Comes Taffy dancing through the fern
    To lead the Surrey spring again.

Her brows are bound with bracken-fronds,
    And golden elf-locks fly above;
Her eyes are bright as diamonds
    And bluer than the sky above.

In moccasins and deer-skin cloak,
    Unfearing, free and fair she flits,
And lights her little damp-wood smoke
    To show her Daddy where she flits.

For far – oh, very far behind,
    So far she cannot call to him,
Comes Tegumai alone to find
    The daughter that was all to him!

# "They"

In September 1902 the Kiplings moved into their last home, the "very-own house" of Bateman's, Burwash, Sussex. They were forced out of Rottingdean by gawping trippers; the Jacobean ironmaster's house of Bateman's offered peace and privacy. Kipling wrote: "It is a good and peaceful place standing in terraced lawns nigh to a walled garden of old red brick, and two fat-headed oast-houses with red brick stomachers, and an aged silver-grey dovecot on top." Kipling had one of the first motor-cars in Sussex, and this story, written in 1904, draws on memories of his house-hunting trips. The story is another attempt to come to terms with Josephine's death. The ending, with its ambivalent warning about the "wrongness" of contact with the other world, may reflect Kipling's concern about his sister, Trix, whose mental breakdown was associated with her cultivation of "psychic" experiences. In *Something of Myself* Kipling writes: "I have seen too much evil and sorrow and wreck of good minds on the road to En-dor to take one step along that perilous track." En-dor is where King Saul consulted a witch; Kipling's poem "En-dor" is a rueful warning against the illusory promises of spiritualism, which tempted so many who lost their children in the Great War.

One view called me to another; one hill top to its fellow, half across the county, and since I could answer at no more trouble than the snapping forward of a lever, I let the county flow under my wheels. The orchid-studded flats of the East gave way to the thyme, ilex, and grey grass of the Downs; these again to the rich cornland and fig-trees of the lower coast, where you carry the beat of the tide on your left hand for fifteen level miles; and when at last I turned inland through a huddle of rounded hills and woods I had run myself clean out of my known marks. Beyond that precise hamlet which stands godmother to the capital of the United States, I found hidden villages where bees, the only things awake, boomed in eighty-foot lindens that overhung grey Norman churches; miraculous brooks diving under stone bridges built for heavier traffic than would ever vex them again; tithe-barns larger than their churches, and an old smithy that cried out aloud how it had once been a hall of the Knights of the Temple. Gypsies I found on a common where the gorse, bracken, and heath fought it out together up a mile of Roman road; and a little farther on I disturbed a red fox rolling dog-fashion in the naked sunlight.

As the wooded hills closed about me I stood up in the car to take the bearings of that great Down whose ringed head is a landmark for fifty miles across the low countries. I judged that the lie of the country would bring me across some westward-running road that went to his feet, but I did not allow for the confusing veils of the woods. A quick turn plunged me first into a green cutting brimful of liquid sunshine, next into a gloomy tunnel where last year's dead

*Washington, Sussex.*

leaves whispered and scuffled about my tyres. The strong hazel stuff meeting overhead had not been cut for a couple of generations at least, nor had any axe helped the moss-cankered oak and beech to spring above them. Here the road changed frankly into a carpeted ride on whose brown velvet spent primrose-clumps showed like jade, and a few sickly, white-stalked bluebells nodded together. As the slope favoured I shut off the power and slid over the whirled leaves, expecting every moment to meet a keeper; but I only heard a jay, far off, arguing against the silence under the twilight of the trees.

Still the track descended. I was on the point of reversing and working my way back on the second speed ere I ended in some swamp, when I saw sunshine through the tangle ahead and lifted the brake.

It was down again at once. As the light beat across my face my fore-wheels took the turf of a great still lawn from which sprang horsemen ten feet high with levelled lances, monstrous peacocks, and sleek round-headed maids of honour – blue, black, and glistening – all of clipped yew. Across the lawn – the marshalled woods besieged it on three sides – stood an ancient house of lichened and weather-worn stone, with mullioned windows and roofs of rose-red tile. It was flanked by semi-circular walls, also rose-red, that closed the lawn on the fourth side, and at their feet a box hedge grew man-high. There were doves on the roof about the slim brick chimneys, and I caught a glimpse of an octagonal dove-house behind the screening wall.

Here, then, I stayed; a horseman's green spear laid at my breast; held by the exceeding beauty of that jewel in that setting.

"If I am not packed off for a trespasser, or if this knight does not ride a wallop at me," thought I, "Shakespeare and Queen Elizabeth at least must come out of that half-open garden door and ask me to tea."

A child appeared at an upper window, and I thought the little thing waved a friendly hand. But it was to call a companion, for presently another bright head showed. Then I heard a laugh among the yew-peacocks, and turning to make sure (till then I had been watching the house only) I saw the silver of a fountain behind a hedge thrown up against the sun. The doves on the roof cooed to the cooing water; but between the two notes I caught the utterly happy chuckle of a child absorbed in some light mischief.

The garden door – heavy oak sunk deep in the thickness of the wall – opened further: a woman in a big garden hat set her foot slowly on the time-hollowed stone step and as slowly walked across the turf. I was forming some apology when she lifted up her head and I saw that she was blind.

"I heard you," she said. "Isn't that a motor car?"

"I'm afraid I've made a mistake in my road. I should have turned off up above – I never dreamed –" I began.

"But I'm very glad. Fancy a motor car coming into the garden! It will be such a treat –" She turned and made as though looking about her. "You – you haven't seen any one, have you – perhaps?"

"No one to speak to, but the children seemed interested at a distance."

"Which?"

"I saw a couple up at the window just now, and I think I heard a little chap in the grounds."

"Oh, lucky you!" she cried, and her face brightened. "I hear them, of course, but that's all. You've seen them and heard them?"

"Yes," I answered. "And if I know anything of children, one of them's having a beautiful time by the fountain yonder. Escaped, I should imagine."

"You're fond of children?"

I gave her one or two reasons why I did not altogether hate them.

"Of course, of course," she said. "Then you understand. Then you won't think it foolish if I ask you to take your car through the gardens, once or twice – quite slowly. I'm sure they'd like to see it. They see so little, poor things. One tries to make their life pleasant, but –" she threw out her hands towards the woods. "We're so out of the world here."

"That will be splendid," I said. "But I can't cut up your grass."

She faced to the right. "Wait a minute," she said. "We're at the South gate, aren't we? Behind those peacocks there's a flagged path. We call it the Peacocks' Walk. You can't see it from here, they tell me, but if you squeeze along by the edge of the wood you can turn at the

*Amberley Castle, Sussex, drawn by Frederick L. Griggs in 1903.*

*"She turned and made as though looking about her", one of the colour illustrations made by F. H. Townsend in 1905.*

first peacock and get on to the flags."

It was sacrilege to wake that dreaming house-front with the clatter of machinery, but I swung the car to clear the turf, brushed along the edge of the wood and turned in on the broad stone path where the fountain-basin lay like one star-sapphire.

"May I come too?" she cried. "No, please don't help me. They'll like it better if they see me."

She felt her way lightly to the front of the car, and with one foot on the step she called: "Children, oh, children! Look and see what's going to happen!"

*Bateman's: "We went through every room and found no shadow of ancient regrets, stifled miseries, nor any menace, though the 'new' end of her was three hundred years old."*

The voice would have drawn lost souls from the Pit, for the yearning that underlay its sweetness, and I was not surprised to hear an answering shout behind the yews. It must have been the child by the fountain, but he fled at our approach, leaving a little toy boat in the water. I saw the glint of his blue blouse among the still horsemen.

Very disposedly we paraded the length of the walk and at her request backed again. This time the child had got the better of his panic, but stood far off and doubting.

"The little fellow's watching us," I said. "I wonder if he'd like a ride."

"They're very shy still. Very shy. But, oh, lucky you to be able to see them! Let's listen."

I stopped the machine at once, and the humid stillness, heavy with the scent of box, cloaked us deep. Shears I could hear where some gardener was clipping; a mumble of bees and broken voices that might have been the doves.

"Oh, unkind!" she said weariedly.

"Perhaps they're only shy of the motor. The little maid at the window looks tremendously interested."

"Yes?" She raised her head. "It was wrong of me to say that. They are really fond of me. It's the only thing that makes life worth living – when they're fond of you, isn't it? I daren't think what the place would be without them. By the way, is it beautiful?"

"I think it is the most beautiful place I have ever seen."

"So they all tell me. I can feel it, of course, but that isn't quite the same thing."

"Then have you never – ?" I began, but stopped abashed.

"Not since I can remember. It happened when I was only a few months old, they tell me. And yet I must remember something, else how could I dream about colours? I see light in my dreams, and colours, but I never see *them*. I only hear them just as I do when I'm awake."

"It's difficult to see faces in dreams. Some people can, but most of us haven't the gift," I went on, looking up at the window where the child stood all but hidden.

"I've heard that too," she said. "And they tell me that one never sees a dead person's face in a dream. Is that true?"

"I believe it is – now I come to think of it."

"But how is it with yourself – yourself?" The blind eyes turned towards me.

"I have never seen the faces of my dead in any dream," I answered.

"Then it must be as bad as being blind."

The sun had dipped behind the woods and the long shades were possessing the insolent horsemen one by one. I saw the light die from off the top of a glossy-leaved lance and all the brave hard green turn to soft black. The house, accepting another day at end, as it had accepted an hundred thousand gone, seemed to settle deeper into its rest among the shadows.

"Have you ever wanted to?" she said after the silence.

"Very much sometimes," I replied. The child had left the window as the shadows closed upon it.

"Ah! So've I, but I don't suppose it's allowed. . . . Where d'you live?"

"Quite the other side of the county – sixty miles and more, and I must be going back. I've come without my big lamp."

"But it's not dark yet. I can feel it."

"I'm afraid it will be by the time I get home. Could you lend me someone to set me on my road at first? I've utterly lost myself."

"I'll send Madden with you to the cross-roads. We are so out of the world, I don't wonder you were lost! I'll guide you round to the front of the house; but you will go slowly, won't you, till you're out of the grounds? It isn't foolish, do you think?"

"I promise you I'll go like this," I said, and let the car start herself down the flagged path.

We skirted the left wing of the house, whose elaborately cast lead guttering alone was worth a day's journey; passed under a great rose-grown gate in the red wall, and so round to the high front of the house which in beauty and stateliness as much excelled the back as that all others I had seen.

"Is it so very beautiful?" she said wistfully when she heard my raptures. "And you like the lead-figures too? There's the old azalea garden behind. They say that this place must have been made for children. Will you help me out, please? I should like to come with you as far as the cross-roads, but I mustn't leave them. Is that you, Madden? I want you to show this gentleman the way to the cross-roads. He has lost his way but – he has seen them."

A butler appeared noiselessly at the miracle of old oak that must be called the front door, and slipped aside to put on his hat. She stood looking at me with open blue eyes in which no sight lay, and I saw for the first time that she was beautiful.

"Remember," she said quietly, "if you are fond of them you will come again," and disappeared within the house.

The butler in the car said nothing till we were nearly at the lodge gates, where catching a glimpse of a blue blouse in a shrubbery I swerved amply lest the devil that leads little boys to play should drag me into child-murder.

"Excuse me," he asked of a sudden, "but why did you do that, Sir?"

"The child yonder."

"Our young gentleman in blue?"

"Of course."

"He runs about a good deal. Did you see him by the fountain, Sir?"

"Oh, yes, several times. Do we turn here?"

"Yes, Sir. And did you 'appen to see them upstairs too?"

"At the upper window? Yes."

"Was that before the mistress come out to speak to you, Sir?"

"A little before that. Why d'you want to know?"

He paused a little. "Only to make sure that – that they had seen the car, Sir, because with children running about, though I'm sure you're driving particularly careful, there might be an accident. That was all, Sir. Here are the cross-roads. You can't miss your way from now on. Thank you, Sir, but that isn't *our* custom, not with –"

"I beg your pardon," I said, and thrust away the British silver.

"Oh, it's quite right with the rest of 'em as a rule. Good-bye, Sir."

He retired into the armour-plated conning tower of his caste and walked away. Evidently a butler solicitous for the honour of his house, and interested, probably through a maid, in the nursery.

Once beyond the signposts at the cross-roads I looked back, but the crumpled hills interlaced so jealously that I could not see where the house had lain. When I asked its name at a cottage along the road, the fat woman who sold sweetmeats there gave me to understand that people with motor cars had small right to live – much less to "go about talking like carriage folk". They were not a pleasant-mannered community.

When I retraced my route on the map that evening I was little wiser. Hawkin's Old Farm appeared to be the Survey title of the place, and the old County Gazetteer, generally so ample, did not

*"Poynings, from the Devil's Dyke", by F. L. Griggs, 1903.*

allude to it. The big house of those parts was Hodnington Hall, Georgian with early Victorian embellishments, as an atrocious steel engraving attested. I carried my difficulty to a neighbour – a deep-rooted tree of that soil – and he gave me a name of a family which conveyed no meaning.

A month or so later – I went again, or it may have been that my car took the road of her own volition. She over-ran the fruitless Downs, threaded every turn of the maze of lanes below the hills, drew through the high-walled woods, impenetrable in their full leaf, came out at the cross-roads where the butler had left me, and a little farther on developed an internal trouble which forced me to turn her in on a grass way-waste that cut into a summer-silent hazel wood. So far as I could make sure by the sun and a six-inch Ordnance map, this should be the road flank of that wood which I had first explored from the heights above. I made a mighty serious business of my repairs and a glittering shop of my repair kit, spanners, pump, and the like, which I spread out orderly upon a rug. It was a trap to catch all childhood, for on such a day, I argued, the children would not be far off. When I paused in my work I listened, but the wood was so full of the noises of summer (though the birds had mated) that I could not at first distinguish these from the tread of small cautious feet stealing across the dead leaves. I rang my bell in an alluring manner, but the feet fled, and I repented, for to a child a sudden noise is very real terror. I must have been at work half an hour when I heard in the wood the voice of the blind woman crying: "Children, oh, children! Where are you?" and the stillness made slow to close on the perfection of that cry. She came towards me, half feeling her way between the tree boles, and though a child, it seemed, clung to her skirt, it swerved into the leafage like a rabbit as she drew nearer.

"Is that you?" she said, "from the other side of the county?"

"Yes, it's me from the other side of the county."

"Then why didn't you come through the upper woods? They were there just now."

"They were here a few minutes ago. I expect they knew my car had broken down, and came to see the fun."

"Nothing serious, I hope? How do cars break down?"

"In fifty different ways. Only mine has chosen the fifty first."

She laughed merrily at the tiny joke, cooed with delicious laughter, and pushed her hat back.

"Let me hear," she said.

"Wait a moment," I cried, "and I'll get you a cushion."

She set her foot on the rug all covered with spare parts, and stooped above it eagerly. "What delightful things!" The hands through which she saw glanced in the chequered sunlight. "A box here – another box! Why you've arranged them like playing shop!"

"I confess now that I put it out to attract them. I don't need half those things really."

"How nice of you! I heard your bell in the upper wood. You say they were here before that?"

"I'm sure of it. Why are they so shy? That little fellow in blue who was with you just now ought to have got over his fright. He's been watching me like a Red Indian."

"It must have been your bell," she said. "I heard one of them go past me in trouble when I was coming down. They're shy – so shy even with me." She turned her face over her shoulder and cried again: "Children, oh, children! Look and see!"

"They must have gone off together on their own affairs," I suggested, for there was a murmur behind us of lowered voices broken by the sudden squeaking giggles of childhood. I returned to my tinkerings and she leaned forward, her chin on her hand, listening interestedly.

"How many are they?" I said at last. The work was finished, but I saw no reason to go.

Her forehead puckered a little in thought. "I don't quite know," she said simply. "Sometimes more – sometimes less. They come and

*"Why, you've arranged them like playing shop!", by F. H. Townsend, 1905.*

stay with me because I love them, you see."

"That must be very jolly," I said, replacing a drawer, and as I spoke I heard the inanity of my answer.

"You – you aren't laughing at me," she cried. "I – I haven't any of my own. I never married. People laugh at me sometimes about them because – because – "

"Because they're savages," I returned. "It's nothing to fret for. That sort laugh at everything that isn't in their own fat lives."

"I don't know. How should I? I only don't like being laughed at about *them*. It hurts; and when one can't see. . . . I don't want to seem silly," her chin quivered like a child's as she spoke, "but we blindies have only one skin, I think. Everything outside hits straight at our souls. It's different with you. You've such good defences in your eyes – looking out – before anyone can really pain you in your soul. People forget that with us."

I was silent reviewing that inexhaustible matter – the more than inherited (since it is also carefully taught) brutality of the Christian peoples, beside which the mere heathendom of the West Coast nigger is clean and restrained. It led me a long distance into myself.

"Don't do that!" she said of a sudden, putting her hands before her eyes.

"What?"

She made a gesture with her hand.

"That! It's – it's all purple and black. Don't! That colour hurts."

"But, how in the world do you know about colours?" I exclaimed, for here was a revelation indeed.

"Colours as colours?" she asked.

"No. *Those* Colours which you saw just now."

"You know as well as I do," she laughed, "else you wouldn't have asked that question. They aren't in the world at all. They're in *you* – when you went so angry."

"D'you mean a dull purplish patch, like port wine mixed with ink?" I said.

"I've never seen ink or port wine, but the colours aren't mixed. They are separate – all separate."

"Do you mean black streaks and jags across the purple?"

She nodded. "Yes – if they are like this," and zig-zagged her finger again, "but it's more red than purple – that bad colour."

"And what are the colours at the top of the – whatever you see?"

Slowly she leaned forward and traced on the rug the figure of the Egg itself.

"I see them so," she said, pointing with a grass stem, "white, green, yellow, red, purple, and when people are angry or bad, black across the red – as you were just now."

"Who told you anything about it – in the beginning?" I demanded.

"About the colours? No one. I used to ask what colours were when I was little – in table-covers and curtains and carpets, you see –

"*It was a trap to catch all childhood*", by F. H. Townsend, 1905.

because some colours hurt me and some made me happy. People told
me; and when I got older that was how I saw people." Again she
traced the outline of the Egg which it is given to very few of us to see.

"All by yourself?" I repeated.

"All by myself. There wasn't anyone else. I only found out
afterwards that other people did not see the Colours."

She leaned against the tree-bole plaiting and unplaiting chance-
plucked grass stems. The children in the wood had drawn nearer. I
could see them with the tail of my eye frolicking like squirrels.

"Now I am sure you will never laugh at me," she went on after a
long silence. "Nor at *them*."

"Goodness! No!" I cried, jolted out of my train of thought. "A
man who laughs at a child – unless the child is laughing too – is a
heathen!"

"I didn't mean that, of course. You'd never laugh *at* children, but I
thought – I used to think – that perhaps you might laugh about *them*.
So now I beg your pardon. . . . What are you going to laugh at?"

I had made no sound, but she knew.

"At the notion of your begging my pardon. If you had done your
duty as a pillar of the State and a landed proprietress you ought to
have summoned me for trespass when I barged through your woods
the other day. It was disgraceful of me – inexcusable."

She looked at me, her head against the tree trunk – long and
steadfastly – this woman who could see the naked soul.

"How curious," she half whispered. "How very curious."

"Why, what have I done?"

"You don't understand ... and yet you understood about the
Colours. Don't you understand?"

She spoke with a passion that nothing had justified, and I faced her
bewilderedly as she rose. The children had gathered themselves in a
roundel behind a bramble bush. One sleek head bent over something
smaller, and the set of the little shoulders told me that fingers were on
lips. They, too, had some child's tremendous secret. I alone was
hopelessly astray there in the broad sunlight.

"No," I said, and shook my head as though the dead eyes could
note. "Whatever it is, I don't understand yet. Perhaps I shall later – if
you'll let me come again."

"You will come again," she answered. "You will surely come again
and walk in the wood."

"Perhaps the children will know me well enough by that time to let
me play with them – as a favour. You know what children are like."

"It isn't a matter of favour but of right," she replied, and while I
wondered what she meant, a dishevelled woman plunged round the
bend of the road, loose-haired, purple, almost lowing with agony as
she ran. It was my rude, fat friend of the sweetmeat shop. The blind
woman heard and stepped forward. "What is it, Mrs. Madehurst?"
she asked.

*"The woman flung her apron over
her head and literally grovelled in
the dust", by F. H. Townsend,
1905.*

The woman flung her apron over her head and literally grovelled in the dust, crying that her grandchild was sick to death, that the local doctor was away fishing, that Jenny the mother was at her wits' end, and so forth, with repetitions and bellowings.

"Where's the next nearest doctor?" I asked between paroxysms.

"Madden will tell you. Go round to the house and take him with you. I'll attend to this. Be quick!" She half supported the fat woman into the shade. In two minutes I was blowing all the horns of Jericho under the front of the House Beautiful, and Madden, in the pantry, rose to the crisis like a butler and a man.

A quarter of an hour at illegal speeds caught us a doctor five miles away. Within the half-hour we had decanted him, much interested in motors, at the door of the sweetmeat shop, and drew up the road to await the verdict.

"Useful things, cars," said Madden, all man and no butler. "If I'd had one when mine took sick she wouldn't have died."

"How was it?" I asked.

"Croup. Mrs. Madden was away. No one knew what to do. I drove eight miles in a tax cart for the doctor. She was choked when we came back. This car 'd ha' saved her. She'd have been close on ten now."

"I'm sorry," I said. "I thought you were rather fond of children from what you told me going to the cross-roads the other day."

"Have you seen 'em again, Sir – this mornin'?"

"Yes, but they're well broke to cars. I couldn't get any of them within twenty yards of it."

He looked at me carefully as a scout considers a stranger – not as a menial should lift his eyes to his divinely appointed superior.

"I wonder why," he said just above the breath that he drew.

We waited on. A light wind from the sea wandered up and down the long lines of the woods, and the wayside grasses, whitened already with summer dust, rose and bowed in sallow waves.

A woman, wiping the suds off her arms, came out of the cottage next the sweetmeat shop.

"I've be'n listenin' in de back-yard," she said cheerily. "He says Arthur's unaccountable bad. Did ye hear him shruck just now? Unaccountable bad. I reckon t'will come Jenny's turn to walk in de wood nex' week along, Mr. Madden."

"Excuse me, Sir, but your lap-robe is slipping," said Madden deferentially. The woman started, dropped a curtsey, and hurried away.

"What does she mean by 'walking in the wood'?" I asked.

"It must be some saying they use hereabouts. I'm from Norfolk myself," said Madden. "They're an independent lot in this county. She took you for a chauffeur, Sir."

I saw the Doctor come out of the cottage followed by a draggle-tailed wench who clung to his arm as though he could make treaty for

*"I saw the Doctor come out of the cottage followed by a draggle-tailed wench", by F. H. Townsend, 1905.*

*East Lavant, Sussex, by F. L. Griggs, 1903.*

**tonneau**: the back seat of an open car

her with Death. "Dat sort," she wailed – "dey're just as much to us dat has 'em as if dey was lawful born. Just as much – just as much! An' God he'd be just as pleased if you saved 'un, Doctor. Don't take it from me. Miss Florence will tell ye de very   ne. Don't leave 'im, Doctor!"

"I know, I know," said the man; "but he'll be quiet for a while now. We'll get the nurse and the medicine as fast as we can." He signalled me to come forward with the car, and I strove not to be privy to what followed; but I saw the girl's face, blotched and frozen with grief, and I felt the hand without a ring clutching at my knees when we moved away.

The Doctor was a man of some humour, for I remember he claimed my car under the Oath of Æsculapius, and used it and me without mercy. First we convoyed Mrs. Madehurst and the blind woman to wait by the sick bed till the nurse should come. Next we invaded a neat county town for prescriptions (the Doctor said the trouble was cerebro-spinal meningitis), and when the County Institute, banked and flanked with scared market cattle, reported itself out of nurses for the moment we literally flung ourselves loose upon the county. We conferred with the owners of great houses – magnates at the ends of overarching avenues whose big-boned womenfolk strode away from their tea-tables to listen to the imperious Doctor. At last a white-haired lady sitting under a cedar of Lebanon and surrounded by a court of magnificent Borzois – all hostile to motors – gave the Doctor, who received them as from a princess, written orders which we bore many miles at top speed, through a park, to a French nunnery, where we took over in exchange a pallid-faced and trembling Sister. She knelt at the bottom of the tonneau telling her beads without pause till, by short cuts of the Doctor's invention, we had her to the sweetmeat shop once more. It was a long afternoon crowded with mad episodes that rose and dissolved like the dust of our wheels; cross-sections of remote and incomprehensible lives through which we raced at right angles; and I went home in the dusk, wearied out, to dream of the clashing horns of cattle; round-eyed nuns walking in a garden of graves; pleasant tea-parties beneath shaded trees; the carbolic-scented, grey-painted corridors of the County Institute; the steps of shy children in the wood, and the hands that clung to my knees as the motor began to move.

I had intended to return in a day or two, but it pleased Fate to hold me from that side of the county, on many pretexts, till the elder and the wild rose had fruited. There came at last a brilliant day, swept clear from the south-west, that brought the hills within hand's reach – a day of unstable airs and high filmy clouds. Through no merit of my own I was free, and set the car for the third time on that known road. As I reached the crest of the Downs I felt the soft air change, saw it glaze under the sun; and, looking down at the sea, in that instant beheld the blue of the Channel turn through polished silver and dulled steel to dingy pewter. A laden collier hugging the coast steered outward for deeper water, and, across copper-coloured haze, I saw sails rise one by one on the anchored fishing-fleet. In a deep dene behind me an eddy of sudden wind drummed through sheltered oaks, and spun aloft the first dry sample of autumn leaves. When I reached the beach road the sea-fog fumed over the brickfields, and the tide was telling all the groins of the gale beyond Ushant. In less than an hour summer England vanished in chill grey. We were again the shut island of the North, all the ships of the world bellowing at our perilous gates; and between their outcries ran the piping of bewildered gulls. My cap dripped moisture, the folds of the rug held it in pools or sluiced it away in runnels, and the salt-rime stuck to my lips.

*Near Tarring Neville, Sussex, by F. L. Griggs, 1903.*

Inland the smell of autumn loaded the thickened fog among the trees, and the drip became a continuous shower. Yet the late flowers – mallow of the wayside, scabious of the field, and dahlia of the garden – showed gay in the mist, and beyond the sea's breath there was little sign of decay in the leaf. Yet in the villages the house doors were all open, and bare-legged, bare-headed children sat at ease on the damp doorsteps to shout "pip-pip" at the stranger.

I made bold to call at the sweetmeat shop, where Mrs. Madehurst met me with a fat woman's hospitable tears. Jenny's child, she said, had died two days after the nun had come. It was, she felt, best out of the way, even though insurance offices, for reasons which she did not pretend to follow, would not willingly insure such stray lives. "Not but what Jenny didn't tend to Arthur as though he'd come all proper at de end of de first year – like Jenny herself." Thanks to Miss Florence, the child had been buried with a pomp which, in Mrs. Madehurst's opinion, more than covered the small irregularity of its birth. She described the coffin, within and without, the glass hearse, and the evergreen lining of the grave.

"But how's the mother?" I asked.

"Jenny? Oh, she'll get over it. I've felt dat way with one or two o' my own. She'll get over. She's walkin' in de wood now."

"In this weather?"

Mrs. Madehurst looked at me with narrowed eyes across the counter.

"I dunno but it opens de 'eart like. Yes, it opens de 'eart. Dat's where losin' and bearin' comes so alike in de long run, we do say."

Now the wisdom of the old wives is greater than that of all the Fathers, and this last oracle sent me thinking so extendedly as I went up the road, that I nearly ran over a woman and a child at the wooded corner by the lodge gates of the House Beautiful.

"Awful weather!" I cried, as I slowed dead for the turn.

"Not so bad," she answered placidly out of the fog. "Mine's used to 'un. You'll find yours indoors, I reckon."

Indoors, Madden received me with professional courtesy, and kind inquiries for the health of the motor, which he would put under cover.

I waited in a still, nut-brown hall, pleasant with late flowers and warmed with a delicious wood fire – a place of good influence and great peace. (Men and women may sometimes, after great effort, achieve a creditable lie; but the house, which is their temple, cannot say anything save the truth of those who have lived in it.) A child's cart and a doll lay on the black-and-white floor, where a rug had been kicked back. I felt that the children had only just hurried away – to hide themselves, most like – in the many turns of the great adzed staircase that climbed statelily out of the hall, or to crouch at gaze behind the lions and roses of the carven gallery above. Then I heard her voice above me, singing as the blind sing – from the soul: –

> In the pleasant orchard-closes.

And all my early summer came back at the call.

> In the pleasant orchard-closes,
> God bless all our gains say we –
> But may God bless all our losses,
> Better suits with our degree.

**the marring fifth line:** "Listen gentle – ay, and simple! Listen, children on the knee!" (E. B. Browning, "The Lost Bower")

She dropped the marring fifth line, and repeated –

> Better suits with our degree!

I saw her lean over the gallery, her linked hands white as pearl against the oak.

"Is that you – from the other side of the county?" she called.

*Rottingdean. The Kiplings lived here, near the Burne-Jones family, from 1897 to 1902, until encroaching building and prying sightseers drove them away. It was from Rottingdean that Kipling made the trips in his steam-driven "Locomobile" which are recalled in "'They'".*

"Yes, me – from the other side of the county," I answered, laughing.

"What a long time before you had to come here again." She ran down the stairs, one hand lightly touching the broad rail. "It's two months and four days. Summer's gone!"

"I meant to come before, but Fate prevented."

"I knew it. Please do something to that fire. They won't let me play with it, but I can feel it's behaving badly. Hit it!"

I looked on either side of the deep fireplace, and found but a half-charred hedge-stake with which I punched a black log into flame.

"It never goes out, day or night," she said, as though explaining. "In case any one comes in with cold toes, you see."

"It's even lovelier inside than it was out," I murmured. The red light poured itself along the age-polished dusky panels till the Tudor roses and lions of the gallery took colour and motion. An old eagle-topped convex mirror gathered the picture into its mysterious heart, distorting afresh the distorted shadows, and curving the gallery lines into the curves of a ship. The day was shutting down in half a gale as the fog turned to stringy scud. Through the uncurtained mullions of the broad window I could see valiant horsemen of the lawn rear and recover against the wind that taunted them with legions of dead leaves.

"Yes, it must be beautiful," she said. "Would you like to go over it? There's still light enough upstairs."

I followed her up the unflinching, wagon-wide staircase to the gallery whence opened the thin fluted Elizabethan doors.

"Feel how they put the latch low down for the sake of the children." She swung a light door inward.

"By the way, where are they?" I asked. "I haven't even heard them to-day."

She did not answer at once. Then, "I can only hear them," she replied softly. "This is one of their rooms – everything ready, you see."

She pointed into a heavily-timbered room. There were little low gate tables and children's chairs. A doll's house, its hooked front half open, faced a great dappled rocking-horse, from whose padded saddle it was but a child's scramble to the broad window-seat overlooking the lawn. A toy gun lay in a corner beside a gilt wooden cannon.

"Surely they've only just gone," I whispered. In the failing light a door creaked cautiously. I heard the rustle of a frock and the patter of feet – quick feet through a room beyond.

"I heard that," she cried triumphantly. "Did you? Children, oh, children! Where are you?"

The voice filled the walls that held it lovingly to the last perfect note, but there came no answering shout such as I had heard in the garden. We hurried on from room to oak-floored room; up a step here, down three steps there; among a maze of passages; always mocked by our quarry. One might as well have tried to work an unstopped warren with a single ferret. There were bolt-holes innumerable – recesses in walls, embrasures of deep slitten windows now darkened, whence they could start up behind us; and abandoned fireplaces, six feet deep in the masonry, as well as the tangle of communicating doors. Above all, they had the twilight for their helper in our game. I had caught one or two joyous chuckles of evasion, and once or twice had seen the silhouette of a child's frock against some darkening window at the end of a passage; but we returned empty-handed to the gallery, just as a middle-aged woman was setting a lamp in its niche.

"No, I haven't seen her either this evening, Miss Florence," I heard her say, "but that Turpin he says he wants to see you about his shed."

"Oh, Mr. Turpin must want to see me very badly. Tell him to come to the hall, Mrs. Madden."

I looked down into the hall whose only light was the dulled fire, and deep in the shadow I saw them at last. They must have slipped down while we were in the passages, and now thought themselves perfectly hidden behind an old gilt leather screen. By child's law, my fruitless chase was as good as an introduction, but since I had taken so much trouble I resolved to force them to come forward later by the simple trick, which children detest, of pretending not to notice them. They lay close, in a little huddle, no more than shadows except when a quick flame betrayed an outline.

"And now we'll have some tea," she said. "I believe I ought to have offered it you at first, but one doesn't arrive at manners somehow when one lives alone and is considered – h'm – peculiar." Then with very pretty scorn, "Would you like a lamp to see to eat by?"

"The firelight's much pleasanter, I think." We descended into that delicious gloom and Madden brought tea.

I took my chair in the direction of the screen ready to surprise or be surprised as the game should go, and at her permission, since a hearth is always sacred, bent forward to play with the fire.

"Where do you get these beautiful short faggots from?" I asked idly. "Why, they are tallies!"

"Of course," she said. "As I can't read or write I'm driven back on the early English tally for my accounts. Give me one and I'll tell you what it meant."

I passed her an unburned hazel-tally, about a foot long, and she ran her thumb down the nicks.

"This is the milk-record for the home farm for the month of April last year, in gallons," said she. "I don't know what I should have done without tallies. An old forester of mine taught me the system. It's out of date now for every one else; but my tenants respect it. One of them's coming now to see me. Oh, it doesn't matter. He has no business here out of office hours. He's a greedy, ignorant man – very

*"I don't know what I should have done without tallies", by F. H. Townsend, 1905.*

greedy or – he wouldn't come here after dark."

"Have you much land then?"

"Only a couple of hundred acres in hand, thank goodness. The other six hundred are nearly all let to folk who knew my folk before me, but this Turpin is quite a new man – and a highway robber."

"But are you sure I shan't be –?"

"Certainly not. You have the right. He hasn't any children."

"Ah, the children!" I said, and slid my low chair back till it nearly touched the screen that hid them. "I wonder whether they'll come out for me."

There was a murmur of voices – Madden's and a deeper note – at the low, dark side door, and a ginger-headed, canvas-gaitered giant of the unmistakable tenant-farmer type stumbled or was pushed in.

"Come to the fire, Mr. Turpin," she said.

"If – if you please, Miss, I'll – I'll be quite as well by the door." He clung to the latch as he spoke like a frightened child. Of a sudden I realised that he was in the grip of some almost overpowering fear.

"Well?"

"About that new shed for the young stock – that was all. These first autumn storms settin' in . . . but I'll come again, Miss." His teeth did not chatter much more than the door latch.

"I think not," she answered levelly. "The new shed – m'm. What did my agent write you on the 15th?"

"I – fancied p'raps that if I came to see you – ma – man to man like, Miss. But –"

His eyes rolled into every corner of the room wide with horror. He half opened the door through which he had entered, but I noticed it shut again – from without and firmly.

"He wrote what I told him," she went on. "You are overstocked already. Dunnett's Farm never carried more than fifty bullocks – even in Mr. Wright's time. And *he* used cake. You've sixty-seven and you don't cake. You've broken the lease in that respect. You're dragging the heart out of the farm."

"I'm – I'm getting some minerals – superphosphates – next week. I've as good as ordered a truck-load already. I'll go down to the station to-morrow about 'em. Then I can come and see you man to man like, Miss, in the daylight. . . . That gentleman's not going away, is he?" He almost shrieked.

I had only slid the chair a little farther back, reaching behind me to tap on the leather of the screen, but he jumped like a rat.

"No. Please attend to me, Mr. Turpin." She turned in her chair and faced him with his back to the door. It was an old and sordid little piece of scheming that she forced from him – his plea for the new cow-shed at his landlady's expense, that he might with the covered manure pay his next year's rent out of the valuation after, as she made clear, he had bled the enriched pastures to the bone. I could not but admire the intensity of his greed, when I saw him out-facing for its

*Josephine Kipling, in about 1895. After her death, the Kiplings found their Rottingdean home almost unbearable because of its associations. Lockwood wrote: "poor Rud told his mother how he saw her when a door opened, when a space was vacant at table, coming out of every green dark corner of the garden, radiant – and heartbreaking."*

sake whatever terror it was that ran wet on his forehead.

I ceased to tap the leather – was, indeed, calculating the cost of the shed – when I felt my relaxed hand taken and turned softly between the soft hands of a child. So at last I had triumphed. In a moment I would turn and acquaint myself with those quick-footed wanderers. . . .

The little brushing kiss fell in the centre of my palm – as a gift on which the fingers were, once, expected to close: as the all-faithful half-reproachful signal of a waiting child not used to neglect even when grown-ups were busiest – a fragment of the mute code devised very long ago.

Then I knew. And it was as though I had known from the first day when I looked across the lawn at the high window.

I heard the door shut. The woman turned to me in silence, and I felt that she knew.

What time passed after this I cannot say. I was roused by the fall of a log, and mechanically rose to put it back. Then I returned to my place in the chair very close to the screen.

"Now you understand," she whispered, across the packed shadows.

"Yes, I understand – now. Thank you."

"I – I only hear them." She bowed her head in her hands. "I have no right, you know – no other right. I have neither borne nor lost – neither borne nor lost!"

"Be very glad then," said I, for my soul was torn open within me. "Forgive me!"

She was still, and I went back to my sorrow and my joy.

"It was because I loved them so," she said at last, brokenly. "*That* was why it was, even from the first – even before I knew that they – they were all I should ever have. And I loved them so!"

She stretched out her arms to the shadows and the shadows within the shadow.

"They came because I loved them – because I needed them. I – I must have made them come. Was that wrong, think you?"

"No – no."

"I – I grant you that the toys and – and all that sort of thing were nonsense, but – but I used to so hate empty rooms myself when I was little." She pointed to the gallery. "And the passages all empty. . . . And how could I ever bear the garden door shut? Suppose – "

"Don't! For pity's sake, don't!" I cried. The twilight had brought a cold rain with gusty squalls that plucked at the leaded windows.

"And the same thing with keeping the fire in all night. *I* don't think it so foolish – do you?"

I looked at the broad brick hearth, saw, through tears I believe, that there was no unpassable iron on or near it, and bowed my head.

"I did all that and lots of other things – just to make believe. Then they came. I heard them, but I didn't know that they were not mine by right till Mrs. Madden told me – "

"The butler's wife? What?"

"One of them – I heard – she saw. And knew. Hers! *Not* for me. I didn't know at first. Perhaps I was jealous. Afterwards, I began to understand that it was only because I loved them, not because – . . . Oh, you *must* bear or lose," she said piteously. "There is no other way – and yet they love me. They must! Don't they?"

There was no sound in the room except the lapping voices of the fire, but we two listened intently, and she at least took comfort from what she heard. She recovered herself and half rose. I sat still in my chair by the screen.

"Don't think me a wretch to whine about myself like this, but – but I'm all in the dark, you know, and *you* can see."

In truth I could see, and my vision confirmed me in my resolve, though that was like the very parting of spirit and flesh. Yet a little longer I would stay since it was the last time.

"You think it is wrong, then?" she cried sharply, though I had said nothing.

*"And yet they love me. They must! Don't they?" by F. H. Townsend, 1905.*

"Not for you. A thousand times no. For you it is right.... I am grateful to you beyond words. For me it would be wrong. For me only...."

"Why?" she said, but passed her hand before her face as she had done at our second meeting in the wood. "Oh, I see," she went on simply as a child. "For you it would be wrong." Then with a little indrawn laugh, "and, d'you remember, I called you lucky – once – at first. You who must never come here again!"

She left me to sit a little longer by the screen, and I heard the sound of her feet die out along the gallery above.

*Amberley Church, Sussex, by F. L. Griggs, 1903.*

# The Land

> "Behold us lawful owners of a grey stone lichened house – A.D. 1634 over the door – beamed, panelled, with old oak staircase, and all untouched and unfaked" exulted Kipling on taking possession of Bateman's. But as this poem, and stories such as "An Habitation Enforced" and "My Son's Wife" show, he used the adjective "lawful" as a limitation of ownership not a confirmation of it. Hobden in this poem and in the Puck stories is based on Isted, a real Burwash labourer and poacher, whose characteristic admonition, "Have it as you're minded. I dunno as I should if I was you," tickled Kipling. But Hobden is also a type of "the English peasant" in a similar sense to George Bourne's Bettesworth in his books based on talks with an old labourer. Kipling's admiration of the licensed lawbreaking of such characters is an important element in his complex understanding of the "Law" by which nature must be shaped and regulated.

When Julius Fabricius, Sub-Prefect of the Weald,
In the days of Diocletian owned our Lower River-field,
He called to him Hobdenius – a Briton of the Clay,
Saying: "What about that River-piece for layin' in to hay?"

And the aged Hobden answered: "I remember as a lad
My father told your father that she wanted dreenin' bad.
An' the more that you neeglect her the less you'll get her clean.
Have it jest *as* you've a mind to, but, if I was you, I'd dreen."

So they drained it long and crossways in the lavish Roman style –
Still we find among the river-drift their flakes of ancient tile,
And in drouthy middle August, when the bones of meadows show,
We can trace the lines they followed sixteen hundred years ago.

Then Julius Fabricius died as even Prefects do,
And after certain centuries, Imperial Rome died too.
Then did robbers enter Britain from across the Northern main
And our Lower River-field was won by Ogier the Dane.

Well could Ogier work his war-boat – well could Ogier wield his brand –
Much he knew of foaming waters – not so much of farming land.
So he called to him a Hobden of the old unaltered blood,
Saying: "What about that River-piece; she doesn't look no good?"

And that aged Hobden answered: " 'Tain't for *me* to interfere,
But I've known that bit o' meadow now for five and fifty year.
Have it *jest* as you've a mind to, but I've proved it time on time,
If you want to change her nature you have *got* to give her lime!"

Ogier sent his wains to Lewes, twenty hours' solemn walk,
And drew back great abundance of the cool, grey, healing chalk.
And old Hobden spread it broadcast, never heeding what was in 't–
Which is why in cleaning ditches, now and then we find a flint.

Ogier died. His sons grew English – Anglo-Saxon was their name–
Till out of blossomed Normandy another pirate came;
For Duke William conquered England and divided with his men,
And our Lower River-field he gave to William of Warenne.

But the Brook (you know her habit) rose one rainy Autumn night
And tore down sodden flitches of the bank to left and right.
So, said William to his Bailiff as they rode their dripping rounds:
"Hob, what about that River-bit – the Brook's got up no bounds?"

And that aged Hobden answered: "'Tain't my business to advise,
But ye might ha' known 'twould happen from the way the valley lies.
Where ye can't hold back the water you must try and save the sile.
Hev it jest as you've a *mind* to, but, if I was you, I'd spile!"

They spiled along the water-course with trunks of willow-trees,
And planks of elms behind 'em and immortal oaken knees.
And when the spates of Autumn whirl the gravel-beds away
You can see their faithful fragments, iron-hard in iron clay.

❖

RIGHT: *A Sussex hedger of the
1930s – such a man as the two
hedgers in Kipling's "Friendly
Brook", whose exact skill he clearly
considered a direct equivalent of his
own writer's craft.*

OPPOSITE: *The Charter of the
River, granting Elsie and John the
river Dudwell for their "private
and particular use behoof
advantage ownership disport and
delight". Kipling derived
considerable pleasure from
constructing such documents, for
instance the fake Chaucerian
manuscript described in his story
"Dayspring Mishandled".*

THE CHARTER of THE RIVER

Know all Men by These Presents that I
The Sieur Rudyard Kipling of Batemans in the County
of Sussex
do grant and confirm and by These Presents have granted and confirmed
To John Kipling and Elsie his Sister [quamdiu se bene gesserint]
The Charter Liberties Freedoms & Benefits all and singular of
all that portion of the Dudwell River lying and situate between Corbie Point
and the Great Ash commonly called Cape Turnagain for their private and
particular use behoof advantage ownership disport and delight
without let hindrance molestation tax toll due fee or Service Excepting always
such Knightly Love and Fealty as already subsists between Us.

That the said John Kipling and Elsie his sister shall be at all times
free to come and go and look and Know — whether shod or barefoot —
between the two points aforesaid and to name and claim and use for
a game all Bays Points Bars Capes Promontories Shingles Shallows
Deeps Ditches Drains Pools and Trees as best shall them please.

And Furthermore by Virtue of These Presents they shall freely enjoy
and exercise The High The Low and The Middle Justice upon and over
all Birds Beasts Reptiles Fishes and Insects as may by custom inhabit
or by accident enter the aforesaid Domain whereof the two aforesaid —
to wit John Kipling and Elsie his Sister — stand accountable and whereof
they are Siezed and possessed.

And the said John Kipling and Elsie his sister shall hold and employ and dig and
enjoy for their sole seisns without tribute to their liege all Gold Precious and
Sub-Precious Stones Metals minerals Mines and Quarries which they may
by art or accident discover within the limits of their Domain aforesaid
And They shall hold further both for her and Sole All rights of Free Forest
Warren and Chase; Turbary: Common; Loppage and Pannage with all such
other Rights and Prerogatives as do vest in the lawful Possessors of such Domains
according to the Custom and Prescription of Old England

Provided Always that the said John Kipling and Elsie his Sister shall in no wise wage War overt or
covert against their Liege Lord but shall always with speed and diligence warn him of all
Plots and Discomfitures against him directed and in his cause shall bear him True and
Knightly Service Nor shall they fortify by Arts or defend with Arms and Engines
any Bank Ford Passage or Pass or any strong place make or suffer to be made
within the length of their dominion. No shall they hold against their Liege Lord or
any of his household or people any bridge by which their Liege-Lord and his Peoples
are used and wonted to cross the River aforesaid at any place; nor shall they
mud Earth Grass or leaves or water throw at or against their Liege Lord or their
Lady Mother but shall in always matters and concerns abide Peaceful Loyal
orderly and discreet as Faithful lieges.

To which Charter I the Sieur Rudyard Kipling
of Batemans in the County of Sussex have set my seal

This Nineteenth Day of June in the Year of our Lord
one thousand nine hundred and six

June: 19: 1906.

*A shepherd on Ditchling Beacon, 1926. Kipling's great feeling for Sussex's rural workers was sometimes warily reciprocated. The Rottingdean shepherd Steve Barrow refused to sing his folksongs to Kipling, on the grounds that "That Rudyard Kipling would send 'em to Lunnon and make a mort of money out of 'em."*

*Georgii Quinti Anno Sexto*, I, who own the River-field,
Am fortified with title-deeds, attested, signed and sealed,
Guaranteeing me, my assigns, my executors and heirs
All sorts of powers and profits which – are neither mine nor theirs.

I have rights of chase and warren, as my dignity requires.
I can fish – but Hobden tickles. I can shoot – but Hobden wires.
I repair, but he reopens, certain gaps which, men allege,
Have been used by every Hobden since a Hobden swapped a hedge.

Shall I dog his morning progress o'er the track-betraying dew?
Demand his dinner-basket into which my pheasant flew?
Confiscate his evening faggot under which my conies ran,
And summons him to judgement? I would sooner summons Pan.

His dead are in the churchyard – thirty generations laid.
Their names were old in history when Domesday Book was made;
And the passion and the piety and prowess of his line
Have seeded, rooted, fruited in some land the Law calls mine.

Not for any beast that burrows, not for any bird that flies,
Would I lose his large sound counsel, miss his keen amending eyes.
He is bailiff, woodman, wheelwright, field-surveyor, engineer,
And if flagrantly a poacher – 'tain't for me to interfere.

"Hob, what about that River-bit?" I turn to him again,
With Fabricius and Ogier and William of Warenne.
"Hev it jest as you've a mind to, *but –*" and here he takes command.
For whoever pays the taxes old Mus' Hobden owns the land.

*Bateman's:*
*Take of English earth as much*
*As either hand may rightly*
*  clutch.*
*In the taking of it breathe*
*Prayer for all who lie beneath –*
*Not the great nor well-bespoke,*
*But the mere uncounted folk*
*Of whose life and death is none*
*Report or lamentation.*
*Lay that earth upon thy heart,*
*And thy sickness shall depart!*

# The Way Through the Woods

"Dan and Una", John and Elsie,
drawn in Puck's field by H. R.
Millar, 1906.

They shut the road through the woods
Seventy years ago.
Weather and rain have undone it again,
And now you would never know
There was once a road through the woods
Before they planted the trees.
It is underneath the coppice and heath
And the thin anemones.
Only the keeper sees
That, where the ring-dove broods,
And the badgers roll at ease,
There was once a road through the woods.

Yet, if you enter the woods
Of a summer evening late,
When the night-air cools on the trout-ringed pools
Where the otter whistles his mate,
(They fear not men in the woods,
Because they see so few.)
You will hear the beat of a horse's feet,
And the swish of a skirt in the dew,
Steadily cantering through
The misty solitudes,
As though they perfectly knew
The old lost road through the woods. . . .
But there is no road through the woods.

Kipling spent his last forty years living in Sussex. Though he could become exasperated – "England is a stuffy little place, mentally, morally and physically", he wrote to Rhodes – he deeply loved the English countryside, and the even tenor of a life he could trace back through time to the Romans and beyond. He writes in *Something of Myself*: "Just beyond the west fringe of our land, in a little valley running from Nowhere to Nothing-at-all, stood the long, over-grown slag-heap of a most ancient forge, supposed to have been worked by the Phoenicians and Romans and, since then, uninterruptedly till the middle of the eighteenth century. The bracken and rush-patches still hid stray pigs of iron, and if one scratched a few inches through the rabbit-shaven turf, one came on the narrow mule-tracks of peacock-hued furnace-slag laid down in Elizabeth's day. The ghost of a road climbed up out of this dead arena, and crossed our fields, where it was known as 'The Gunway', and popularly connected with Armada times. Every foot of that little corner was alive with ghosts and shadows." These verses, expressing this feeling, were written in autumn 1909.

# The Irish Guards in the Great War

On 4 August 1914, Carrie Kipling wrote in her diary, "My cold possesses me". Rudyard added his own note: "incidentally Armageddon begins". He had stridently warned of the war to come; now it had arrived, there was little practical he could do. He gave recruiting speeches, he visited France as a war correspondent, he stirred up correspondents on both sides of the Atlantic with his belief that the Germans were determined to destroy civilisation. In January 1917, Kipling was approached to write *The History of the Irish Guards in the Great War*, which appeared in two volumes in 1923. The title page claims that the work is simply "edited and compiled from their diaries and papers by Rudyard Kipling". His secretary Dorothy Ponton confirmed: "Some of the material for the book was collected from the diaries of officers – mere scraps of paper stained with the mud of the trenches – or even flecked with blood." However, it forms a continuous narrative with very little direct quotation. It is one of the least known of Kipling's works, but by no means the least interesting. Kipling's characteristic economy of expression and his habit of implying what he does not wish to say directly are both powerful tools in constructing such a painful chronicle. The following extract is from his introduction.

As evidence is released, historians may be able to reconstruct what happened in or behind the battle-line; what motives and necessities swayed the actors; and who stood up or failed under his burden. But a battalion's field is bounded by its own vision. Even within these limits, there is large room for error. Witnesses to phases of fights die and are dispersed; the ground over which they fought is battered out of recognition in a few hours; survivors confuse dates, places and personalities, and in the trenches, the monotony of the waiting days and the repetition-work of repairs breed mistakes and false judgements. Men grow doubtful or oversure, and, in all good faith, give directly opposed versions. The clear sight of a comrade so mangled that he seems to have been long dead is burnt in on one brain to the exclusion of all else that happened that day. The shock of an exploded dump, shaking down a firmament upon the landscape, dislocates memory throughout half a battalion; and so on in all matters, till the end of laborious enquiry is too often the opening of fresh confusion. When to this are added the personal prejudices and misunderstandings of men under heavy strain, carrying clouded memories of orders half given or half heard, amid scenes that pass like nightmares, the only wonder to the compiler of these records has been that any sure fact whatever should be retrieved out of the whirlpools of war.

It seemed to him best, then, to abandon all idea of such broad and balanced narratives as will be put forward by experts, and to limit himself to matters which directly touched the men's lives and fortunes. Nor has he been too careful to correct the inferences of the

*Kipling appealing for recruits in Southport in June 1915.*

time by the knowledge of later events. From first to last, the Irish Guards, like the rest of our Armies, knew little of what was going on round them. Probably they knew less at the close of the War than at the beginning when our forces were so small that each man felt himself somebody indeed, and so stood to be hunted through the heat from Mons to Meaux, turned again to suffer beneath the Soupir ridges, and endured the first hideous winter of The Salient where, wet, almost weaponless, but unbroken, he helped in the long miracle of holding the line.

But the men of '14 and '15, and what meagre records of their day were safe to keep, have long been lost; while the crowded years between remove their battles across dead Belgian towns and villages as far as the fights in Homer.

Doubtless, all will be reconstructed to the satisfaction of future years when, if there be memory beyond the grave, the ghosts may laugh at the neatly groomed histories. Meantime, we can take it for granted that the old Regular Army of England passed away in the mud of Flanders in less than a year. In training, morale, endurance, courage and devotion the Earth did not hold its like, but it possessed neither the numbers, guns, nor equipment necessary for the type of war that overtook it. The fact of its unpreparedness has been extolled as proof of the purity of its country's ideals, which must be great consolation to all concerned. But, how slowly that equipment was furnished, how inadequate were our first attempts at bombs, trench-mortars, duck-boards, wiring and the rest, may be divined through the loyal and guarded allusions in the Diaries. Nor do private communications give much hint of it, for one of the marvels of that marvellous time was the silence of those concerned on everything that might too much distress their friends at home. The censorship

*A recruiting poster reflects the popular mood of patriotism and sentimental sacrifice. F. H. Townsend's* Punch *cartoon of an under-age boy at a recruiting office has a darker edge: "Do you know where boys go who tell lies?" "To the Front, Sir."*

had imposed this as a matter of precaution, but only the spirit of the officers could have backed the law so completely; and, as better days came, their early makeshifts and contrivances passed out of remembrance with their early dead. But the sufferings of our Armies were constant. They included wet and cold in due season, dirt always, occasional vermin, exposure, extreme fatigue, and the hourly incidence of death in every shape along the front line and, later, in the farthest back-areas where the enemy aeroplanes harried their camps. And when our Regular troops had been expended, these experiences were imposed upon officers and men compelled to cover, within a few months, the long years of training that should go to the making of a soldier – men unbroken even to the disturbing impact of crowds and like experiences, which the conscript accepts from his youth. Their short home-leaves gave them sudden changes to the tense home atmosphere where, under cover of a whirl of "entertainment", they and their kin wearied themselves to forget and escape a little from that life, on the brink of the next world, whose guns they could hear summoning in the silences between their talk. Yet, some were glad to return – else why should youngsters of three years' experience have found themselves upon a frosty night, on an iron-bound French road, shouting aloud for joy as they heard the stammer of a machine-

*Life in the trenches, of which Kipling wrote: "They speculated on all things in Heaven and earth as they worked in piled filth among the carcasses of their fellows, lay out under the stars on the eve of open battle, or vegetated through a month's feeding and idleness between one sacrifice and the next."*

gun over the rise, and turned up the well-known trench that led to their own dug-out and their brethren from whom they had been separated by the vast interval of ninety-six hours? Many have confessed to the same delight in their work, as there were others to whom almost every hour was frankly detestable except for the companionship that revealed them one to another till the chances of war separated the companions. And there were, too, many, almost children, of whom no record remains. They came out from Warley with the constantly renewed drafts, lived the span of a Second Lieutenant's life and were spent. Their intimates might preserve, perhaps, memories of a promise cut short, recollections of a phrase that stuck, a chance-seen act of bravery or of kindness. The Diaries give their names and fates with the conventional expressions of regret. In most instances, the compiler has let the mere fact suffice; since, to his mind, it did not seem fit to heap words on the doom.

RIGHT: *An Irish Guardsman's kit, laid out for inspection.*

OPPOSITE: *F. H. Townsend's* Punch *cartoon about the sack of Warsaw reflects Government black propaganda exaggerating German atrocities, which Kipling firmly believed. In 1918, he wrote a vindictive poem, "The Death-Bed", about the Kaiser's rumoured throat cancer (a disease Kipling himself feared):*

*Some die shouting in gas or fire;*
*Some die silent, by shell and shot.*
*Some die desperate, caught on*
*    the wire;*
*Some die suddenly. This will not.*

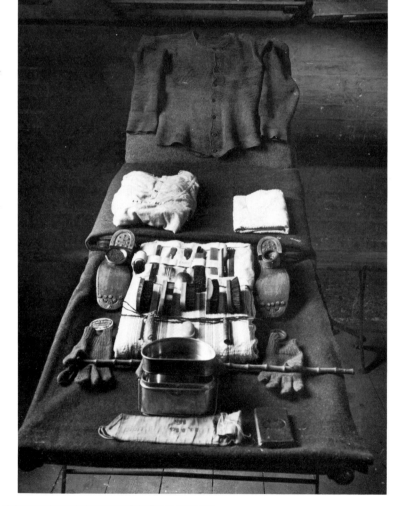

WORDS—AND DEEDS.

# Gethsemane

Kipling anticipated the Great War, and when it came he threw himself into propaganda activities. But he remained a poet, not a politician, and his deepest response to the war was troubled and introspective. "Gethsemane", partly because its "story" is so obscure, is perhaps his most potent distillation of the horror of the gas and slaughter of the trenches. A passage from his friend Rider Haggard's diary for 22 May 1918 is relevant: "I happened to remark that I thought that this world was one of the hells. He replied that he did not *think*, he was *certain* of it. He went on to show that it had every attribute of a hell, doubt, fear, pain, struggle, bereavement, almost irresistible temptations springing from the nature with which we are clothed, physical and mental suffering, etc., etc., ending in the worst fate that man can devise for man. Execution! As for the future he is inclined to let the matter drift. He said, what he has often said to me before, that what he wants is a 'good long rest'."

The Garden called Gethsemane
  In Picardy it was,
And there the people came to see
  The English soldiers pass.
We used to pass – we used to pass
  Or halt, as it might be,
And ship our masks in case of gas
  Beyond Gethsemane.

The Garden called Gethsemane,
  It held a pretty lass,
But all the time she talked to me
  I prayed my cup might pass.
The officer sat on the chair,
  The men lay on the grass,
And all the time we halted there
  I prayed my cup might pass.

It didn't pass – it didn't pass –
  It didn't pass from me.
I drank it when we met the gas
  Beyond Gethsemane!

ABOVE: *A soldier writing, perhaps filling in one of the uninformative field postcards, a series of set sentences which could be left or erased, but to which no personal message could be added.*

OPPOSITE: *The point of "breaking strain".*

# The Battle of Loos

The battle of Loos in September 1915 was a typically inconclusive, muddled and wasteful clash, with thousands dying for a few yards won or lost. As Kipling shows in this further extract from his *History of the Irish Guards in the Great War*, the chief theme of the war, especially in its early stages, was the slaughter of innocence at the behest of incompetence. For Kipling, however, the true test of the war was not success or failure of particular strategies, or victory or defeat in particular battles: it was the individual's discovery of his own point of "breaking strain", and mastery of it to achieve self-ownership. By this test there could be no vain death. Necessary or not, the sacrifice of the soldiers was a real one, and Kipling gave it its true value. The terrible new realities of trench warfare were not lost on him, and after the war he wrote some fine stories about the effects of shell shock. But he had always understood the underlying truths of men in war:

> An' now the ugly bullets come peckin' through the dust,
> An' no one wants to face 'em, but every beggar must;
> So, like a man in irons which isn't glad to go,
> They moves 'em off in companies uncommon stiff an' slow.

The attack of their Brigade developed during the course of the day. The four C.O.s of the Battalions met their Brigadier at the 1st Grenadier Guards Headquarters. He took them to a point just north of Loos, whence they could see Chalk-Pit Wood, and the battered bulk of the colliery head and workings known as Puits 14 bis, together with what few small buildings still stood thereabouts, and told them that he proposed to attack as follows: at half-past two a heavy bombardment lasting for one hour and a half would be delivered on that sector. At four the 2nd Irish Guards would advance upon Chalk-Pit Wood and would establish themselves on the north-east and south-east faces of it, supported by the 1st Coldstream. The 1st Scots Guards were to advance echeloned to the right rear of the Irish, and to attack Puits 14 bis moving round the south side of Chalk-Pit Wood, covered by heavy fire from the Irish out of the Wood itself. For this purpose, four machine-guns of the Brigade Machine-Gun Company were to accompany the latter Battalion. The 3rd Grenadiers were to support the 1st Scots in their attack on the Puits. Chalk-Pit Wood at that time existed as a somewhat dishevelled line of smallish trees and brush running from north to south along the edge of some irregular chalk workings which terminated at their north end in a deepish circular quarry. It was not easy to arrive at its precise shape and size, for the thing, like so much of the war-landscape of France, was seen but once by the men vitally concerned in its features, and thereafter changed outline almost weekly, as gun-fire smote and levelled it from different angles.

The orders for the Battalion, after the conference and the short view of the ground, were that No. 3 Company (Captain Wynter) was to advance from their trenches when the bombardment stopped, to the southern end of Chalk-Pit Wood, get through and dig itself in in the tough chalk on the farther side. No. 2 Company (Captain Bird), on the left of No. 3, would make for the centre of the Wood, dig in too, on the far side, and thus prolong No. 3's line up to and including the Chalk-Pit – that is to say, that the two Companies would hold the whole face of the Wood.

Nos. 1 and 4 Companies were to follow and back up Nos. 3 and 2 respectively. At four o'clock the two leading Companies deployed and advanced, "keeping their direction and formation perfectly". That much could be seen from what remained of Vermelles water-tower, where some of the officers of the 1st Battalion were watching, regardless of occasional enemy shell. They advanced quickly, and pushed through to the far edge of the Wood with very few casualties, and those, as far as could be made out, from rifle or machine-gun fire. (Shell-fire had caught them while getting out of their trenches, but, notwithstanding, their losses had not been heavy till then.) The rear Companies pushed up to thicken the line, as the fire increased from the front, and while digging in beyond the Wood, 2nd Lieutenant Pakenham-Law was fatally wounded in the head. Digging was not easy work, and seeing that the left of the two first Companies did not seem to have extended as far as the Chalk-Pit, at the north of the

*Men returning to the Front, 1916. A posed photograph, it is nonetheless graphic. The song they are singing may be any of the gruesome parody anthems of the troops:*

> *If you want to find the old battalion,*
> *I know where they are, I know where they are,*
> *I know where they are.*
> *They're hanging on the old barbed wire.*
> *I've seen 'em, I've seen 'em,*
> *Hanging on the old barbed wire.*

171

Wood, the C.O. ordered the last two platoons of No. 4 Company which were just coming up, to bear off to the left and get hold of the place. In the meantime, the 1st Scots Guards, following orders, had come partly round and partly through the right flank of the Irish, and attacked Puits 14 bis, which was reasonably stocked with machine-guns, but which they captured for the moment. Their rush took with them "some few Irish Guardsmen", with 2nd Lieutenants W. F. J. Clifford and J. Kipling of No. 2 Company who went forward not less willingly because Captain Cuthbert commanding the Scots Guards party had been Adjutant to the Reserve Battalion at Warley ere the 2nd Battalion was formed, and they all knew him. Together, this rush reached a line beyond the Puits, well under machine-gun fire (out of the Bois Hugo across the Lens–La Bassée road). Here 2nd Lieutenant Clifford was shot and wounded or killed – the body was found later – and 2nd Lieutenant Kipling was wounded and missing. The Scots Guards also lost Captain Cuthbert, wounded or killed, and the combined Irish and Scots Guards party fell back from the Puits and retired "into and through Chalk-Pit Wood in some confusion". The C.O. and Adjutant, Colonel Butler and Captain Vesey, went forward through the Wood to clear up matters, but, soon after they had entered it the Adjutant was badly wounded and had to be carried off. Almost at the same moment, "the men from the Puits came streaming back through the Wood, followed by a great part of the line which had been digging in on the farther side of it."

Evidently, one and a half hour's bombardment, against a country-side packed with machine-guns, was not enough to placate it. The Battalion had been swept from all quarters, and shelled at the same time, at the end of two hard days and sleepless nights, as a first experience of war, and had lost seven of their officers in forty minutes. They were re-formed somewhat to the rear along the Loos–Hulluch road. ("Jerry did himself well at Loos upon us innocents. We went into it, knowing no more than our own dead what was coming, and Jerry fair lifted us out of it with machine-guns. That was all there was to it *that* day.") The watchers on the Vermelles water-

*A trench scene.*

tower saw no more than a slow forward wave obscured by Chalk-Pit Wood; the spreading of a few scattered figures, always, it seemed, moving leisurely; and then a return, with no apparent haste in it, behind the Wood once more. They had a fair idea, though, of what had happened, and guessed what was to follow. The re-formed line would go up again exactly to where it had come from. While this was being arranged, and when a couple of Companies of the 1st Coldstream had turned up in a hollow on the edge of the Loos–Hulluch road, to support the Battalion, a runner came back with a message from Captain Alexander saying that he and some men were still in their scratch-trenches on the far side of Chalk-Pit Wood, and he would be greatly obliged if they would kindly send some more men up, and with speed. The actual language was somewhat crisper, and was supplemented, so the tale runs, by remarks from the runner addressed to the community at large. The demand was met at once, and the rest of the line was despatched to the near side of the Wood in support. The two Companies of the Coldstream came up on the left of the Irish Guards, and seized and settled down in the Chalk-Pit itself. They all had a night's energetic digging ahead of them, with but their own entrenching tools to help, and support-trenches had to be made behind the Wood in case the enemy should be moved to counter-attack. To meet that chance, as there was a gap between the supporting Coldstream Companies and the 1st Guards Brigade on the left, the C.O. of the 2nd Battalion collected some hundred and fifty men of various regiments, during the dusk, and stuffed them

Officer: *"You fool! Come back at once!"* Tommy: *"Not me, Sir! There's a wasp in the trench."* Punch *cartoons by artists such as L. Raven Hill and F. H. Townsend were an accurate and disturbing reflection of the realities of war; the jocular captions frequently held a sting in their tail.*

into an old German communication-trench as a defence. No counter-attack developed, but it was a joyless night that they spent among the uptorn trees and lumps of unworkable chalk. Their show had failed with all the others along the line, and "the greatest battle in the history of the world" was frankly stuck. The most they could do was to hang on and wait developments. They were shelled throughout the next day, heavily but inaccurately, when 2nd Lieutenant Sassoon was wounded by a rifle bullet. In the evening they watched the 1st Coldstream make an unsuccessful attack on Puits 14 bis, for the place was a well-planned machine-gun nest – the first of many that they were fated to lose their strength against through the years to come. That night closed in rain, and they were left to the mercy of Providence. No one could get to them, and they could get at nobody; but they could and did dig deeper into the chalk, to keep warm, and to ensure against the morrow (29th September) when the enemy guns found their range and pitched the stuff fairly into the trenches "burying many men and blowing a few to pieces". Yet, according to the count, which surely seems inaccurate, they only lost twenty dead in the course of the long day. The 3rd Guards Brigade on their right, sent in word that the Germans were massing for attack in the Bois Hugo in front of their line. "All ranks were warned", which, in such a situation, meant no more than that the experienced among them, of whom there were a few, waited for the cessation of shell-fire, and the inexperienced, of whom there were many, waited for what would come next. ("And the first time that he is under *that* sort of fire, a man stops his thinking. He's all full of wonder, sweat, and great curses.") No attack, however, came, and the Gunners claimed that their fire on Bois Hugo had broken it up. Then the Brigade on their left cheered them with instructions that Chalk-Pit Wood must be "held at all costs", and that they would not be relieved for another two days; also, that "certain modifications of the Brigade line would take place". It turned out later that these arrangements did not affect the Battalions. They were taken out of the line "wet, dirty, and exhausted" on the night of the 30th September when, after a heavy day's shelling, the Norfolks relieved them, and they got into billets behind Sailly-Labourse. They had been under continuous strain since the 25th of the month, and from the 27th to the 30th in a punishing action which had cost them, as far as could be made out, 324 casualties, including 101 missing. Of these last, the Diary records that "the majority of them were found to have been admitted to some Field Ambulance wounded". The number of known dead is set down officially as not more than 25, which must be below the mark. Of their officers, 2nd Lieutenant Pakenham-Law had died of wounds; 2nd Lieutenants Clifford and Kipling were missing, Captain and Adjutant the Hon. T. E. Vesey, Captain Wynter, Lieutenant Stevens, and 2nd Lieutenants Sassoon and Grayson were wounded, the last being blown up by a shell. It was a fair average for the day of a debut,

**Sassoon**: Reginald Ellice Sassoon M.C., not the war poet

"*Well done, the New Army*", a Townsend cartoon from Punch, 1916. The soldier is applying a field dressing.

and taught them somewhat for their future guidance. Their Commanding Officer told them so at Adjutant's Parade, after they had been rested and cleaned on the 2nd October at Verquigneul; but it does not seem to have occurred to any one to suggest that direct Infantry attacks, after ninety-minute bombardments, on works begotten out of a generation of thought and prevision, scientifically built up by immense labour and applied science, and developed against all contingencies through nine months, are not likely to find a fortunate issue. So, while the Press was explaining to a puzzled public what a far-reaching success had been achieved, the "greatest battle in the history of the world" simmered down to picking up the pieces on both sides of the line, and a return to autumnal trench-work, until more and heavier guns could be designed and manufactured in England. Meantime, men died.

*Going over the top, a still from moving film of the Battle of the Somme. A few frames later, the man climbing the rise on the right is lying still, as the others disappear from view.*

# My Boy Jack

John Kipling, born at Rottingdean in 1897, grew into a happy, untroubled young man, with little of his father's dark brooding side. The Kiplings were quietly very proud of him. His death at Loos on 27 September 1915, just six weeks after his eighteenth birthday, was a terrible blow. It was made worse because John was simply reported missing during the fighting at Chalk-Pit Wood. Rudyard held out no hope – "I've seen what shells can do" – but Carrie nurtured fruitless hopes of his survival. The news brought Kipling many messages of consolation, but also a number of gloating accusatory letters, charging him with personal responsibility for the war, and for his only son's death. And indeed Kipling had been hot for war, and had pulled strings to secure John a commission despite his poor eyesight. The Kiplings kept their grief in check – perhaps damagingly so – but thoughts such as these must have added one more load to the freight of bitterness of their later years. "My Boy Jack", set in the mouth of the grieving mother of a dead sailor, was published the following year.

"Have you news of my boy Jack?"
  *Not this tide.*
"When d'you think that he'll come back?"
  *Not with this wind blowing, and this tide.*

"Has any one else had word of him?"
  *Not this tide.*
*For what is sunk will hardly swim,*
  *Not with this wind blowing, and this tide.*

"Oh, dear, what comfort can I find?"
  *None this tide,*
  *Nor any tide,*
*Except he did not shame his kind –*
  *Not even with that wind blowing, and that tide.*

*Then hold your head up all the more,*
  *This tide,*
  *And every tide;*
*Because he was the son you bore,*
  *And gave to that wind blowing and that tide!*

ABOVE: *John Kipling playing soldiers.*

OPPOSITE: *Second Lieutenant J. Kipling, 1915.*
  *My son died laughing at some*
  *jest. I would I knew*
  *What it were, and it might serve*
  *me at a time when jests are*
  *few.*

# The Gardener

Despite, perhaps partly because of, Carrie's continuing staunch but over-protective support, Kipling's last years were lonely, especially after his remaining daughter Elsie's marriage in 1924; he also suffered badly from an undiagnosed duodenal ulcer. But he continued to break new ground in his writing, and produced some of his finest work. "The Gardener", showing his complete mastery of the nuances of English village life, was written in March 1925. It draws not only on the Kiplings' private loss, but also on Rudyard's work for the War Graves Commission. He devised the inscription seen in each cemetery, "Their Name Liveth for Evermore", and was largely responsible for the reports *The Graves of the Fallen* (1919) and *War Graves of the Empire* (1928). He wrote to Rider Haggard while working on this story, after a visit to the Rouen War Cemetery, "One never gets over the shock of this Dead Sea of arrested lives." The final sentence of the story alludes to the Gospel of St. John, chapter 20 verse 15, but the use here and in "Gethsemane" of Christian imagery is not evidence of Kipling's own beliefs. He simply used the fittest material for the task, as he used the symbols and beliefs of Hinduism, Islam, Buddhism, Freemasonry, even Mithraism, elsewhere. His faith is more basic than any creed. In one of his last letters he wrote: "He who put us into this life does not abandon His work for *any* reason or default at the end of it. That is all I have come to learn out of my life."

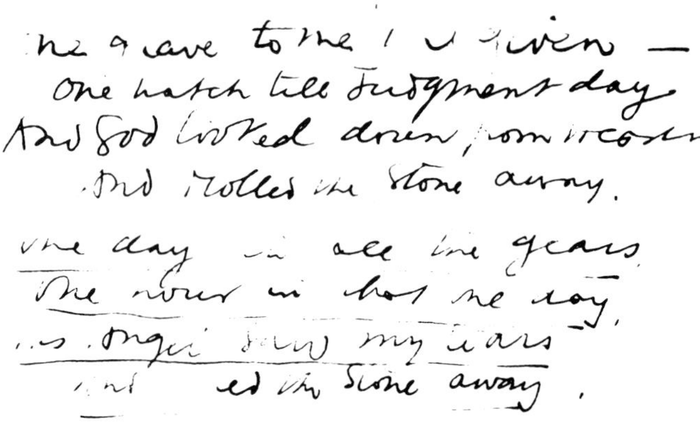

One grave to me was given,
One watch till Judgement Day;
And God looked down from Heaven
And rolled the stone away.

*One day in all the years,*
*One hour in that one day,*
*His Angel saw my tears,*
*And rolled the stone away!*

Every one in the village knew that Helen Turrell did her duty by all her world, and by none more honourably than by her only brother's unfortunate child. The village knew, too, that George Turrell had tried his family severely since early youth, and were not surprised to be told that, after many fresh starts given and thrown away, he, an Inspector of Indian Police, had entangled himself with the daughter of a retired non-commissioned officer, and had died of a fall from a horse a few weeks before his child was born. Mercifully, George's father and mother were both dead, and though Helen, thirty-five and independent, might well have washed her hands of the whole disgraceful affair, she most nobly took charge, though she was, at the time, under threat of lung trouble which had driven her to the South of France. She arranged for the passage of the child and a nurse from Bombay, met them at Marseilles, nursed the baby through an attack of infantile dysentery due to the carelessness of the nurse, whom she had had to dismiss, and at last, thin and worn but triumphant, brought the boy late in the autumn, wholly restored, to her Hampshire home.

All these details were public property, for Helen was as open as the day, and held that scandals are only increased by hushing them up. She admitted that George had always been rather a black sheep, but things might have been much worse if the mother had insisted on her right to keep the boy. Luckily, it seemed that people of that class would do almost anything for money, and, as George had always turned to her in his scrapes, she felt herself justified – her friends agreed with her – in cutting the whole non-commissioned officer connection, and giving the child every advantage. A christening, by the Rector, under the name of Michael, was the first step. So far as she knew herself, she was not, she said, a child-lover, but, for all his faults, she had been very fond of George, and she pointed out that little Michael had his father's mouth to a line; which made something to build upon.

As a matter of fact, it was the Turrell forehead, broad, low, and well-shaped, with the widely spaced eyes beneath it, that Michael had most faithfully reproduced. His mouth was somewhat better cut than the family type. But Helen, who would concede nothing good to his mother's side, vowed he was a Turrell all over, and, there being no one to contradict, the likeness was established.

In a few years Michael took his place, as accepted as Helen had always been – fearless, philosophical, and fairly good-looking. At six, he wished to know why he could not call her "Mummy", as other boys called their mothers. She explained that she was only his auntie, and that aunties were not quite the same as mummies, but that, if it gave him pleasure, he might call her "Mummy" at bedtime, for a pet-name between themselves.

Michael kept his secret most loyally, but Helen, as usual, explained the fact to her friends; which when Michael heard, he raged.

*"I won't call you 'Mummy' any more", a drawing by J. Dewar Mills from the story's first publication in the* Strand *magazine, May 1926.*

"Why did you tell? *Why* did you tell?" came at the end of the storm.

"Because it's always best to tell the truth," Helen answered, her arm round him as he shook in his cot.

"All right, but when the troof's ugly I don't think it's nice."

"Don't you, dear?"

"No, I don't, and" – she felt the small body stiffen – "now you've told, I won't call you 'Mummy' any more – not even at bedtimes."

"But isn't that rather unkind?" said Helen softly.

"I don't care! I don't care! You've hurted me in my insides and I'll hurt you back. I'll hurt you as long as I live!"

"Don't, oh, don't talk like that, dear! You don't know what–"

"I will! And when I'm dead I'll hurt you worse!"

"Thank goodness, I shall be dead long before you, darling."

"Huh! Emma says, ''Never know your luck.'" (Michael had been talking to Helen's elderly, flat-faced maid.) "Lots of little boys die quite soon. So'll I. *Then* you'll see!"

Helen caught her breath and moved towards the door, but the wail of "Mummy! Mummy!" drew her back again, and the two wept together.

At ten years old, after two terms at a prep school, something or somebody gave him the idea that his civil status was not quite regular. He attacked Helen on the subject, breaking down her stammered defences with the family directness.

"''Don't believe a word of it," he said, cheerily, at the end. "People wouldn't have talked like they did if my people had been married. But don't you bother, Auntie. I've found out all about my sort in English Hist'ry and the Shakespeare bits. There was William the Conqueror to begin with, and – oh, heaps more, and they all got on first-rate. 'Twon't make any difference to you, my being *that* – will it?"

"As if anything could–" she began.

"All right. We won't talk about it any more if it makes you cry." He never mentioned the thing again of his own will, but when, two years later, he skilfully managed to have measles in the holidays, as his temperature went up to the appointed one hundred and four he muttered of nothing else, till Helen's voice, piercing at last his delirium, reached him with assurance that nothing on earth or beyond could make any difference between them.

The terms at his public school and the wonderful Christmas, Easter, and Summer holidays followed each other, variegated and glorious as jewels on a string; and as jewels Helen treasured them. In due time Michael developed his own interests, which ran their courses and gave way to others; but his interest in Helen was constant and increasing throughout. She repaid it with all that she had of affection or could command of counsel and money; and since Michael was no fool, the War took him just before what was like to have been a most promising career.

He was to have gone up to Oxford, with a scholarship, in October. At the end of August he was on the edge of joining the first holocaust of public-school boys who threw themselves into the Line; but the captain of his O.T.C., where he had been sergeant for nearly a year, headed him off and steered him directly to a commission in a battalion so new that half of it still wore the old Army red, and the other half was breeding meningitis through living overcrowdedly in damp tents. Helen had been shocked at the idea of direct enlistment.

"But it's in the family," Michael laughed.

"You don't mean to tell me that you believed that old story all this time?" said Helen. (Emma, her maid, had been dead now several years.) "I gave you my word of honour – and I give it again – that – that it's all right. It is indeed."

"Oh, *that* doesn't worry me. It never did," he replied valiantly. "What I meant was, I should have got into the show earlier if I'd enlisted – like my grandfather."

"Don't talk like that! Are you afraid of it's ending so soon, then?"

"No such luck. You know what K. says."

"Yes. But my banker told me last Monday it couldn't *possibly* last beyond Christmas – for financial reasons."

" 'Hope he's right, but our Colonel – and he's a Regular – says it's going to be a long job."

Michael's battalion was fortunate in that, by some chance which meant several "leaves", it was used for coast-defence among shallow trenches on the Norfolk coast; thence sent north to watch the mouth of a Scotch estuary, and, lastly, held for weeks on a baseless rumour of distant service. But, the very day that Michael was to have met Helen for four whole hours at a railway-junction up the line, it was hurled out, to help make good the wastage of Loos, and he had only just time to send her a wire of farewell.

In France luck again helped the battalion. It was put down near the Salient, where it led a meritorious and unexacting life, while the Somme was being manufactured; and enjoyed the peace of the Armentières and Laventie sectors when that battle began. Finding that it had sound views on protecting its own flanks and could dig, a prudent Commander stole it out of its own Division, under pretence of helping to lay telegraphs, and used it round Ypres at large.

A month later, and just after Michael had written Helen that there was nothing special doing and therefore no need to worry, a shell-splinter dropping out of a wet dawn killed him at once. The next shell uprooted and laid down over the body what had been the foundation of a barn wall, so neatly that none but an expert would have guessed that anything unpleasant had happened.

❁

By this time the village was old in experience of war, and, English fashion, had evolved a ritual to meet it. When the postmistress handed her seven-year-old daughter the official telegram to take to Miss Turrell, she observed to the Rector's gardener: "It's Miss Helen's turn now." He replied, thinking of his own son: "Well, he's lasted longer than some." The child herself came to the front-door weeping aloud, because Master Michael had often given her sweets. Helen, presently, found herself pulling down the house-blinds one after one with great care, and saying earnestly to each: "Missing *always* means dead." Then she took her place in the dreary procession that was impelled to go through an inevitable series of unprofitable emotions. The Rector, of course, preached hope and prophesied word, very soon, from a prison camp. Several friends, too, told her perfectly truthful tales, but always about other women, to whom, after months and months of silence, their missing had been miraculously restored. Other people urged her to communicate with infallible Secretaries of organisations who could communicate with benevolent neutrals, who could extract accurate information from the most secretive of Hun prison commandants. Helen did and wrote

K.: Kitchener

OPPOSITE *and* ABOVE: *Michael and Helen, drawn by J. Dewar Mills in 1926.*

*Men of the 7th Northamptonshire Regiment, 9 April 1917; eight days earlier at Ypres they had lost their C.O., 11 officers and 246 men. Kipling's "Epitaphs of the War" are unequivocal:*
*If any ask you why we died,*
*Tell them, because our fathers lied.*

and signed everything that was suggested or put before her.

Once, on one of Michael's leaves, he had taken her over a munition factory, where she saw the progress of a shell from blank-iron to the all but finished article. It struck her at the time that the wretched thing was never left alone for a single second; and "I'm being manufactured into a bereaved next of kin", she told herself, as she prepared her documents.

In due course, when all the organisations had deeply or sincerely regretted their inability to trace, etc., something gave way within her and all sensation – save of thankfulness for the release – came to an end in blessed passivity. Michael had died and her world had stood still and she had been one with the full shock of that arrest. Now she was standing still and the world was going forward, but it did not concern her – in no way or relation did it touch her. She knew this by the ease with which she could slip Michael's name into talk and incline her head to the proper angle, at the proper murmur of sympathy.

In the blessed realisation of that relief, the Armistice with all its bells broke over her and passed unheeded. At the end of another year she had overcome her physical loathing of the living and returned young, so that she could take them by the hand and almost sincerely wish them well. She had no interest in any aftermath, national or personal, of the war, but, moving at an immense distance, she sat on various relief committees and held strong views – she heard herself delivering them – about the site of the proposed village War Memorial.

Then there came to her, as next of kin, an official intimation, backed by a page of a letter to her in indelible pencil, a silver identity-disc, and a watch, to the effect that the body of Lieutenant Michael Turrell had been found, identified, and re-interred in Hagenzeele Third Military Cemetery – the letter of the row and the grave's number in that row duly given.

So Helen found herself moved on to another process of the manufacture – to a world full of exultant or broken relatives, now strong in the certainty that there was an altar upon earth where they might lay their love. These soon told her, and by means of time-tables made clear, how easy it was and how little it interfered with life's affairs to go and see one's grave.

"*So* different," as the Rector's wife said, "if he'd been killed in Mesopotamia, or even Gallipoli."

The agony of being waked up to some sort of second life drove Helen across the Channel, where, in a new world of abbreviated titles, she learnt that Hagenzeele Third could be comfortably reached by an afternoon train which fitted in with the morning boat, and that there was a comfortable little hotel not three kilometres from Hagenzeele itself, where one could spend quite a comfortable night and see one's grave next morning. All this she had from a Central Authority who lived in a board and tar-paper shed on the skirts of a razed city full of whirling lime-dust and blown papers.

"By the way," said he, "you know your grave, of course?"

"Yes, thank you," said Helen, and showed its row and number typed on Michael's own little typewriter. The officer would have checked it, out of one of his many books; but a large Lancashire woman thrust between them and bade him tell her where she might find her son, who had been corporal in the A.S.C. His proper name, she sobbed, was Anderson, but, coming of respectable folk, he had of

*Tyne Cot Cemetery. Many of the graves here are of unidentified men; on each of their headstones are Kipling's words, "A Soldier of the Great War Known Unto God".*

course enlisted under the name of Smith; and had been killed at Dickiebush, in early '15. She had not his number nor did she know which of his two Christian names he might have used with his alias; but her Cook's tourist ticket expired at the end of Easter week, and if by then she could not find her child she should go mad. Whereupon she fell forward on Helen's breast; but the officer's wife came out quickly from a little bedroom behind the office, and the three of them lifted the woman on to the cot.

"They are often like this," said the officer's wife, loosening the tight bonnet-strings. "Yesterday she said he'd been killed at Hooge. Are you sure you know your grave? It makes such a difference."

"Yes, thank you," said Helen, and hurried out before the woman on the bed should begin to lament again.

Tea in a crowded mauve and blue striped wooden structure, with a false front, carried her still further into the nightmare. She paid her bill beside a stolid, plain-featured Englishwoman, who, hearing her enquire about the train to Hagenzeele, volunteered to come with her.

"I'm going to Hagenzeele myself," she explained. "Not to Hagenzeele Third; mine is Sugar Factory, but they call it La Rosière now. It's just south of Hagenzeele Three. Have you got your room at the hotel there?"

"Oh yes, thank you. I've wired."

"That's better. Sometimes the place is quite full, and at others there's hardly a soul. But they've put bathrooms into the old Lion d'Or – that's the hotel on the west side of Sugar Factory – and it draws off a lot of people, luckily."

"It's all new to me. This is the first time I've been over."

"Indeed! This is my ninth time since the Armistice. Not on my own account. *I* haven't lost any one, thank God – but, like every one else, I've a lot of friends at home who have. Coming over as often as I do, I find it helps them to have some one just look at the – the place and tell them about it afterwards. And one can take photos for them, too. I get quite a list of commissions to execute." She laughed nervously and tapped her slung Kodak. "There are two or three to see at Sugar Factory this time, and plenty of others in the cemeteries all about. My system is to save them up, and arrange them, you know. And when I've got enough commissions for one area to make it worth while, I pop over and execute them. It *does* comfort people."

"I suppose so," Helen answered, shivering as they entered the little train.

"Of course it does. (Isn't it lucky we've got window-seats?) It must do or they wouldn't ask one to do it, would they? I've a list of quite twelve or fifteen commissions here" – she tapped the Kodak again – "I must sort them out to-night. Oh, I forgot to ask you. What's yours?"

"My nephew," said Helen. "But I was very fond of him."

"Ah, yes! I sometimes wonder whether *they* know after death? What do you think?"

"Oh, I don't – I haven't dared to think much about that sort of thing," said Helen, almost lifting her hands to keep her off.

"Perhaps that's better," the woman answered. "The sense of loss must be enough, I expect. Well, I won't worry you any more."

Helen was grateful, but when they reached the hotel Mrs. Scarsworth (they had exchanged names) insisted on dining at the same table with her, and after the meal, in the little, hideous salon full of low-voiced relatives, took Helen through her "commissions" with biographies of the dead, where she happened to know them, and sketches of their next of kin. Helen endured till nearly half-past nine, ere she fled to her room.

Almost at once there was a knock at her door and Mrs. Scarsworth entered; her hands, holding the dreadful list, clasped before her.

"Yes – yes – *I* know," she began. "You're sick of me, but I want to tell you something. You – you aren't married, are you? Then perhaps you won't . . . But it doesn't matter. I've *got* to tell some one. I can't go on any longer like this."

"But please –" Mrs. Scarsworth had backed against the shut door, and her mouth worked dryly.

"In a minute," she said. "You – you know about these graves of mine I was telling you about downstairs, just now? They really *are* commissions. At least several of them are." Her eye wandered round the room. "What extraordinary wall-papers they have in Belgium, don't you think? . . . Yes. I swear they are commissions. But there's *one*, d'you see, and – and he was more to me than anything else in the world. Do you understand?"

Helen nodded.

"More than any one else. And, of course, he oughtn't to have been. He ought to have been nothing to me. But he *was*. He *is*. That's why I do the commissions, you see. That's all."

"But why do you tell me?" Helen asked desperately.

"Because I'm *so* tired of lying. Tired of lying – always lying – year in and year out. When I don't tell lies I've got to act 'em and I've got to think 'em, always. *You* don't know what that means. He was everything to me that he oughtn't to have been – the one real thing – the only thing that ever happened to me in all my life; and I've had to pretend he wasn't. I've had to watch every word I said, and think out what lie I'd tell next, for years and years!"

"How many years?" Helen asked.

"Six years and four months before, and two and three-quarters after. I've gone to him eight times, since. To-morrow'll make the ninth, and – and I can't – I *can't* go to him again with nobody in the world knowing. I want to be honest with some one before I go. Do you understand? It doesn't matter about *me*. I was never truthful,

*Rudyard and Carrie Kipling at Loos Cemetery in 1920. The waste of a generation on the Great War battlefields was, said Kipling, "a bitter and sad business, even for such as know where their boys are laid." John Kipling's body was never found.*

even as a girl. But it isn't worthy of *him*. So – so I – I had to tell you. I can't keep it up any longer. Oh, I can't!"

She lifted her joined hands almost to the level of her mouth, and brought them down sharply, still joined, to full arms' length below her waist. Helen reached forward, caught them, bowed her head over them, and murmured: "Oh, my dear! My dear!" Mrs. Scarsworth stepped back, her face all mottled.

"My God!" said she. "Is *that* how you take it?"

Helen could not speak, and the woman went out; but it was a long while before Helen was able to sleep.

Next morning Mrs. Scarsworth left early on her round of commissions, and Helen walked alone to Hagenzeele Third. The place was still in the making, and stood some five or six feet above the metalled road, which it flanked for hundreds of yards. Culverts across a deep ditch served for entrances through the unfinished boundary wall. She climbed a few wooden-faced earthen steps and then met the entire crowded level of the thing in one held breath. She did not know that Hagenzeele Third counted twenty-one thousand dead already. All she saw was a merciless sea of black crosses, bearing little strips of stamped tin at all angles across their faces. She could distinguish no order or arrangement in their mass; nothing but a waist-high wilderness as of weeds stricken dead, rushing at her. She went forward, moved to the left and the right hopelessly, wondering by what guidance she should ever come to her own. A great distance away there was a line of whiteness. It proved to be a block of some two or three hundred graves whose headstones had already been set, whose flowers were planted out, and whose new-sown grass showed green. Here she could see clear-cut letters at the ends of the rows, and, referring to her slip, realised that it was not here she must look.

A man knelt behind a line of headstones – evidently a gardener, for he was firming a young plant in the soft earth. She went towards him, her paper in her hand. He rose at her approach and without prelude or salutation asked: "Who are you looking for?"

"Lieutenant Michael Turrell – my nephew," said Helen slowly and word for word, as she had many thousands of times in her life.

The man lifted his eyes and looked at her with infinite compassion before he turned from the fresh-sown grass toward the naked black crosses.

"Come with me," he said, "and I will show you where your son lies."

When Helen left the Cemetery she turned for a last look. In the distance she saw the man bending over his young plants; and she went away, supposing him to be the gardener.

# Further Reading

## Biography

Amis, Kingsley, *Rudyard Kipling and his World* (1975)
Birkenhead, Lord, *Rudyard Kipling* (1978)
Brown, Hilton, *Rudyard Kipling: A New Appreciation* (1945)
Carrington, Charles, *Rudyard Kipling: His Life and Work* (1955)
Kipling, Rudyard, *Something of Myself* (1937)
Orel, Harold, ed., *Kipling: Interviews and Recollections* (2 vols., 1983)
Wilson, Angus, *The Strange Ride of Rudyard Kipling* (1979)

## Criticism

Bratton, J. S., *The Victorian Popular Ballad* (1975)
Cornell, Louis L., *Kipling in India* (1966)
Dobree, Bonamy, *Rudyard Kipling: Realist and Fabulist* (1967)
Gilbert, Elliot, ed., *Kipling and the Critics* (1966)
Green, Roger Lancelyn, ed., *Kipling: The Critical Heritage* (1971)
Green, Roger Lancelyn, *Kipling and the Children* (1965)
Gross, John, ed., *Rudyard Kipling: The Man, His Work and His World* (1972)
Keating, P. J., *The Working Classes in Victorian Fiction* (1971)
Mason, Philip, *Kipling: The Glass, the Shadow and the Fire* (1975)
Rutherford, Andrew, ed., *Kipling's Mind and Art* (1964)
Tompkins, J. M. S., *The Art of Rudyard Kipling* (1959)

## Bibliography

Harbord, R. E., *The Reader's Guide to Rudyard Kipling's Work* (1963–1972)
Livingston, Flora V., *Bibliography of the Works of Rudyard Kipling* (1927; *Supplement* 1938)
Stewart, James McG. & Yeats, A. W., *Rudyard Kipling: A Bibliographical Catalogue* (1959)
University of Sussex Library, *The Kipling Papers* (1979)

## Works

*Complete Works* (35 vols., Sussex Edition, 1937–39)
*Rudyard Kipling to Rider Haggard: The Record of a Friendship*, ed. Morton Cohen (1965)
*"O Beloved Kids!": Rudyard Kipling's Letters to his Children*, ed. Elliot Gilbert (1983)
*Early Verse by Rudyard Kipling 1879–1889*, ed. Andrew Rutherford (1986)
*Kipling's India: Uncollected Sketches 1884–88*, ed. Thomas Pinney (1986)

# Picture Credits

BBC Hulton Picture Library: 28, 112
Berg Collection, New York Public Library: 37
Collection Viollet: 187
East Sussex County Library: 137, 150, 158, 160
Hampshire County Library, Portsmouth: 32
Illustrated London News: 13
Imperial War Museum: 164, 165, 166, 168, 169, 171, 172, 175, 184
India Office: 115
Mansell Collection: 8, 11, 12, 31, 71, 118
National Portrait Gallery, London: 34
National Trust/University of Sussex Library: 9, 14, 17, 18, 23, 25, 38, 39, 40, 45, 47, 48, 50, 51, 54,
    60, 72, 87, 90, 105, 106, 107, 108, 111, 119, 126, 127, 129 (top), 131, 133, 143, 154, 163, 176, 177,
    178, 192
National Trust/Weidenfeld & Nicolson Archives: 159
Punch: 5, 10, 167, 173
The Times Picture Library/University of Sussex Library: 140
Weidenfeld & Nicolson Archives: 41
All other pictures are from private collections

# Acknowledgements

The Albion Press would like to thank the librarians and archivists of all the institutions named
above for their help in producing this book, and also the London Library and the Bridgeman Art
Library. They would also like to thank John Burt of the University of Sussex Library and
Margaret Willes of The National Trust for their particular help. Copyright material from
*Something of Myself* and the letters of Rudyard Kipling is here reproduced by kind permission of
A. P. Watt Ltd. on behalf of The National Trust and Macmillan London Ltd.

For help in various ways, the editor would like to thank Dr J. S. Bratton, Alan Peacock and
Barry Smith; Emma Bradford, Jane Havell and Elizabeth Loving at the Albion Press; and Dan
Franklin at William Collins. He would also like to record his indebtedness to the Kipling scholars
whose work is listed under "Further Reading".